Treasure in Three Acts

Palmyrton Estate Sale Mystery Series

S.W. Hubbard

Published by S.W. Hubbard, 2022.

TREASURE IN THREE ACTS

First edition. November 7, 2022.

Written by S.W. Hubbard.

Chapter 1

S o. Much. Stuff.

It's been a while since Another Man's Treasure has held an estate sale in a house like this—a recently built executive home with five bedrooms (each with a cavernous closet), a kitchen like the set for a Food Network show, and a three-bay garage. Six thousand square feet of American over-consumption.

Usually, we work in the homes of old people.

Living ones, downsizing to a condo or assisted living.

Or dead ones, whose heirs are emptying out the family home.

We traffic in heirlooms, antiques, kitsch, and collectibles of bygone eras.

Today's project is one hundred percent 21st century.

Ethan and Everly Corrigan are in their late thirties, with three young children. This huge house doesn't contain anything older than Esme, age eight. Nevertheless, it's filled from basement to attic with possessions that will not be making the move to Singapore, where Ethan Corrigan has taken a high-level job in international finance. And where the rest of the thematically E-named family is obliged to accompany him.

Where the breadwinner goes, the bread-eaters must follow.

Ethan trails me around the house as I work on pricing. In theory, he's a handsome man: tall and muscular, thick dark hair, blue eyes, straight nose, strong chin. In practice, he's unattractive: his thinly veiled contempt for every human who's not him undermines his physical attributes.

"You're pricing this sofa at only a thousand bucks? We paid fifteen grand! It's Fendi."

It's not my fault you foolishly overpaid for a status label is what I want to say. Instead, I adopt the imperturbable expression of a Buddhist monk and murmur, "Unfortunately, sofas are worse than cars. They lose most of their value as soon as they leave the showroom." I could get more for this one if it were in pristine condition. But there's a snag in the fabric, probably

1

from Elvis, the Corrigans' big, goofy Labradoodle, and a pinkish stain on one cushion that looks suspiciously like raspberry Juicy Juice.

I don't point out these flaws to my client because I don't want the kids and the dog, and by extension, their mom, to get in trouble with Ethan, who's about as forgiving as a judge at the Salem witch trials.

I keep working the family room, pricing the stylish barrel chairs, the big, sharp-edged coffee table that looks like stitches waiting to happen for these active kids, and the shelves, filled with bowls and vases and statuettes of animals, all acquired from Pottery Barn and Restoration Hardware. Less interesting than the collection of southeast Asian fertility goddesses I had to sell at our last sale, but probably easier to unload.

I move on to the gargantuan TV, where bright colored cartoon characters cavort across the screen.

"What's the name of this show, Elodie?" I ask the four-year-old staring slack-jawed at the antics of an anteater and a sloth.

She doesn't answer. Doesn't seem to notice my presence at all.

Is this what I have to look forward to when my own kids are four? Right now, Aiden and Thea are only eight months old, and we're careful to keep them away from the TV. My sisters-in-law laugh at Sean and me, assuring us we'll soon cave to demands for screen time, just to gain some peace and quiet for ourselves.

I'm sure we will, but we're trying hard to postpone that day. The first two months of life with premature twins were exhausting, but now that they're robust eight-month-olds, they greet us with squeals of delight. Their bright eyes—Aiden's blue, Thea's brown—study everything they see with curiosity. And they keep each other endlessly amused without the narcotic of TV.

I hope my kids will never be dazed and sedated by electronics like poor little Elodie.

I move across the hall to a room that contains more toys than the high-end toy shop on the Palmyrton green.

"Everything in here goes," Ethan declares.

From nowhere, a small projectile enters the room, prostrating himself on top of a stuffed moose big enough to double as a bean bag chair. "Nooooo! Moosey is coming with us. I won't leave him!"

Six-year-old Eamon sobs into the moose's brown pelt, kicking his heels and pounding his fists in a full-body tantrum. I know this poor child doesn't want consolation from a stranger, so I head to the other side of the room to let the father handle it. But Ethan follows me, leaving his son behind with a scowl.

"I've already explained to the kids that they each get to take three reasonably sized toys with them. We'll buy more...."

"...when you get to Singapore." I finish the sentence I've already heard dozens of times in the two days I've been prepping this sale. Everyone in the Corrigan family except Ethan is having trouble with this move. Everly keeps trying to promote it as a grand adventure, but the kids aren't buying that line, probably because they can tell their mother doesn't believe it herself.

I attempt to stare down Ethan. Surely, he doesn't intend to follow me around this room, second-guessing the prices I assign to every action figure, Barbie accessory, and Lego set? My glare doesn't drive him away although it stifles some of his commentary.

Eamon's wails bring Everly to the scene. I expect her to wrap her son in a comforting embrace, but instead she walks toward her husband holding out a vibrating cell phone. "It's Larsen."

He grabs the phone, presses it to his ear, and stalks from the room shouting the foreign language of high finance. Only then does Everly sink to her knees next to her despairing child. She rubs his back, murmuring, "It's okay, Eam. It'll be okay."

I keep working silently, used to carrying on in the face of homeowners' unhappiness. Emptying a house is never joyful. Almost every item marked for sale comes with a memory attached—some happy, some miserable. At times, my clients are consoled by the thought of their possessions finding a second life with new owners. But a child can't be comforted by picturing his beloved stuffed animal in another kid's room.

Eamon's meltdown bothers me more than it should. The protective layer I've developed to shield me from clients' misery has worn thin, perhaps by motherhood or perhaps because I've been away from work for a while. This is the biggest sale I've run since returning from maternity leave. My assistants, Donna and Ty, held the business together for over three months in the dark days of winter. But now we're in the summer high season. I have to work if

I'm going to preserve the success of the business I spent fifteen years building.

The problem has been finding reliable childcare. At first, either my parents or Sean's parents would watch the kids while Sean and I worked but minding the twins has become more demanding as the kids get heavier and more active. Twins are too much work for grandparents in their seventies, especially because the lion's share of the work falls upon the female half of each duo. So we started interviewing nannies sent by an agency, women Sean regarded as if they were all serial killers out on parole. Disregarding the agency's background checks, my detective husband launched his own investigations of each candidate. Finally, he agreed to entrust the kids to a woman with twenty years' experience as long as she agreed to constant surveillance by a nannycam. I was mortified, but Roseline seemed to take it in stride, inured to the demands of working for dual-career couples.

However, I must admit, the nannycam was a good idea. We like being able to see the kids during the day and observing Roseline's gentle care and unflappable patience has set both our minds at ease. I glance at the still screaming Eamon from the corner of my eye. The Corrigan kids could benefit from what Roseline has to offer.

Eventually, Eamon's wails subside into choked hiccups. At that moment, my phone chirps with a text from my husband.

What time will you be home? We have a bit of a situation here.

Chapter 2

It's nearly five and I've finished pricing everything on the first floor. Donna has been upstairs handling the bedrooms, while Ty has tackled the garage and huge finished basement. If they're as far along as I am, we can wrap up in half an hour and be ready to open the sale tomorrow morning at 8AM. I text Sean to clarify, but his only reassurance is that no one's sick and the "situation" is too complicated to discuss by phone.

With this bomb ticking in the back of my mind, I set off to confer with my staff. I find Donna in the spare bedroom contemplating a walk-in closet filled from floor to ceiling with labeled plastic bins: 0-3 mos, 3-6 mos, 6mos-1yr. And that's just the first shelf.

"Wouldja look at all these kids' clothes, Audrey?" She shakes her head and opens a bin to reveal neatly folded onesies, rompers, and tiny dresses. "It looks like Mrs. Corrigan bought all new clothes for each kid, so I don't get why she saved all these. If she has another baby, it won't wear hand-me-downs."

I'm not planning to have more kids, but I admit to being unable to part with the itty-bitty outfits the twins wore home from the hospital. But their everyday outfits I ship off as fast as they outgrow them. "Look on the bright side, Donna—Everly has these clothes so well organized, all you need is a price label for each bin."

"Yep—that's my last task up here," Donna agrees. So I head out to the garage to find Ty.

Unlike most suburban garages, the Corrigan garage doesn't contain any tools or lawn care products. Ethan clearly doesn't do his own weed-whacking. Instead, it's filled with more kids' toys and equipment. I find Ty shaking his head over a contraption that looks like a brightly colored Conestoga wagon.

"Any idea how to price this? They go for six hundred large brand new."

I look at the screen of his phone where he's called up a description of the deluxe all-terrain stroller-cruiser that seats four kids and holds a cooler. You'd need a team of oxen to pull it fully loaded. "Price it high," I advise. "I bet it'll get snapped up by one of the neighborhood moms."

Ty glances out the open garage door at the silent development of widely spaced McMansions. "Don't they all already have their own?"

I agree with an unamused laugh. "You're probably right. Maybe not so high—some mother from a regular middle class neighborhood will buy it. It's aspirational."

As Ty prepares to close the garage doors, he squints at a beat-up minivan slowly cruising the cul de sac. "Damn early birds circling already."

I grin at him as the door slides closed. "You know that's a sign this sale will be a big success."

<hr />

HALF AN HOUR LATER, I pull into my own driveway. Can I make it into the house without Mrs. Bannerman spotting me?

Since the arrival of the twins, Sean and I have become one of those shameful families who have too much junk in the garage to permit parking two cars. In my defense, motherhood forced me to get rid of my tiny Honda Civic and replace it with a larger, safer, Toyota RAV 4. And once I find a willing recipient for the two outgrown bassinets that were passed down to me, and Sean finds time to break down all the cardboard boxes from our daily Amazon deliveries, I should be able to once again park inside.

Until then, I must run the gauntlet that is Alma Bannerman.

The Bannermans have lived on our street for forty years, arriving as newlyweds, raising their two sons, and settling into a contented retirement of bridge games, cruises, and bus trips to Broadway matinees. As all the other older residents moved away, replaced by young couples like Sean and me, the Bannermans assumed the role of elder statesmen, dispensing wisdom about Japanese beetle infestations, reliable plumbers, and the town's arcane garbage collection restrictions. Mr. Bannerman would not only loan you a tool but would also come over and help with the project. Mrs. Bannerman could be relied upon to have the missing ingredient for any recipe you might have gone into unprepared. They would take in your mail when you were on vacation, sign for packages while you were at work, and water your hanging baskets when they shriveled on hot days.

Then Mr. Bannerman died.

Without him, Alma drifts. She's let go of the activities they used to do together, unwilling or unable to join in as a solo participant. But she hasn't lost interest in the neighborhood. God forbid you're in the shower when a delivery lands on your porch because Alma will snatch it up if it stays there for more than five minutes. She brings it back later with an apology. "Oh, I didn't realize you were home. I didn't want it to be stolen." Then she settles in for a fifteen-minute chat.

As I park in my driveway, I glance in my rearview mirror. Sure enough, Alma's front window drapes twitch. She'll be over here in a flash, bearing fresh-baked muffins, craning her neck at the back door to catch a glimpse of the twins.

I can't snatch the muffins and push her out the door. I can't decline the muffins and push her out the door. Kindness requires me to eat a blueberry crumble and give her a cup of tea and let her bounce Aiden on her knee.

And I'd do that gladly.

Just not every day.

Every. Single. Day.

Today, I need to make it inside unobserved so I can find out what's going on with the situation. Glancing over my shoulder, I slip into the house. Sean is chopping vegetables for dinner. "How was the sale prep?"

"Exhausting." The twins pull themselves up in their playpen and squeal for me. Immediately, I feel my breasts swell with milk, so I pick them both up and stagger toward the family room to nurse. "What's the situation?"

Sean opens his mouth to answer just as a knock sounds at the back door.

"That must be Alma. I tried to slip in unobserved, but clearly I failed."

"Oh, geez. She was already here once today." Sean assumes his sternest cop expression and heads to the door.

I get the kids settled to nurse and listen as Sean accepts the muffins while firmly deflecting Alma's request to visit with me.

For about a minute.

After which Alma pops into the family room, her permed hair bobbing above her thick glasses.

"There you are!" Alma settles on the couch across from me, unperturbed by the fact I'm practically naked from the waist up. I've given up on modesty around her. If she's going to intrude, she's going to get an eyeful.

Alma takes Thea when she's done nursing and regales me with the convoluted tale of her encounter with the gas meter reader. All I need to do is smile and nod. Meanwhile, my mind is churning with the questions I long to ask my husband.

Finally, after Sean makes the oven timer go off, Alma leaves, the twins are satisfied, and I can talk to my husband.

"I'm dying. What's the situation?"

Sean sits beside me and takes my hand. "Don't panic. But Roseline is quitting."

I snatch my hand away. "She's resentful about that nannycam. I knew it!"

"No, it's nothing to do with that. Her daughter in Houston has been diagnosed with cancer. Roseline has to go there for a while to take care of her."

I gaze down at Thea, blissfully examining her own toes. What could be worse than finding out your daughter has cancer? "But she's only in her early thirties, right?" Roseline has proudly showed us pictures of her grown children: the son a teacher on Long Island, the daughter a computer programmer in Texas.

"Roseline says they caught the cancer early and the prognosis is good, but her daughter needs support while she's going through the treatment."

"Of course she does. Roseline has to be with her." After the shock of the illness subsides, my empathy is nudged aside by panic.

We're without childcare. Again.

I massage my temples where a headache has started to pulse. Roseline was so good with the kids, so reliable. Why has this calamity befallen her...and us? "When is she leaving? Please don't tell me today was her last day."

"No, she's giving us three days' notice because her daughter doesn't start treatment right away. She thinks she'll only be gone for two or three months." Sean pulls me into a hug. "If we could go back to using our parents for a while, we could keep the job open for Roseline."

I fling my head back on the sofa cushion. "But we both agreed that watching the twins full-time is too hard on our folks." I feel my eyes itch with tears of frustration. Before I had kids, I secretly suspected people of over-dramatizing their childcare problems. Karma is biting me back. I have to start from scratch again looking for a reliable person to watch the children I gave birth to, so I don't destroy the business I built from nothing.

Sean squeezes my hand. "We have a little time. Something will come up."

Chapter 3

Despite the "no early birds" warning we printed in the ad for the Corrigan sale, the line awaiting me in the morning snakes down the driveway and into the cul-de-sac. This is the kind of neighborhood where homeowners would call the cops to complain about trespassers, especially ones that look like the gaggle of mothers and grandmothers chatting in Spanish while their babies lean out of strollers and pluck leaves from the shrubs. I'd like to open the doors to the sale early, but when I enter the house, Everly Corrigan is still meandering around her vast kitchen imploring the kids to eat their breakfast. Her giant SUV is packed to the gills, awaiting their departure to the Jersey Shore for a week, after which they leave for Singapore.

The kids will never see this house again, but the reality of that hasn't sunk in, and I'm sure not going to point it out.

"My waffle doesn't have enough syrup," Esme whines.

"I want different cereal," Eamon demands.

I grab a bottle of Log Cabin from the island and squirt a blob onto the waffle. Then I hold up two boxes of ostensibly organic cereal that I suspect were produced on the same factory line as Sugar Pops and Cocoa Krispies and tell Eamon to choose.

Surprisingly, the kids comply under my supervision, and within twenty minutes, I've hustled the Corrigans out the door.

Donna grins at me as the garage door rumbles shut behind Everly, while I open the front door to the hordes of customers. "You've got this motherhood thing down pat, Audrey."

"Ha! Don't bet on it." In between the initial hectic spurt of selling lamps and toys and dishes and clothes, I tell Donna the bad news about Roseline. "I was all set to coast through four years of expert nanny-ing until the kids go off to pre-school. Now I'm back to square one."

"You take two dollar for dis?" A woman waves one of Everly's designer blouses under my nose.

"Absolutely no price reductions today." I decline to meet her eye to avoid arguments.

The woman drops the silk like it's on fire and stalks away.

Donna re-hangs the blouse, talking to me over her shoulder. "Can't your folks help out again?"

"In a pinch. But it's not ideal. Sean's mother can't go up and down our steps, and my dad and Natalie have a vacation planned. I don't know where—"

"I could help you out."

The voice is soft, with a southern twang. I turn around to see a thin young woman, maybe nineteen or twenty, who's been picking through items from the under five dollars box. "I love watching kids," she tells me in a rural drawl. "I'm the second oldest of eight. I took care of all my little brothers and sisters." She pronounces eight as eye-tuh.

"Eight! Wow, your mom was busy." Donna offers a chipper response to humor our young customer.

Although the girl is plain and meek, she's persistent. "Yes, ma'am, Ah'd love to babysit your kids. Kids really like me. Ah play games with them, and ah sing. Ah'm not like those girls who stare at their phones and ignore the little ones."

I smile to be polite. "I'm sure you're not. But I need someone, er—" *Qualified... experienced...above reproach...not random.* "—uhm, someone older."

"Ahm twenty-one. Why, most girls I know back home have two kids of their own now."

"Where are you from?" Donna asks. "Not New Jersey."

The girl laughs, revealing a small gap between her two front teeth. "Oh, lawd no. Ahm from West Virginia." She steps closer to the checkout table. "Ah heard y'all say you have twins. That takes a lot of energy. My brothers Petey and Perry are twins. They were a handful, but I managed them just fine." She grabs a pen from the table and slides a pad of post-it notes away from Donna. "Here. I'll leave you my phone number." She hands me the note on which a name and number are written in round, loopy printing. "God willing, you'll give me a call."

Starla Douglas.

Starla?

"Okay—thanks." I shoo her aside. "If you don't mind, I have customers to wait on here."

"Yes, ma'am. I understand." Starla waves and backs away. "Y'all think on it. Ah'll come back tomorrow."

The post-lunch lull ends, and business picks up as people returning home from work or picking up their kids decide to stop by the sale. Donna and I barely exchange a word that's not related to products or pricing. As the clock creeps closer to four, I leave Donna on her own and make a pass through the house to urge people to take their selections to the check-out table. When I get to the garage, I hear raised voices.

"Hey!" There's a stern edge in Ty's voice. "Don't be tearin' through that trash."

A tall, thin man looks up from his task of pawing through the two white garbage bags lined up on the Corrigans' driveway. He peers at Ty through crooked glasses, his curly hair pinned up in a man-bun, his jeans both too large and too short for his rangy frame. "If you're discarding these items, why can't I have them?"

I know Ty doesn't care about the contents of the bags—the remnants of our hastily eaten lunch plus some unsellable broken toys and mismatched kids' shoes. He simply doesn't want the man making a mess he'll have to clean up.

Ty's patience has been pushed to the limit today by over-privileged housewives under the mistaken impression they're shopping at Bloomingdales. He's had to restrain his irritation against our core constituency, so I fear this hapless dude is about to pay the price. Ty steps towards him with a fierce glare that would make any sane man back down. "There's nuthin' in those sacks anyone can use." Ty yanks the bag from the man's hand. "And I don't want trash dumped all over this driveway."

But the skinny guy is not intimidated. He points to a bulge in the semi-transparent plastic. "I can see two children's rainboots in there. They're perfectly serviceable and should not be added to a landfill."

Ty puts his hands on his hips and speaks slowly and distinctly. "One is red and one is blue. They're not a pair. We couldn't find the other two."

"One is left and one is right," the man insists. "The color is immaterial. They still work to keep a child's feet dry."

Ty cocks his head. "You seriously tellin' me you gonna send your kid to school wearin' two different color boots?"

The man takes the garbage bag and slings it over his shoulder like Santa Claus. "What my children wear is no concern of yours." And he marches down the driveway.

Now I notice the beat-up blue minivan that had been circling yesterday, parked behind several other cars at the curb.

"I better not see that bag of trash tossed out the door of your van when I leave tonight," Ty shouts after him. "Imma take down your plate number."

The man keeps walking, refusing to be goaded into a response. "Let him go," I say to Ty. "One less bag of trash for us to dispose of."

"Whack job," Ty mutters as he closes the garage door and begins straightening up for tomorrow. "Not bad enough his poor kids gotta wear other people's clothes? He's so cheap he won't even buy a matched pair of used boots!"

Having been on the receiving end of a lot of hand-me-downs as a child, Ty is super-sensitive to the stress kids feel when their clothes set them apart from their friends. "I saw that guy lurking around the house all day," I tell Ty, "but he never bought anything. I guess our prices were too steep for him."

Ty doesn't comment. Just continues reorganizing Everly Corrigan's seemingly bottomless supply of children's clothes. I know we sold a lot, but there's still so much left to be sold tomorrow. Suddenly, I feel just as sad and angry as Ty that the skinny guy's kid has to wear mismatched boots when the Corrigan kids have so much that they can lose their boots with impunity, knowing their mom will always buy them another pair. I pat Ty on the back. "Maybe tomorrow we can give him some better stuff from the items left at the end of the sale."

I rejoin Donna inside to help her get ready for tomorrow. As we're consolidating everything into the family room, Donna plucks the post-it note with Starla's number out of the trash. "You know, Audrey, maybe you shouldn't be so quick to throw this away."

I face her with my hands on my hips. "Are you kidding me? You want me to leave my children with some random redneck who shows up at a sale? When Aiden and Thea start talking, they'll sound like characters from *Duck Dynasty*."

"She seemed nice." Donna keeps talking as she positions the unsold kitchenware for maximum effect. "You could try her out by having her help your mother-in-law while we're setting up next week's sale. If she seems good, you could let her fly solo."

Donna holds out the post-it note to me, and reluctantly I put it in my fannypack. It's hard for me to imagine Little Miss Cornpone working alongside my mother-in-law, the Queen of Galway. But the "God willing" and the "yes, ma'ams" are sure to go over big with Sean's mother. And Starla could do the lifting and the running up and down stairs while my mother-in-law barks out instructions.

Maybe this could work. That is, if Starla passes Sean's security clearance.

Chapter 4

That night after we put the kids to bed, Sean and I discuss our options. I don't want to lead with Starla until I see what he's got.

He's got nothing.

Sean called three nanny agencies earlier today and they all have a months-long waiting list. "Looks like we've got no choice but to fall back on our parents for a while."

So I tell him about Starla. I expect an outraged response from Mr. Background Check, but Sean is intrigued. "Well, as long as we never left the kids alone with her, she'd be handy to help my mother. Couldn't hurt to interview her."

"Really? She won't have references. She sounds like she just moved here from some holler in Appalachia."

Sean arches his eyebrows. "You accused me of turning the nannycam on Roseline because she's Black. Now who's biased?"

Direct hit. I pick up my phone and tap in the numbers from the post-it note.

The phone rings endlessly and I finally hang up.

"Why didn't you leave a message?" Sean asks.

"Must be a landline with no answering machine. Don't you think that's weird? What kind of twenty-year-old doesn't have a cellphone?"

"If she stops back at the sale tomorrow, invite her to come here for an interview." Sean calls our dog Ethel to go out one last time before bed. "I'll find out everything there is to know about young Starla."

———————————

BUT DAY TWO OF THE Corrigan sale passes with no sign of the girl.

Instead, I have a steady stream of challenges. A gaggle of ladies who always shop my sales together have items in their hands but refuse to check out, hoping that I'll declare half-off soon.

I can outlast them.

A tall, handsome older gentleman with thick silver hair and a beaky nose paces from room to room, looking at everything but selecting nothing. I can't figure him out. Well-dressed older men sometimes come to sales with antiques, but the Corrigans have only 21st century consumer goods. And this fellow doesn't look like a grandpa hoping to get a used highchair for when his grandkids come to visit. But he doesn't look suspicious either.

Not like my shoplifter. She's wearing designer yoga pants and an engagement ring with a pigeon-egg sized diamond, but I see her slip a Crate and Barrel candlestick into her deep, Louis Vuitton tote, while holding a small carved owl in the other hand. Glancing around, she grabs a set of cork drink coasters and comes up to the check-out table. "This owl is so precious," she says smiling to reveal her dazzling dentistry. "And I can always use extra coasters."

"And an extra candlestick." I gesture toward her bag. "Let me wrap that for you so it doesn't get scratched." My smile matches hers for boundless good cheer.

Her cheeks flush and she tosses her honey-blond ponytail. "Oh, right. I stuck it in there because I couldn't carry everything."

"Always a challenge at a sale," I agree, and collect payment for all three items. When she flounces off, I notice that my gentleman shopper observed the entire interaction. I think I notice a slight smile on his severe face, but he says nothing and I soon lose track of him.

We sell and sell and sell. In the afternoon, I cut prices. The crowd never lets up. But still, when we close the doors at four, there's much more than the usual vanload of leftovers to be donated to charity.

"I will never again be envious of people who live in houses like this," Donna grumbles as we clean up after the sale. "The more space they have, the more stuff they accumulate. I'm glad I live in a two-bedroom condo."

We could've run this sale for three full days, but the Corrigans weren't willing to let us start earlier.

Donna waves at the unsold items in the kitchen. "This is good stuff. Stuff that definitely would have sold at a smaller sale. It's just that here, there was so much of everything people could afford to be picky." She holds up a perfectly good garlic press. "I mean, how many kitchens have four of these, all different styles?"

"I agree. How much garlic does one woman need to crush?"

Ty staggers past carrying an unwieldy box destined for Sister Alice in Newark. "Especially a woman who doesn't even cook."

Ty's being a little harsh. While it's true that since we've been here, we haven't seen Everly Corrigan cook anything other than Easy Mac, no one can expect a woman to churn out gourmet meals when she's in the process of moving halfway across the globe. "I hope Sister Alice knows people who can use what we didn't sell." I hold up a gadget for removing the seeds from pomegranates. "Somehow, I don't think newly arrived refugees and people recently released from prison are going to have a need for this."

"Or this." Donna holds up an apron imprinted with instructions for opening various varieties of oysters.

Through the door leading to the garage, we hear Ty's voice. "So, you're back."

A customer having second thoughts about something he passed up during the day? I poke my head out the door and see Ty talking to Mr. Skinny Man-Bun, the trash-picker from yesterday. I can tell from the look on Ty's face he's having some inner conflict, an uncommon condition for such a decisive man.

"You got kids?" Ty asks the man. He wants to be generous, but I can see there's something about Man-Bun that rubs Ty the wrong way.

"There are children in my community."

"What's that mean?" Ty's voice takes on an edge. "There are children in every community."

I think Man-Bun should watch his step if he hopes to get any freebies from Ty.

The guy holds his hand to his chest. "I have not contributed my DNA to the children who live in our home, but I am still responsible for their welfare."

Ty turns his back. "So that's a long way of sayin' you're their stepdad."

"I'm part of the village required to raise good humans."

If this is meant to be clarification, it falls far short. I can see the molten lava of exasperation rising up in Ty. It's late. We've been working hard all day. The end still isn't in sight.

Ty spins and takes a step closer to Man Bun, dropping a bag of kids' clothes at his feet. My assistant has his patented "you don't want to run into me in a dark alley" look on his face. "Yesterday, you were taking mismatched boots for your kids. If they need clothes that bad, you can have these. But if you're handing me some line of BS...if you're plannin' on selling this stuff at a flea market or on eBay...." The twitch of Ty's head indicates the consequences for betrayal are too horrible to be spoken aloud.

But the guy is not so easily intimidated. He knows damn well Ty has no way to enforce his threat. "You're planning on casting these clothes into the waste stream. I'll keep them on the backs of children, one way or another. Any items children in my community can't use will be shared."

Now Ty is curious despite himself. "Shared how?"

"Shared with anyone who has more of something that we might need. We're freegans. We live beyond the taint of capitalism."

"Say what?"

"We limit our participation in the conventional economy by never buying anything." Man Bun throws back his shoulders and extends his arms. "We forage for all we need."

Ty scratches his head. "Forage? How do you forage for gas for that van of yours?" Ty nods toward the dilapidated van parked at the curb, which definitely looks like it could've been given away for free.

"It's been retro-fitted to burn bio-diesel. We collect discarded cooking oil from fast food restaurants to power it."

Ty squirms and curls his lip—he's got a low bar for revulsion. But he's not giving in.

"What about electricity at your house? I don't see Con Ed bein' down with *foraging* that."

I'm curious too. But Man Bun realizes he's said too much. He wraps his arms around the bulging bag of clothes and heads toward the garage door. "Do you hold sales like this every weekend?" he asks me as he passes. "Does your website have a schedule?"

"Yes." The truthful answer comes out of me automatically even though I'm not enthusiastic about having this guy foraging at all our events.

"Wait," Ty objects as the man staggers down the driveway. "How do you forage for a computer and internet access?"

But our freegan is gone with a wave of his hand.

"I think I've just been had." Ty returns to work with a shake of his head. "Freegans. Now I've heard everything."

"If everyone were a freegan, we'd be out of business," I say with a laugh. "Still, when I see how much totally unnecessary crap the Corrigans own, I think the freegans might be onto something."

"The Corrigans make the freegans possible. If everybody rejected capitalism, there wouldn't be anybody for that guy..." Ty waves at the sputtering van spewing French-fry scented exhaust..." to forage *from*."

I pat Ty's shoulder. "Sounds like somebody was paying attention in economics class."

"Damn straight."

As I load a box of unsold kitchen items into the Another Man's Treasure van, a soft voice behind me calls out, "Hi, Audrey. Remember me?"

I bring my head up, banging it on the roof of the van. "Ow!"

"I'm so sorry! Did y'all hurt yourself?"

Starla.

I back out of our van, and there she is, looking even skinnier and more pathetic than I remembered. The idea of hiring her as a helper for my mother-in-law immediately vacates my mind. Is she even strong enough to heft my sturdy twins all day?

"Hi." She waves her childlike hand. "You didn't call, so I thought I'd drop by...uhm, you know...just in case y'all lost my number."

I choose not to mention that her phone has no answering machine. "Look, Starla—" As I'm about to blow her off, my phone rings with Sean's special ringtone. I hold a finger up. "Excuse me. I have to take this."

Sean starts talking before I even say hello. "Audrey, guess what? I got accepted for the domestic terrorism training program. I'll be away for three days next week. Did you talk to that girl about helping my mom with the kids?"

Chapter 5

At six o'clock, Starla arrives at our house for her interview. Apparently, a friend had given her a ride to the sale, but she comes to the house on a rickety bike. It's close to the twins' bedtime, so we introduce her to the kids before Sean starts his high-intensity interrogation.

"Oh! They're just cuter than Christmas." Starla's face lights up as soon as she sees Thea and Aiden. She drops down next to them on their play blanket and pulls them both onto her lap, cooing and clapping her hands. Thea squirms away, as usual, but Aiden embraces this new friend with enthusiasm. I'm impressed that Starla doesn't push too hard with Thea. She lets my suspicious daughter observe her from the far corner of the blanket. But when Starla breaks into a verse of "There is a Balm in Gilead" in a pure, clear soprano, Thea drops her stuffed lamb and comes closer to listen. Before long, she's in Starla's lap.

Sean's eyes meet mine in approval.

Soon I take the kids off to nurse and go to bed, while Starla stays in the family room with Sean for her interview. As I rock the twins to sleep, I can hear low voices downstairs, but not the words they're saying. My phone is on silent, but I feel it vibrating a few times as I rock. I finally lay Thea in her crib just as I hear Sean saying good-bye and closing the front door.

I trot downstairs without even looking at my phone. "Well?"

"I told her to start on Monday."

My jaw drops as I stare at my husband. "Shouldn't we have discussed this?"

"Sorry, but I didn't want to disturb you and the twins at bedtime. Starla has another interview tomorrow. I didn't want to lose her." Sean waves me onto the sofa. "She seems like a great young woman. She left her town in West Virginia because there's no jobs there. She's only been here two weeks. She doesn't have a car or a phone yet. She's living with an elderly lady in exchange for doing light chores, but she's totally flexible with her time. I explained that she'd be helping my mother, and she's fine with that. Says she likes old folks just as much as babies."

"What about a background check?"

Sean lifts his hands palms up. "She really doesn't have any paper trail. She told me she doesn't have a West Virginia driver's license although she knows how to drive. The DMV was 30 miles from their house, and no one would ever take her for the test. Poor kid. They didn't have internet at home, so she doesn't know a thing about social media. I'll check for an arrest record, but I doubt she has one."

"So that's it?" My voice rises with indignation. "You hired her because she seems like a nice kid? You put Roseline through an investigation worthy of a national security clearance and she had sterling references. We don't know Starla from Adam."

Sean has the good grace to look sheepish. "I admit, I went overboard with Roseline because she was the first non-family person to watch our kids. She turned out to be great, so I'm relaxing a little. The kids really took to Starla, and she'll be here with my mom, so I think we can be more flexible."

"We?"

"I'm going to go talk to the old lady she's living with...Mrs. Karpinski, 34 Clover Lane." Sean lays a reassuring hand on my knee. "We're not turning the kids over to her. You'll be here with her the first few days of next week before she even meets my mother."

My phone vibrates again, and this time I take the call. It's the same number that tried to reach me twice before. Sean watches me with growing curiosity as I listen to the man talking rapidly on the other end of the line. My heart pounds with excitement.

I end the call with my hand shaking.

"What's up?" Sean asks.

"You know that old mansion on the road between Palmyrton and Mendham?"

"The insane asylum? I got called out there a few times when I was a patrolman."

"The Toliver mansion, Villa Aurora, was a private psychiatric clinic, and a girls' school after the Toliver family moved out. Now a developer bought it, and it's going to be remodeled as a wedding venue. And guess who just got asked to bid on holding a sale to empty it out?" I pull Sean into an impromptu dance around the kitchen. "The profits from a sale like this will give us the deposit money we need to put the twins on the Happy Explorers pre-school waiting list. Assuming I clinch the deal."

I have Sean's attention now. He does a spin and a dip to the music playing on our sound system. "That's a lucky break. What do you have to do to clinch the deal?"

I stop dancing and squeeze Sean's hands. "The developer, Alex Agyros, is showing us around on Monday. They want to start the renovations ASAP. The new owner wants to empty the mansion quickly, so he doesn't have to pay for the contents to be hauled away. He also thinks the sale will bring out tons of curiosity seekers, which will be good publicity for his wedding venue plans. Another Man's Treasure is his first choice for the job as long as we can meet his strict timeline."

"How did he hear about you? Through Isabelle?"

My friend Isabelle is Palmyrton's most successful residential real estate agent. She often throws business my way, but I'm not sure if she knows Alex Agyros or not. She's never mentioned him. "Possibly. I didn't ask."

Sean opens his mouth to speak, but I plow right over him, talking faster and faster. "And this sale will be great for my business, too. I can sign up lots of new customers to the Another Man's Treasure newsletter list. And get lots of publicity among real estate brokers by working with Alex Agyros."

Sean scratches his head. "You have to be there in person on Monday?"

"Yes." I put my hands on my hips. "You're going to have to take the morning off to supervise your mom and Starla together. I can't let this job slip away."

I see the indecision pulling him in two directions. He was enthusiastic about Starla because he thought I'd be breaking her in. Now, it's all on him. "Ok-a-a-y. I guess I can take the morning off. Nothing big is happening at work."

Now it's my turn to hesitate. Am I letting my excitement over this job cloud my maternal judgment? "Forget it. I'll call Alex back and tell him I can't take on this job right now."

Sean takes the phone away from me and tosses it on the sofa. With his hands on my shoulders, he looks me in the eye. "No. We're in this together. We'll make this work. Starla's got limitless energy, and she seemed totally open to working with my mom. And my mother will enjoy having a new audience for her pearls of wisdom."

Through the baby monitor, I hear Aiden coo in his sleep. It sounds like he's saying, "La, la, la."

Chapter 6

"I did some research on Villa Aurora yesterday," I tell Ty and Donna as we drive to our potential new project on Monday morning. I left Sean home alone with the kids; Starla and my mother-in-law hadn't shown up yet.

"Why does that not surprise me?" Ty murmurs.

"Don't listen to him, Audrey. I want to hear all about it," Donna assures me.

"The mansion was built over two years, from 1916 to 1918, in the Italianate Revival style. Phineas Toliver built it for his new wife after they took a three-month tour of Europe and fell in love with Italy. By the time they moved in during the summer of 1918, Camille Toliver was seven months pregnant. Phineas hired several maids and cooks and nannies to keep the house running while his delicate young wife prepared to deliver."

Donna chews her thumb. "Why do I have the feeling this doesn't end well?"

I forge ahead with the story. "On September 16, baby Thomas Toliver was born. Unfortunately, the Spanish Flu was racing through New York, New Jersey, and Philadelphia at the time. Two of Toliver's maids got sick and died within days. Then Mrs. Toliver got sick."

"Oh, no! How horrible," Donna gasps.

"It gets worse. The remaining staff fled the house in fear, leaving Phineas to care for his wife and newborn. Camille Toliver died three days after giving birth. Phineas was unable to hire a wet nurse to feed the baby because everyone thought the house was contaminated."

"Wait," Ty interrupts. "What's a wet nurse?"

"In those days, if a new mother couldn't breastfeed her child, a woman who had recently given birth would hire herself out to feed the other woman's child in addition to her own. It was a way for poor women to make a few extra bucks."

"They didn't have formula or bottles in those days?" Ty asks. "I guess I never thought about it—when was all that invented?"

"I wasn't sure myself, so I googled it. Formula that actually met the nutritional needs of human infants wasn't developed until the 1950s. But desperate people had tried to come up with substitutes for mother's milk for centuries. They offered babies cow milk diluted with water and mixed with sugar. They let the babies suck it off a rag or through a cork nipple. They knew nothing about sterilization. Needless to say, only the toughest babies survived that treatment."

"This is really depressing, Audrey," Donna wails.

"Believe me, this story sent chills down my spine. I think it's hard caring for babies in the 21st century. Ha—it's nothing compared to the past. Babies died all the time."

"So little Thomas Toliver didn't survive?" Ty asks.

"No, he died a few days after his mother. Starvation, infection—who knows? Phineas was utterly devastated. He moved out of Villa Aurora—left it with every stick of furniture, all the housewares, all the art. Apparently, he didn't even take his clothes with him when he departed."

"What happened to Phineas?"

"He died in a train crash when he was in his early forties. Left all his money to charity."

"And who bought the house?"

"It was empty for over a decade. People really believed it was a house of death. By the time the legend faded in the public's memory, rich people wanted houses with more modern amenities. Finally, in the late 1930s, the Episcopal Diocese of Palmer County established a school there, Saint Anselm's Academy for Girls."

I drum my fingers on the steering wheel as we stop for a light. "But so far as I can tell, all the original Toliver furniture was included in the sale. So we might find some great old antiques there."

"And a bunch of desks and blackboards?" Ty asks.

"Maybe. It was a school from 1938 to 1967. Then the school closed, and eventually Villa Aurora was repurposed as The Center for Mindful Living."

"And that's when it became a nut house," Ty clarifies.

"They prefer the term "private psychiatric facility specializing in intractable patients."

"What does intractable mean?" Donna asks.

"People so bad nobody else will take 'em."

"I'm afraid you're right, Ty. The Center had a rather sketchy reputation, and it finally closed down when the state department of health launched an investigation. The last patient was moved out four years ago." I make the final turn demanded by the GPS. "Sean says he remembers being called out there when he was a patrolman. Some of the patients were aggressive, and it sounds like the staff wasn't much better."

"Bad jobs attract bad people." Ty stretches his long legs as best he can in the passenger seat of my new SUV. "Whereas good jobs, like workin' for Another Man's Treasure, attract the best people, right Donna?"

"Absolutely!" She presses her nose against the rear passenger window. "Ooo, look—I can see the top of the mansion's tower through the trees."

We all turn expectantly, and as the road bends, there it is: Villa Aurora. The gray stone mansion has a central, four-story tower that looms over the three-story main house. There's a large veranda that wraps around two sides, and a covered portico where guests can pull up in their limousines. Tall windows march across the front of the house, each topped with carved cornices.

"Huh," Ty says. "I've always heard about this place, but I've never been this close before. Just caught glimpses of it from the main road. It's a beast, for sure."

"Kinda romantic and creepy at the same time." Donna jumps out of the car and tilts her head to take in the full expanse of the mansion. "It would definitely be a dramatic setting for a wedding."

Ty stands with his hands on his hips surveying the place. "Meet your prince charming and tie the knot in a castle."

Donna snorts. "Meeting Prince Charming is the hard part."

"Looks like our real estate developer dude hasn't shown up yet." Ty brushes a grasshopper from his pants leg as he wades through the weeds sprouting from the deserted gravel driveway. "Let's look around the back."

Donna and I follow him around the veranda to the wild, sweeping meadow behind the house. We can make out the traces of what once must have been formal gardens—walls and pathways, a crumbling fountain, a row of overgrown hedges, and a gazebo supporting the weight of two cascading pink rosebushes.

"Wow, imagine having this as a backyard to play in," Donna says.

Ty steps closer to the fountain, then jumps back. "Eeew—there's some big ol' frogs hopping in the rainwater there."

"Scaredy cat!" Donna elbows him. "I bet your nephew would get a kick out of trying to catch them."

I bend down to sniff a flower struggling to hold its own against the crush of weeds in the border. "Sad that it's gotten so overgrown. It'll take a ton of work to restore this."

"Fabulous, isn't it?"

The voice causes all three of us to spin around. A tall, handsome man in an open-necked shirt and snappy Ray-Bans waves to us as he approaches. "Alex Agyros," he announces. Glancing between me and Donna, he settles on me. "You must be Audrey Nealon."

I shake the hand he offers and introduce my staff.

Alex's eyebrows shoot up when he hears Donna's last name. "Frascatelli? You're Italian! I'm Greek." He crosses his index and middle fingers. "We're like that, eh? Just switch out the Parmesan for some feta!"

Donna grins. "I love Greek food!"

Alex turns back to me. "And to answer your question, yes, it will take a lot of work to restore this, but by next summer, it will be the premier location in New Jersey for weddings and events, both indoor and outdoor. I've hired a fabulous, up-and-coming landscape architect, and get this—he's the great-grandson of the Italian immigrant who built all these stone walls and walkways for Phineas Toliver. How cool is that!"

Alex barely pauses for our agreement before continuing with his sales pitch. "The landscape architect will be starting the design back here in the next few days. Of course, he can't plant the borders or reseed the lawn until we're done with the trucks and dumpsters needed for the interior demolition." Alex grins at me. "And we can't start that until you hold the sale and empty everything out of the mansion."

"Sounds like Another Man's Treasure is the critical path," I say, glad that he's talking like this is a done deal.

"Indeed, you are." Alex leads us towards the front door. "Let's go inside and see what you're up against, shall we?"

Despite his expensive Italian loafers, Alex steps nimbly through the weeds. He exudes energy and enthusiasm even when he's not talking. Taking a large ring of keys from his messenger bag, he heads for the back door. But he waves us away from following him. "I want you to experience entering through the grand foyer. Go around to the front door. I have to unlock it from inside."

Ty makes a face at the drama, but Donna and I are in for the thrill. By the time we troop around to the front porch, Alex has the grand double doors open, and stands on the threshold to usher us in.

Before us, a grand curving staircase ascends from a wide black and white marble foyer. Even though it's dusty and the wallpaper is peeling, the space's dramatic appeal is undeniable.

"Imagine a bride descending that staircase, her train trailing behind her, her face illuminated by the thousands of crystals in that chandelier." Alex lowers his hand from the staircase to the ground floor. "And her captivated groom and guests wait here below." Alex drops his voice from enthusiastic to reverent.

Donna's mouth drops open.

Ty's eyes roll.

"Yep, lots of potential," I agree before Ty can offer a smart comeback. "But there's nothing to sell here. Show us the rooms where we'll be working."

"Right this way." Alex opens a tall wooden door and leads us into a formal sitting room furnished in elegant, if dusty, antiques. "This parlor has remained unchanged through all the different uses of the house. Mr. Toliver furnished it as a reception room to welcome guests to his home. Unfortunately, he hardly had a chance to use it for that before tragedy struck. When the school took over the house, they used this room to greet parents considering St. Anselm's to educate their daughters. And then when the clinic took over, they used this space to interview the families of prospective patients."

A large oil landscape painting hangs on one wall; the brass plate attached to the frame informs me it's Mt. Vesuvius. I step forward to examine some of the furniture. There's a tall cabinet with a curved front topped with delicate water lily carvings, and some chairs with curved arms and worn velvet upholstery that was once a deep moss green. "It just needs to be cleaned up. We can sell this easily. I know several antique dealers especially interested in Art Nouveau and Traditional Revival."

"I told my partner this furniture was too valuable to toss in the Dumpster." Alex looks gratified that I've validated his position. "It's beautiful, just not right for the vibe we want for a 21st century event venue." He turns toward pocket doors dividing the front parlor from what I assume is the back parlor. "My plan is to remove these doors and make this one large reception space." He opens them and leads us through to a room lined with lovely built-in cabinetry surrounding a beautifully tiled fireplace but furnished with cheap plastic chairs and card tables. "I think the clinic used this room for recreation or occupational therapy or something. The original furniture has been moved out. We might find it in the basement or attic."

I step up to look more closely at the shelves, which are full of board games, art supplies, and sewing and knitting projects. "No worries. We can sell all this."

Donna shivers and I hear her mutter to Ty, "Kinda sad in here. I can imagine the patients filling their days with pointless activities."

She's right. There's something jarring about imagining mentally ill people doing soothing, simple tasks while sitting in an elegant room with high ceilings, parquet floors, and three sets of French doors.

If Alex heard what Donna said, he doesn't acknowledge it. He marches briskly into the hall and leads us to rooms that face the sweeping rear lawn. "Here is the library," he announces at the door of the first room.

"Wow!" Finally, Ty is impressed and willing to show it. Floor-to-ceiling bookshelves, all packed with books, line the paneled walls. Two rolling ladders provide access to the upper shelves, which contain old, leather-bound volumes. But the lower shelves hold dog-eared paperbacks as well as some old textbooks. "This room stayed a library throughout the life of the house," Alex explains, "and we plan to continue the tradition."

"A library for weddings?" Donna enquires.

"We plan to market Villa Aurora as a business event venue as well. This room will be ideal for educational break-out sessions or smaller meetings." Alex points to the upper shelves. "I understand you folks have some knowledge of rare books. If any of those are very valuable, they should be sold, but if they're only worth five or ten bucks a piece, then we'll keep them as decorative pieces. They give the room a nice intellectual atmosphere, don't you think?" He lowers his pointing hand to the paperbacks. "All those should be sold, of course."

Ty leafs through a dusty geography reference book he pulled from a middle shelf. "This is full of out-of-date maps. It shows Ukraine as part of the Soviet Union and refers to Zimbabwe as Rhodesia. It might actually sell as a novelty item. Usually, old textbooks have to be trashed."

"Of course, I realize some of the items in the house will end up in a Dumpster," Alex says. "But we want to limit the amount that has to be hauled away to a landfill, both for financial and environmental reasons."

"Don't you worry." Donna pats his arm. "We'll be able to sell most of this stuff, if for no other reason than people want a little souvenir of this grand old house."

Alex beams at her. "That's what I told my partner! He wanted to haul everything away, but I said we'd be missing a big marketing opportunity if we took that approach. I plan to be here throughout the sale, passing out information on the event venue and answering people's questions."

"Oh, joy," Ty mutters under his breath.

I have to agree that running a sale with the owner hanging around is not optimal, but I don't sense Alex will be a problem. He has no emotional attachment to the items we're selling, and if his partner was willing to haul the house's contents to the dump, presumably Alex won't be arguing with me on pricing strategies. Besides, he's very cute and seems to have taken an interest in Donna. I'd love for Donna to come out of this sale with a date lined up with a handsome, successful businessman.

We quickly move through the other rooms on the first floor: the dining room, where the original banquet table has been supplemented with utilitarian round tables to feed a crowd; the study, maintained as an office; and the kitchen, full of commercial grade equipment. Then Alex invites us to go upstairs.

"Do you want to go around to the main staircase, or can you manage these back stairs?" Alex points to the servants' staircase leading up from the butlers' pantry. "They're very narrow and steep."

"Oh, no problem." Donna heads for the back staircase. "I'm sure we'll go up and down these a million times during the sale."

Alex grabs her elbow. "Let me go first and light the way with my flashlight. I don't want you to stumble."

Ty makes a face at me as we follow behind Donna and her valiant knight.

Upstairs, the house feels darker and decidedly creepier. Alex leads us along a corridor lined with mis-matched doors, some beautiful, paneled wood; some flimsy hollow core. "Each of the original seven bedrooms has been subdivided into two and sometimes three rooms," Alex explains. "This is where the students boarded and where the patients lived. We'll be tearing down these walls." He raps on a plasterboard interior wall. "And restoring the bedrooms to their original grandeur. Especially the master bedroom, which will become the bridal suite."

I peek inside a bedroom: two twin beds with thin mattresses, a scratched dresser, and a battered nightstand. "They're all the same," Alex explains. "Some of them still have old clothes in drawers and closets. I think they vacated the clinic patients on very short notice."

I open a closet door, where a few sad polyester tops hang droopily over a line of stretched out sneakers. No souvenirs of a grand past life here.

We reach the middle of the hall and Alex rubs his hands together. "And now, for the tower!"

Chapter 7

Alex pulls out his keys again and unlocks a sturdy Yale deadbolt. "I think they were very concerned to keep the clinic patients out of the tower," Alex explains. "The views are magnificent," he calls over his shoulder as we follow him up a dizzying spiral staircase. "But the potential for, er, self-harm, is certainly there."

After a climb that leaves all of us, even Ty, huffing, we arrive in an empty, square room lined with windows on all four sides. Sunshine pours in, and I feel like I'm standing in the sky.

"Legend has it that Toliver built the tower so he could come up here and watch the sunrise. Aurora means 'dawn' in Italian," Alex tells us.

"I'd love to be up here for the sunrise." Donna turns in a circle. "Which way is east?"

"This way." Alex guides Donna to the east-facing window. "You can see part of the Manhattan skyline on the horizon."

"Wow! That's amazing!"

"And at night, it's even more spectacular. The area around the mansion is dark, so you can see the stars, and then you see all the lights of civilization in the distance."

Donna looks up at Alex. "What will you do with this room when the venue opens?"

He grins. "I think we'll promote it as a love nest. We'd never get a bed up that spiral staircase, but we could line this floor with big cushions. Imagine making love with the stars and the moon so close you could practically touch them!"

Donna blushes. "Oooo, romantic!"

Ty looks out the west-facing window over the driveway. "It's a long way straight down. Splat. No wonder they wanted to keep the kids and the patients outta here." He turns to face Alex. "So there's nuthin' for us to sell up here. You mentioned attic and basement areas that might contain some of the original furniture?"

Alex snaps his fingers. "Right, right! I'm so captivated by this space, I want to show it to everybody."

"We loved seeing it," Donna says with a sweet smile for Alex. Then she hisses at Ty. "No need to be so rude."

"Just tryin' to keep us on schedule is all."

Alex leads us back to the spiral staircase. "Let's go back down and I'll show you the two attic areas off the third floor."

We pick our way back down the twisting metal staircase and follow Alex back to the servants' staircase on the second floor. "We need to go up to the third floor where the servants' quarters used to be," he explains. Once we're on the dark, low-ceilinged third floor, Alex pulls out the keys again and unlocks a heavy wooden door. We follow him into a dim, unfinished space full of boxes and sheet-draped furniture.

"This space is over the kitchen wing, and there's another space on the other end of the hall over the portico. Things the previous owners couldn't use got pushed in here."

I lift a sheet to reveal a surprisingly nice mahogany dresser with a beautiful, curved mirror. Ty nods his approval of an inlaid drum table. "I guess this furniture was too nice for dorm rooms or patient rooms," he remarks. "I'm surprised they never tried to sell it."

"The school was run by an order of Episcopal nuns overseen by the Diocese of Palmer County. Maybe there was a lot of bureaucracy involved in selling things," I speculate. "Maybe it was just easier to store it."

Alex makes a sweeping gesture. "It's all mine now, and I say, 'sell it all!'"

When we emerge from the attic, I quickly check my phone. Still no messages from Sean or my mother-in-law. No news is good news, I suppose, but I feel anxious about how they're managing with Starla.

While Ty and Donna discuss how they plan to rearrange the furniture so the antiques can be displayed in the best light, I fire off a quick text to Sean.

How's it going?

I spent an hour with Mom and Starla. Got called in to work. Can't talk now.

What?! Sean already left them on their own? Quickly, I text my mother-in-law.

How's it going with Starla? Are you all okay?

Mary answers immediately. *We're grand! This lass is a marvelous worker.*

Hmmm. That's a good report...I guess. I hope Mary isn't making poor Starla mop floors and scrub toilets.

But there's no time for further questions. Alex is ready to lead me down to the basement while Donna and Ty explore the second attic area at the other end of the hall. "Have you been in the real estate business many years?" I ask Alex as we descend the grand staircase, trying to sound chatty but really dying to know where he's getting the money to buy and refurbish this place.

"Oh, yes—I grew up in the business. My father, Constantine Agyros, built five of the largest housing developments in Palmer County in the eighties and nineties. He's retired now, but he's taken a great interest in this project."

Ah, that explains the deep pockets and the confidence. I remember seeing, "Realize your Dreams in a Constantine Home" billboards all around Palmer County when I was a teenager.

"I guess real estate development is in your blood, eh?" I comment as we descend into the depths of the basement.

"Absolutely," he agrees. "My grandfather, my father, and now, me."

A dank, mushroomy smell rises to greet us.

"Hmmm—seems we might have a mold issue down here. Do you have allergies?" Alex asks with concern.

"Oh, I'm immune to all the spores floating around in old houses," I assure him. "Let's see if there's anything valuable down here."

The basement is a vast, gloomy space illuminated by three widely spaced, dangling lightbulbs. Alex pulls out a flashlight to provide light between the dim pools of illumination.

The first thing his beam crosses is a network of sagging metal shelves loaded with industrial-sized cans of vegetables with peeling labels.

"Yuck! All that can go in the Dumpster," Alex says.

The thought of the psychiatric patients eating dreary meals of canned green beans and mashed potatoes makes me shudder. I push the vision out of my mind with a fantasy of happy couples eating wedding banquets in the grand rooms above us. "I suppose you'll be hiring trendy chefs to prepare the food here when you reopen?" I ask Alex as I trail him further into the basement's interior.

"Nothing but the best farm-to-table cuisine," he assures me. "The landscaper will plant an herb garden right here on the property." Then he stumbles against something and lets out a yelp.

His flashlight shines upon a messy clutter of old trunks and leather suitcases. I run my hand over the dusty surface of the nearest one and uncover a name tag inscribed with spidery script: Miss Emmeline Hartnett, 1564 Larch Avenue, Summit, NJ. "These must date back to the days of St. Anselm's Academy. But why would the girls' suitcases still be here? Didn't they take them back when they graduated?"

"Mmmm—no clue. We can dump those too," Alex says.

"Actually, old trunks and vintage luggage have value. I'll have Ty come down here and check through these."

Next, we encounter gardening supplies and a tool bench and then, further on, a pile of old-fashioned classroom desks.

"Can I ask a personal question?" Alex continues talking before I have a chance to respond. "Is your colleague Donna...er...attached?"

"She's divorced." The truth shoots out of me like popcorn in a microwave, and I immediately wish I'd been more discreet. "Uhm, why do you ask?"

"I find her very appealing." Alex grins at me, holding up both hands to ward off my objections. "But I'll wait until our business is concluded to ask her out."

Should I be worried? I've been encouraging Donna to start dating now that her abusive marriage is more than a year behind her. Alex is handsome and successful—a much better catch than the losers circulating on the dating apps. But is he a player?

I'm torn between wanting to protect Donna and wanting her to get back out in the dating scene. She definitely showed Alex more than her usual level of friendliness. I suspect Ty noticed their mutual interest as well. That explains his crankiness. In his eyes, no man will ever be good enough for Donna. Or for his sister, Charmaine.

While my mind chews over the romantic possibilities, my eyes aren't watching where we're going. Alex stops in his tracks, and I plow into him. "Good Lord, what's that?"

His flashlight beam cuts into the far corner of the cobwebbed basement.

A rusty chain and padlock dangle from the bars of a cage big enough to hold a person.

Chapter 8

Alex grabs my elbow and turns me around toward the stairs. "It was probably used as a lockable storage area for valuable items."

"Jeez, I hope you're right. Because the alternative is just too awful to think about."

Once we're upstairs in the bright, utilitarian kitchen, I can see Alex looks as rattled as I feel. "Do you think it's been there from the era of the school or from the clinic?" I muse aloud. "Should we tell someone about it?"

Alex waves this idea away. "What would be the point? Both the school and the clinic have been closed for years. I'll have someone break it up and haul it away."

I realize a scandal surrounding students or patients being locked in the basement of Villa Aurora would cast a pall over Alex's business plan. No one wants to think they're dancing their wedding waltz over some terrified victim's prison cell. And I suppose he's right. The health department closed the clinic down for a reason, so they must be aware of what went on here.

At that moment, Ty and Donna join us in the kitchen. "Anything good in the basement?" Ty makes a move toward the basement steps.

"Nothing much down there." Alex smiles brightly. "So, what do you think? How soon can you start the sale?"

I'd prefer to discuss this with my staff in private, but the truth is, we only have two options—the weekend after this coming weekend, or two weeks after that—since we have sales booked for the intervening weeks. And I already know that Alex won't want to wait that long. "What do you think, team? Can we pull it together for the weekend of the twentieth?"

Ty purses his lips. "We'll need some extra help to be ready that fast. I'll see if Charmaine can work the days of the sale, but I could also use a pair of strong hands to help move some of that heavy furniture outta the attic."

"Eight hours for two days at $15 an hour would be two hundred forty dollars out of our bottom line." I do the mental math aloud, so Alex realizes his demands are costing me.

"Deduct that from my share of the profits," he says, reaching for my hand to shake. "I have total faith in Another Man's Treasure to pull this off." After Alex shakes my hand, he pumps Ty's hand vigorously and gives Donna a lingering hand-squeeze and a wink.

"I'll have the house opened up for you first thing tomorrow morning," Alex assures me. "Of course, I have other business to attend to, but I'll be popping in an out throughout the week to check on your progress."

Ty is smart enough to turn his head so Alex doesn't notice his pained expression, but Donna looks delighted. We all leave the house together, and it's not until Donna and Ty are in my car that we can talk candidly.

I turn off the radio and start down the long driveway. "What do you think?"

"There's some good stuff in those attics," Ty says. "Furniture, statues, paintings. And you know people gonna turn out for this sale just so they can get a look at Villa Aurora."

"And we don't even have to clean up after the sale," Donna adds. "We sell what we can, and Alex's workers put everything else in the Dumpster on the Monday after."

They make this job sound like a no-brainer. My hands clench the steering wheel and I stare straight ahead.

"Why you worried, Audge?"

I glance sideways at Ty. "This job will be a huge amount of work for the three of us. If we screw it up, our mistakes will be very visible. Alex Agyros is a prominent figure in New Jersey real estate. Working for someone famous in a famous location can bring us great publicity...or terrible public humiliation."

Ty snorts. "We ain't about to be humiliated. Not on my watch."

"We can do it, Audrey," Donna pipes from the back seat. "Why are you doubting us? That's not like you."

"I'm not doubting you. I guess I'm doubting myself. Now that I'm a mother, I can't just forget my personal life and work all night."

"Who said anything 'bout workin' all night?" Ty rears his head in dismay. "The good thing about this job is all the items are large. We're not going to be screwin' around pricin' every little doll and flowerpot and knick-knack like we were at the Corrigan sale."

As always, Ty cheers me up. His hatred of knick-knacks is legendary. "I suppose you're right..."

He thumbs his chest. "I know I'm right. Once we drag all the good stuff outta the attics, you can take pictures of it and research the prices from home. You won't have to be onsite every day."

"I can't leave all this work for you and Donna. I'll be at Villa Aurora every day...as long as this babysitting deal with Starla and my mother-in-law holds up." Before pulling out onto the main road, I check my phone again. Still no messages from Mary. Does that mean things are going well? Or is she so furious she can't express her rage via text?

After dropping off Ty and Donna at the office, I arrive home at 5:15, which is usually melt-down time for the twins. But I enter the back door to total silence. My antennae rise in alarm, but soon I hear the low murmur of voices in the kitchen.

Aiden and Thea are swinging in their swings, each absorbed with a toy, while my mother-in-law and Starla sit at the kitchen table playing cards. There's a basket of folded laundry waiting to go upstairs and a pot of something wonderful-smelling bubbling on the stove.

Mary catches sight of me standing in stunned silence in the doorway. "Well, there's our Audrey! How was your workday, love?"

"Fine, I guess." I sit down at the table with them. "Er, there's good news and bad news. We landed a big, profitable new job. But it's a rush, so I'll have to work on-site at the house every day between now and a week from Thursday, then a three-day sale over the weekend."

Starla perks up like Ethel when a steak comes off the barbeque. "I can work all those days, no problem. And Mrs. Coughlin is so nice." Starla beams at Mary. "She taught me the right way to make real Irish tea."

"And Starla taught me a few new tricks in gin rummy." Mary taps Starla's hand. "We're havin' a grand time here, aren't we pet?"

Starla offers her endearing gap-toothed smile and bobs her head in agreement.

Love? Pet? What's going on here? I know my mother-in-law well enough to know she never gushes to be polite. Indeed, she rarely gushes at all, so Starla clearly has impressed her. I glance from the young woman to the old. "So

Starla, you're willing to come back and help Mary with the twins every day this week and next?"

"Oh, yes, ma'am. I would purely love that."

We agree on a time for tomorrow, and Starla politely declines Mary's offer of a ride home but accepts a container of stew from the pot on the stove. Mary and I stand side-by-side at the kitchen window and watch as Starla hops on her rickety bike and pedals off.

"She's a hard worker, Audrey." My mother-in-law turns toward the stove. "She did that laundry of her own accord and chopped all the vegetables for the stew." Mary raises the lid on the pot, and a scent much better than that emitted by her usual bland Irish stew rises into the air. "The girl convinced me to add some garlic and bay leaf and some other spice she found in your cabinet. Said she learned about herbs from her great-aunt." Mary scrunches her face as she tastes the results. "Hmm. Not bad."

Mary is accepting cooking advice from a twenty-year-old West Virginia girl? What solar system have I been transported to?

The twins have finally noticed I'm home, and I sit with them on my lap as Mary continues to bustle around the kitchen talking to me. "Starla had a hard life growing up, I think, but she doesn't complain. Skinny as she is, she ate like a sailor at lunch. That's why I sent her home with some stew. I don't think she gets enough to eat."

I let this remark pass. Mary doesn't think any of her sons gets enough to eat either. "You like working with her? She's not getting on your nerves?"

Mary dismisses this with a wave of her hand as if she can't imagine where I came up with such an idea. "No, she's good company. And she does all the heavy lifting with the bairns." Mary gathers up her purse and her knitting, pausing to caress Aiden's golden red curls. "I'm happy to keep working with her this week. But honestly, I think Starla can manage just fine on her own. She's great with the wee ones. Sings them songs and plays with them. Never a cross word."

"La!" Thea shouts.

"That's right, you enjoyed playing with La-La today, didn't you, pet?" Mary kisses her grand-daughter's forehead.

This week? I contemplate my mother-in-law's sturdy back. Is she trying to back away from long-term babysitting? "Did you have something planned for the week after next?"

"Ach, it's nothing. A bus trip to Pennsylvania Dutch Country that Joe and I signed up for when we thought you were all set with Roseline. But we don't have to go."

Now I feel guilty. They rarely travel anywhere. "We don't want you to cancel your plans for us. But do you really think Starla would be okay on her own? We hardly know the girl."

Mary squeezes my arm. "Give me a few more days with Starla and I'll find out all there is to know. And you can go off to work at your sale, no worries."

Chapter 9

"You're here early." Donna drops her purse on her desk at 8:15 and looks at me with googly eyes.

Since the birth of the twins, I'm usually the last person to arrive in the morning, staggering in with excuses about diaper explosions and lost blankies that slowed my exit from home. "I sailed out the door this morning. Starla showed up early and kept the kids distracted while I left."

"So she's working out?" Donna rolls her chair closer to my desk for a chat.

"I'm astonished, but Starla and my mother-in-law are getting along like two Labradors at the dog park. Mary thinks Starla is a hard worker, and Starla told me this morning she's learning a lot from Mary."

Donna wrinkles her brow. She's met my mother-in-law. "Like what?"

"Yesterday they covered how to brew a perfect pot of Barry's Irish Breakfast tea and how one should never buy cheap, store-brand tea bags. I believe they also covered stain removal techniques and silverware drawer reorganization. But on the plus side, Starla slipped some wicked good herbs into Mary's Irish stew. Delicious!"

"They're working together again today?"

"Yep, I'm totally covered for this entire week." I rub my hands together. "As soon as Ty gets here, we'll head over to Villa Aurora and get to work pricing."

"Have you heard from Alex?" Donna busies herself with sorting the mail as she asks.

"In fact, I have. Why? Are you hoping he'll be there when we arrive?" I narrow my eyes. "Those are awfully nice jeans and boots for a workday."

Donna blushes and her eyes dart toward a stuffed tote bag beside her desk. I march over and peer inside. "You little schemer! You brought trash clothes to change into after he leaves."

Donna tosses her hair. "It doesn't hurt for Another Man's Treasure to make a good impression on our first day on the job."

"I think Alex is handsome and nice and successful. And he's definitely interested in you. Have you googled him?"

"Audrey!" Donna does her best to act shocked.

"Oh come on, everyone googles people they're interested in these days. What did you discover?"

"He graduated from Boston University in 2001, which makes him 43. He's divorced. One son who's five."

"Perfect! If he were 43 and never married, there would be something wrong with him. How long has he been divorced?"

"I couldn't tell. I found one picture of him and his ex at some kind of fancy fundraiser four years ago." Donna hesitates. "She was just okay-looking." Clapping her hand over her mouth, Donna squeals, "OMG! That was so mean! I can't believe I said that!"

I laugh and toss an eraser at her head. "Donna, your concept of mean is radically different from everyone else's on the planet. Except maybe Mother Teresa. I'm confident you're sexier than Alex's ex, and there's nothing wrong with that."

"Who sexy?" Ty demands as he strides through the door.

The two of us giggle like middle-schoolers. "Never mind."

Ty scowls, well aware he's being left out of something. "Listen up, y'all. I got my man Lamar comin' to help move furniture from noon to five today and all day tomorrow. So let's get over to Villa Aurora and figure out what's goin' where."

"Okay, I'll be ready in a minute." Donna swivels to face her computer. "Let me send this email announcing the sale to our newsletter list."

"Alex said he'd meet us there at nine to open up," I tell Ty. "We'll leave here in twenty minutes."

Ty fixes himself a cup of coffee at our office machine. "We gonna hafta wait for that dude every morning? Can't he give you the key?"

"I'll make an access plan with him today," I assure Ty. "Who's Lamar? Have I met him?"

"He played football for Palmyrton High back in the day. Got a scholarship to a D3 school and tore up his knee. Keeps sayin' he's gonna play for the European League." Ty taps his temple. "He's livin' in fantasyland, but he's strong as an ox. And he needs some scratch. I told him you'd pay cash."

"Sure. No worries."

Ty sits down with his coffee and keeps chatting. "I talked to my grams about Villa Aurora. She said she knows a lady at church who used to work in the kitchen there when it was the psychiatric clinic." Ty stretches out his long legs. "Grams said her friend hated that job. The food she had to prepare was horrible. Only stayed 'cause she needed the work." Ty takes a final swig of coffee. "Now she cooks in the cafeteria at the Bumford-Stanley School. Says the food's a lot better, but the people are just as crazy."

I laugh at the thought of Grandma Betty's friend trading a job serving mentally ill patients and their families for a job serving privileged prep school kids and their families and feeling the only improvement is better quality ingredients. Thinking about the cage in the basement, I enquire, "Did the friend have any inside info about why the clinic was shut down?"

"Grams didn't say. I'll tell her to ask her friend at church on Sunday."

"Okay, I'm ready," Donna announces. "Let's get this sale started."

Chapter 10

With Ty driving the AMT van, Donna and I are free to gawk at the view of Villa Aurora as it gradually becomes visible through the trees. First the tower appears, then the sunlight sparkles off the second story windows, and finally the grand double door and portico face us as the van lumbers up the long, twisting driveway.

"Think how gorgeous it will look at night with every window glowing," Donna gushes.

While Donna fantasizes about how Villa Aurora will look to arriving party guests, I'm wondering how mental patients felt rolling up to this big, gray fortress of a house. And what about little girls being sent to boarding school here? Were they excited or anxious?

Donna rattles on happily. "And maybe Alex will string fairy lights through the trees. Wouldn't that be a pretty touch?"

"I bet if you make the suggestion, he'll hop right on it," Ty says.

Donna thumps his shoulder from the backseat. "Why are you being so mean about Alex? He's a nice man."

"Maybe he's nice, but he's not very punctual." Ty frowns at the parking area. "It's past nine, and he's still not here."

We tumble out of the van, and by the time we get our supplies unloaded, Alex waves to us cheerily from inside the huge double front door.

"See, he was here all along," Donna mutters to Ty. "He must've parked in the back."

Ty ignores her and marches up the wide front steps. "Morning." He peers over Alex's shoulder. "Mind if I head straight up to the attic? I gotta helper coming at noon and I want to be ready for him."

"Sure. I unlocked both attic doors."

"C'mon, Donna." Ty waves her forward.

"Good morning, Alex." Donna offers her best smile. "Don't mind Ty. He's eager to get his hands on those antiques!"

"Well, I can't see what we've got to work with unless you help me move some stuff out into the hall." Ty points to Donna's feet. "What're you wearing those shoes for? You're likely to break your neck with all these steps."

"I'm fine," Donna nudges Ty forward, and the two of them make the climb up the curving staircase.

Alex stands silently watching Donna's ass disappear overhead.

"The house key?" I prompt him.

He snaps to attention. "Right. Right." Alex pats his pockets. "I have it here somewhere."

Finally, he produces a newly cut, shiny key and hands it over. "This opens the back door leading into the utility room behind the kitchen. Let's keep the big front doors locked until the days of the sale. They can only be unlocked from inside. I've unlocked the two attic spaces for you, but not the Tower since there's nothing up there."

I accept the key and put it in my pocket. Then Alex reviews the contract I've prepared for him and signs it with a flourish.

"Bye, Audrey. I'll stop back to check on you later in the week. Don't hesitate to call if you need anything." He heads for the back door but stops when he's halfway across the foyer. "And don't work Donna too hard."

After Alex leaves, I head into the grand front parlor to assess the furniture there. Soon I'm absorbed in my work, taking photos, evaluating damage to the finish of some of the pieces, and checking to see if drawers and cabinet doors work. I've got my head deep inside an etagere when I hear voices coming from the foyer.

That's not Ty. It sounds like Alex, but he left fifteen minutes ago. I get up from my hands and knees in time to see Alex following a tall, fierce-looking older man into the parlor.

"Sorry to disturb you, Audrey." Alex seems flustered. "This is my father. He's curious to see how things are going."

"Constantine Agyros." The older man extends his hand for me to shake. As I'm announcing my name, I have the sensation I've met this man before. But where?

"Nice to meet you." He acknowledges my greeting, but immediately turns his attention to the etagere, running his hand over the surface. "You think this is worth something?" With an attitude that goes well beyond parental curiosity, his dark eyes challenge me to make a case for this art deco antique.

I launch into a mini lecture of the attributes of art deco furniture, pointing out the inlaid wood finish and the shiny, geometric drawer pulls. "It's a nice piece," I conclude. "I think I can sell it for three thousand dollars."

Constantine spins to face his son. "See, that's a classy piece of furniture. Not like the junk they sell nowadays. Why get rid of it? You should use it in this room."

Alex's cheerful expression darkens. "We discussed this, Dad." He speaks through a clenched jaw. "That's not our vision for the venue. Today's young couples—"

Constantine stalks further into the room, dismissing his son with a flap of his hand. "Vision, schmision. Good taste never goes out of style, right Audrey?"

Whoa, boy—I'm not getting pulled into this father-son squabble. "I don't know anything about decorating a wedding venue. I had a very small, casual wedding."

Now Constantine is studying one of the paintings on the wall. Seeing him in profile, something clicks in my memory. He was the tall gentleman at the Corrigan sale who hung around watching the sale but didn't buy anything. Alex's father was scoping me out before his son hired me! I wonder if Alex sent him, or if Constantine took on the project himself.

Alex shifts impatiently from foot to foot as his father makes a circuit of the parlor. I go back to making notes about the antiques that surround us although having both Agyros men watching me work makes me feel like an exotic animal at the zoo. Finally, Alex can no longer restrain himself. "C'mon, Dad—let's get out of Audrey's way. She has a lot of work to do."

Constantine acts like he didn't even hear this plea. He points to one of the Italian landscape paintings that Phineas Toliver brought back from his European tour. "Is this by a famous artist?" he asks me.

"The artist's name is Enrico Porfiri. The painting isn't museum quality, but I know some collectors who might be interested."

"You hear that?" Constantine raises his voice and turns on his son. "Your stupid partner wanted to toss this in the Dumpster like it was shlock from Walmart! What kinda fool does that? Yet you trust this guy, cave into him at every turn." Constantine gazes up to the heavens at the lunacy of Alex's partner. "Good thing I got you to hire this girl." He juts his chin at me. "She'll get you some cash to put toward your bottom line. You don't know what your margins are going to be."

I'm starting to feel sorry for Alex and not just because I don't appreciate being referred to as "this girl."

"That's enough!" Alex raises his voice to match his father's. "I've run the numbers on this project, and we're on solid ground. I'm done discussing it with you." He checks his gold watch. "I have a meeting to get to. Your car is blocking me in the driveway. Let's go." Alex holds the parlor door open until his father reluctantly passes through. Then he looks back over his shoulder at me. "Sorry you got pulled into that."

I lift my hand in reassurance. "No worries. Parents always think they know best."

Alex glances into the foyer to make sure his father is out of earshot. "Dad retired so he and Mom could spend a few months every year in Greece. But he's having trouble totally letting go of the business. I let him have a little input to keep him busy while he's in New Jersey, and he ends up trying to micromanage the whole project."

Before I can reply, I hear Constantine shouting, "I thought you were in a big hurry," and Alex trots off.

I can't help smiling as I return to my work. I've had my disagreements with my own father, who strongly disapproved of my decision to go into the estate sale business instead of choosing a career related to his field, mathematics. But over the past few years, Dad has come to trust my judgment, and I've grown less resistant to his advice. I hope Alex and his father can learn to strike the same balance.

The morning passes quickly. Once Donna and Ty move some of the smaller furniture out of the attic, I'm able to get in and take photos of the larger pieces. I start researching prices for the best quality furniture and let Ty and Donna handle pricing on the more run-of-the-mill pieces. We agree that the best furniture needs to come down to the main level so it can be displayed to the greatest advantage. "Besides" Ty adds. "We don't want people way up here in these little attic rooms. There'll be no way to keep an eye on them during the sale."

"Will you and Lamar be able to move all this?" I ask, surveying the chairs, dressers, and tables that must be relocated.

"Don't worry 'bout it. Lamar be able to carry half this stuff single-handed."

At noon, Ty's phone chirps announcing Lamar's arrival outside. A few minutes later, he reappears upstairs with his friend. Ty makes the introductions while I struggle to act like I'm meeting any average person. Ty is 6' 1, and Lamar is easily four inches taller and three times as broad. His neck is thicker than my thigh. Ty's muscular biceps look like Barbie's spindly appendages in comparison to Lamar's massive upper arms. He fills the narrow attic hallway from wall to wall.

Gingerly, I extend my hand to shake, but I needn't have worried. The big man is surprisingly gentle, his voice calm and low. "Hi, Miss Audrey. I've heard so many good things about you from Ty. I'm real happy to have this chance to work with you."

"We're grateful you were available on short notice. Ty will show you what to do. Donna and I are going to work in the library for a while to stay out of your way."

Donna and I have been sorting and pricing books for a while when we hear voices in the hall. I stick my head out the library door in time to see Lamar descending the stairs carrying a sizeable mahogany desk as if it were a flimsy item from Ikea. "Wow," Donna murmurs in my ear. "If I'd have been carrying that with Ty, I would have had to stop and rest three times."

"I think Lamar is going to be a godsend on this job," I agree.

At five, we all meet in the kitchen to review our progress and make plans for tomorrow. Ty and Lamar will spend another full day in the attic, while Donna focuses on the dining room and I sort through the paintings and other artwork.

"What about the basement?" Donna rattles the locked door.

"Oh, geez—I forgot to ask Alex to unlock that for us."

Ty takes a long draw from his Gatorade. "I thought he said there was nothing worth selling down there?"

"Those suitcases and trunks have value," I say. "Also the tools and gardening equipment. Alex says he wants as much sold as possible. But I don't know if he plans to come back here before the sale. I hate to ask him to make a special trip."

Lamar sizes up the old lock on the basement door. "You wanna go down there? I get you in."

Ty lays a hand on the big man's arm. "Don't go bustin' anything up."

"What kinda fool you take me for?"

While Lamar searches through a few kitchen drawers, my gaze locks with Ty's. How does Lamar know how to open locked doors?

Ty arches his eyebrows and grins when Lamar returns with a thin skewer and a flat spatula. He sets to work on the lock, and within two minutes we hear a click and a creak, and the door swings open. Lamar steps back with a grin and ushers us across the threshold.

Who am I to complain? I follow him down the basement stairs.

"Let's bring a few of the suitcases and trunks upstairs," I tell Lamar and Ty as we stumble through the dimly lit basement toward the pile of luggage. "It was too dark down there for me to tell if they were any good."

"This here, Miss Audrey?" Lamar hoists a stack of five suitcases, while Ty lifts a trunk and Donna and I each take two suitcases by their handles. We bring them up into the bright light of the kitchen.

"Ooo! Some of these are cute," Donna says, assessing a square, cream-colored suitcase with navy blue leather trim. "We can definitely sell this."

Lamar's expansive brow furrows. "Really? 'Cause I've seen better suitcases than that at Walmart."

All three of us laugh. "People won't buy these for traveling," I explain. "They're popular as decorative pieces."

Lamar still looks dubious.

"Suitcases like these are all the rage on Vintage TikTok and Instagram," Donna says. "Let's carry these three out to the dining room where I can get a good background and I'll put up a post right now."

Lamar carries the suitcases as directed, and we all follow Donna to watch her impromptu photo shoot. "Donna's our social media expert," I tell Lamar.

"Instagram...TikTok." Lamar wags his head. "I don't do none of that nonsense."

"I used to think it was nonsense," Ty agrees, "until one of her posts brought in two ladies who fought each other over old half-empty perfume bottles that I was sure were headed to the dump. We let them bid against each other and cleared five hundred bucks."

Donna smiles at the memory as she fusses with arranging and rearranging the suitcases for each photo. "That's why our motto is..."

We all finish in unison "...you never know what will sell!"

Donna clicks the camera on her phone a few more times. Then her fingers fly across the screen as she writes a clever description. I used to ask to approve these social media posts, but now I trust her totally. She knows what attracts interest and brings in customers.

"Okay—all posted." Donna looks around at the dining room. "Should we set up the luggage in here, or move it somewhere else?"

"We can set up some of the smaller bags on these round tables...until we sell the tables," Ty offers.

While Lamar and Ty bring up the rest of the suitcases and trunks, Donna and I display the best ones. "I still don't understand why the suitcases were left here," I say as I examine the faded name tags and chipped monograms on the bags. Something shifts as I move one small leather suitcase. "This one has something in it." I flip open the latch and a musty smell arises from the satin-lined interior. "Look—a bundle of letters."

Chapter 11

"Audrey, what's wrong?" Sean extends his arm across our bed and pulls me closer. "You've been thrashing back and forth for half-an-hour."

"I'm sorry. I don't mean to keep you up." I burrow into his side. "It's those letters. I can't get that poor little girl out of my mind."

Donna and I had glanced at the letters while we were at Villa Aurora, but the spidery handwriting was hard to read, and we had work to do. So I stuffed them in my tote bag and brought them home, where I forgot about them in the excitement of seeing the twins after a long day of separation and marveling that Starla and Mary had another successful day of co-nannying.

But after dinner and putting the twins to sleep, I pulled the letters out of my bag. My mistake was reading them right before my bedtime.

"They're pathetic, for sure." Sean strokes my cheek. "But that little girl is an old woman by now. She either recovered from her experience at St. Anselm's or she didn't. There's nothing you can do for her."

I flip on my back and stare at the ceiling. Of course, Sean is right, but his logic doesn't stop the churning in my brain. "I can't stop imagining Thea shipped off to a boarding school when she's just a child...writing letters home about how miserable she is. Can you fathom reading a letter like that from your daughter...a letter that says she's not getting enough to eat... and ignoring it? Tossing it away like it was junk mail selling you replacement windows? Or worse, responding and telling her to buck up, buttercup?"

"Audrey, your imagination is too vivid. We're not shipping our kids off to boarding school at any age." Sean rolls over and pulls up the covers. "Get some sleep. You have a busy day tomorrow."

Soon my husband is softly snoring, but I'm still agonizing over the letters I found in little Emmeline's suitcase. They call to me like a mournful loon wailing from a dark lake. Slipping out of bed, I go downstairs to look at the bundle again.

There are five letters in identical, heavy cream envelopes with a crest printed in the upper left corner. Slanted, swooping handwriting takes up half the front of each envelope, addressing the letter to Miss Emmeline Hartnett, St. Anselm's Academy.

I open the one I found most disturbing and re-read it.

Dear Emmeline,

Your father and I were deeply disappointed to receive your last letter. Your behavior is not becoming to a young lady of your fortunate position. Your lack of gratitude for the fine education you are receiving shocks us deeply. Since reading your missives is so upsetting to us, we will no longer open any letters from you, nor will we come to St. Anselm's on visitation day.

If your behavior improves and we receive good reports from the head-mistress, you may be permitted to visit us at Christmastime. However, if this baseless complaining continues, you will not return home until the end of the school year.

Sincerely,

Mother and Father

My hands shake as I drop the expensive letterhead on my kitchen table. The tone of the letter makes it seem like Emmeline is a teenage delinquent with a long string of screw-ups. But having read the other letters, I know that Emmeline is nine years old.

Nine.

Who even sends a kid away to boarding school at age nine?

Sean says that standards among wealthy parents in the 1950s were different from what we expect today, and he's probably right, but when your daughter writes to you and tells you she's hungry every day, do you ignore that? Call her a whiner?

What kind of monstrous parents are these?

But the most heartbreaking letter is one that was never mailed. Unlike the others, the small, plain white envelope hasn't been slit at the top. Instead, the glue has disintegrated over time and the flap is open. It's addressed to Mr. and Mrs. Curtis Hartnett in neat but childish handwriting.

I slide out the single sheet of cheap, ruled paper and read the child's note again.

Dear Mama and Papa,

I am trying so hard to be good and to do all my asinemants exactly right. But this morning Sister Esther said I was wispering during morning prayers, but

I wasn't. She must have herd some other girl. My punishmant was to have no breakfast, not even water. During read aloud time, my mouth and throte were so dry, I couldn't speak clear and Sister Esther got mad and told me I would have to sit alone in the classroom wile the others went to lunch. That is where I am writing this letter. I feel dizzy. The words I am writing are moving on the page. I am worried I will not do a good job in my classes this afternoon. I don't know what to do. I am trying so hard, but I keep making mistakes.

I am sorry for being such a trubblesome girl.

Regretfully,

Emmeline

The first time I read this letter, I cried. But this time, I'm angry. How dare that school treat a child this way? Depriving her of food and water is barbaric, no matter what the era. And then making her feel she was to blame for her own abuse!

How could poor little Emmeline endure seven more years of torture at that school? Did she graduate or escape? Did her parents come to their senses? Did a more compassionate school administrator take over?

I'll never fall back asleep unless I make stab at trying to find out what happened to her.

If Emmeline was nine in 1952, she'd be eighty today. She could still be alive, or she could be long dead. I google "Emmeline Hartnett New Jersey" and tense, waiting for an obituary to pop up.

But instead, the first article to appear is from a local newspaper, dated six years ago. The headline reads, "Retired Summit Librarian Honored for Work Promoting Literacy." A petite, silver-haired woman is pictured accepting a framed award certificate. She looks lively, but she could certainly be approaching eighty.

The lump of pity that's been choking me dissolves a little. If this is my Emmeline, she seems to have survived her stint at St. Anselm's. I carry my laptop to the family room sofa and settle back to read. The article explains how Miss Hartnett worked as a children's librarian at the Summit Public Library for forty years, then continued to volunteer as a tutor for children who struggled with reading. It lists her many accomplishments and ends with a quote from Emmeline herself. "I struggled with reading as a child. No one knew anything about dyslexia or other reading disabilities in the 1950s when

I was in elementary school. My teachers thought I was dumb or uncooperative. When I was fifteen, I met a teacher who unlocked the mystery and the beauty of reading for me. She changed my life. For the rest of my career, I tried to be a life-changer for other children."

Wow! She suffered until she was fifteen before someone finally helped her. Imagine enduring all that trauma and being strong enough to use your suffering to help others.

I close my laptop knowing I'll be able to sleep now.

And I know something else. As long as Miss Hartnett hasn't died in the six years since that article was written, I'm going to find her and return her suitcase to her.

Chapter 12

I sit in front of Aiden and Thea shoveling rice cereal into their little bird mouths. Sean brings me a plate of whole wheat toast and a mug of coffee, and I speak without looking away from my task. "Did you ever talk to that old lady that Starla lives with?"

"I stopped by yesterday on my way home from work and rang the bell, but no one answered." Sean intercepts Aiden's cereal-encrusted hand before the baby has a chance to rub it into his hair. "I can try again today if you want me to. But I figured it didn't really matter since Starla and my mom are getting along so well."

I decide that the early morning rush is not the best time to launch into a discussion of his parents' travel plans. I'll see what intel Mary can wrangle out of Starla today, and I'll talk over with Sean the possibility of Starla flying solo after dinner tonight. "I think it couldn't hurt to find out the old gal's impressions just in case Starla ever has to watch the kids on her own."

Sean agrees just as Starla shows up at the door. The morning is drizzly and the poor kid's jeans are soaked from her bike ride over here. "I could come and pick you up on rainy days," Sean offers.

"Oh, no—I'm fine." Starla immediately starts bustling around the kitchen cleaning up our morning mess while playing peek-a-boo with the twins.

"Do you have a lot of chores to do for Mrs. Karpinski?" I ask her.

"Nah. She's got a cleaning lady and a guy who mows the grass. I just unload the dishwasher and get things down from high shelves." Starla opens cabinets and puts away our breakfast food. She already seems to know where everything belongs.

"Is she nice?" I persist.

"She surely is. Just a little hard of hearing." Starla tugs at her ear and grins. "I hafta shout at her. My voice is all wore out by the time I go to bed."

I glance at Sean. That might explain why the old gal didn't answer the door yesterday.

Starla lifts Aiden from his highchair. "Hoo-ee! Someone's pretty stinky!" And she takes him off to do the dirty work.

I could get used to this. Once again, it looks like I'll be early for work.

***

AT VILLA AURORA, WORK has kicked into high gear. We need to get all the antiques organized today because on Friday, Donna and Ty will move over to prepping the small sale we'd previously booked for this weekend. Meanwhile, I'll finish pricing and start sending out photos to collectors on our customer list. Next week, we'll tackle all the utilitarian items left behind by the school and the clinic.

"Do you think Alex wants us to sell these lighting sconces?" Donna asks me as she examines how the glass-globed lights are attached to the dining room wall. "If he wants them sold, we might need help taking them down."

"I'll text Alex and ask him." We move on to some other work.

The text goes unanswered for so long that I've almost forgotten about it. Then my phone rings with a call from Alex.

I answer and immediately start asking about the light fixtures.

"Yeah—do whatever you think is best." His voice sounds hoarse and shaky.

"Is something wrong?" I ask.

"Yes. That's why I called. I-I've had some bad news. Terrible news. My father died last night."

"Oh, no! I'm so sorry for your loss."

Donna stops working and watches me.

"Had your dad been ill?" I continue, although the old man certainly looked fine when I met him.

"Not at all—he was in perfect health. That's why I'm so shocked. My mom was out with her bridge group last night. When she got home at 9:30 dad was already asleep, which was a little unusual. She got into bed beside him and when she woke up this morning, he was—" Alex's voice chokes with a sob.

I'm not sure how to respond. I don't know Alex that well, and my entire experience of him has been cheerful and upbeat. "Is there anything I can do to help?" I ask. Because that's what everyone asks in these situations even if they can't possibly help. But as the words leave my mouth, I wonder if Alex will want to postpone the sale.

"No, no, thank you. Just carry on. But I won't be stopping by Villa Aurora this week as I planned. I wanted to let you know you're on your own."

"No problem," I assure him. "Are we proceeding with the sale? Did you want me to postpone it?"

"No. Absolutely not. Carry on." And he hangs up.

The news of Constantine Agyros's death sends Donna into a tizzy. "Will there be a viewing? When do you think it will be? Should I go? Will you go with me?"

"I don't know, Donna. I told you every word of our conversation. I'm sure there will be an obituary with services listed soon."

"I want to offer him my condolences." Donna paces, wringing her microfiber dust cloth. "But I can't call him. I don't know him well enough for that. And he's busy. I'll send him a card. Do we know his home address? Or should I send it to his office? But he probably won't be going in to work this week, so—"

"Audge? Hey, Audge! C'mere a minute."

Ty and Lamar have been moving furniture, and Ty's call is a welcome distraction from Donna's agonizing.

I follow Ty's voice into the dining room where he and Lamar stand contemplating the items they moved in here yesterday.

"Did you move any of this stuff?" Ty asks me.

"No. This is the first time I came into this room today."

Ty and Lamar exchange a glance. "We know we put that desk there," Ty points, "in front of that table with the suitcases. And now, it's over there, under the window."

"You're sure you didn't move it later?"

"Positive." Ty speaks with authority. "And there's drag marks on the floor. We don't drag. We lift and carry."

I know that's true. An estate sale organizer only has to break a leg off a piece of furniture once to learn that dragging is never a good idea.

Lamar shifts his huge body uneasily. "You think this place is haunted?"

I laugh at the idea of the big man being afraid of ghosts. But a flesh and blood thief is no joking matter. "Is anything missing?"

Ty shrugs. "All the big furniture is here. But I don't remember how many suitcases we brought up from the basement."

Donna wanders in from the kitchen to see what's going on. When Ty explains, she pulls out her phone. "I took pictures in here to post on Instagram, remember? Let's compare the pictures with how the room looks now."

We all crowd around her. The desk must've been moved to provide easier access to the suitcases. The suitcases are now stacked in a different order than they were in the photos, but when we count and compare, all the suitcases are still here.

"Freaky," Donna says.

"Why break into this fancy house just to look over those suitcases?" Lamar asks. "And then he didn't even steal none of 'em."

"Unl-e-s-ss…" Donna's gaze meets mine.

"He wanted something from inside the suitcases. Like those letters we found. I took them home with me because I wanted to read them. Or maybe one of the other suitcases had something valuable in it. We didn't check them all carefully."

Lamar scratches his head. "But those suitcases been down in that basement for years. Why did he come lookin' for the letters now?"

Donna waves her phone. "Because I posted these pictures on Instagram and Facebook with the caption, "Claim a little piece of Villa Aurora history with a few of these vintage suitcases. Stack three to make an end table or use an open one to display your prized collections."

Ty furrows his brow. His voice is dubious. "And someone saw that and came clear out here to break in and get at them?"

Donna traces her fingertips over the suitcases of different sizes and shapes. "I cleaned them all up on the outside so the picture would look good. But I didn't open each one to check the interior. Audrey only opened that small blue one because she heard the letters shifting around. There could've been something small hidden in one of the other bags or trunks."

Donna's speculations make sense. Someone could've seen the social media post, recognized a bag, and come looking for something they considered to be rightfully theirs. "Have you checked the doors and windows for signs of a break-in?"

"Not yet," Ty says, moving toward the big dining room windows. "I wanted to make sure it wasn't you moving stuff around."

We all separate to check the windows in the room, but they're all locked tight. Ty tries to unlock and lift one, but it's jammed shut. "I think these windows are nailed shut," he says, examining the sills and trim. "Didn't want any patients escaping."

We check the front door and the other first floor windows, but there's no sign of forced entry.

Now I'm flummoxed. "So they got in with a key. That means it can't be some random person who saw the social media post." We're in the foyer, and I point to the front door, which has a formidable bar lock which can only be opened from in the inside. "The thief must've entered through the back door, just as we and Alex have been doing. That's the only door with a modern lock that can be opened from the outside."

"Who all has a key beside you and Alex?" Donna asks.

"Presumably, Alex's partner would have a key."

"Which is who?" Ty asks.

"I don't know. Alex never mentioned his name." I plant my hands on my hips. "This is weird. But since nothing valuable is missing, so far as we know, I'm not going to call Alex. Not today, when he's so distraught about his dad."

When Ty looks confused, Donna explains the bad news about Constantine's death.

Ty scratches his head. "Kind of a weird coincidence the old man died on the night someone was sneakin' around in here."

"Let's not get paranoid," I say. "Constantine is in his seventies, and he died in his sleep."

"Yeah," Donna shivers. "His poor wife woke up next to a corpse."

Still, Ty's remark unsettles me. Is something going on that's beyond my understanding? Constantine Agyros has been a property developer in New Jersey for forty years. It's a cut-throat business—no doubt he's picked up some enemies along the way. Could the publicity around the re-development of Villa Aurora have brought some of them out of the woodwork? But what could they hope to find in these old suitcases?

Ty pats me on the back. "Don't sweat it, Audge. Before we leave at the end of the day, we'll set a little booby trap inside that back door."

Chapter 13

The remainder of our workday passes without incident. Donna pauses mid-afternoon to see if Constantine Agyros's obituary has appeared, but all she finds is a small blurb on the PalmyrtonNow.com news site that seems to have been taken from a press release. "With deep sadness, Agyros Property Management announces the death of its founder, Constantine Agyros. The family asks for privacy at this difficult time. Funeral arrangements will be announced at a future date."

Donna studies the dignified, formal photograph of Constantine Agyros that appears with the article. "He looks familiar. When would I have met him?" Then she snaps her fingers and answers her own question. "He's the handsome older man who didn't buy anything at the Corrigan sale." She looks at me, puzzled. "What was Alex's father doing there?"

"I think he must've come to observe how we work. He seems to not have been fully retired."

Donna frowns in frustration as she re-reads the article aloud to me. " 'The family is asking for privacy.' I guess that means I can't call or text, huh?"

She's a woman of action and doesn't like not knowing how to proceed with her condolences. "Relax, Donna. They probably have a big family, maybe even relatives in Greece. It's not surprising they haven't announced the viewing yet." A nugget of knowledge I've gleaned from Sean pops into my head. "And you know, when a healthy person dies at home, there's always an autopsy."

Donna shudders. "Can the family say no? I'd hate to think of my dad being cut up and his organs weighed like they show on CSI."

"An autopsy isn't optional. The process might be gruesome, but if it were my dad, I'd want to know what caused his death."

"I suppose."

We've finished sorting and pricing books in the library when Ty calls us to see his improvised security system. He and Lamar have moved a huge armoire in front of the dining room door. Unless the thief is as strong as those two, he won't be able to return to the dining room tonight.

And Ty has strung up an ingenious system that will bring down a stack of pots and utensils in the kitchen when the back door is opened. "The noise could work to scare them off. They'll think someone else is also in here."

"Or they'll think it's a ghost," Lamar says, slapping his knee.

"Good work, Ty. At the very least, they'll realize we're on to them and lay off." I lock the door behind us.

"I hope."

———— ◦ ————

I ARRIVE HOME BEFORE five to once again find my home spotless, my children happy, and my dinner emitting delicious aromas from the oven. I could really get used to this!

"Where's Mary?" I ask Starla, who's sitting cross-legged on the family room floor playing with the twins.

"She left half an hour ago. She's going to bingo with her lady friends tonight, so she had to get dinner made for Joe."

Hmmm. Shouldn't she have cleared that with me? But how can I be mad? I pick up Aiden, who's laughing and clean and reaching for the toy Starla's waving at him. Hard to believe he's been neglected in any way.

Starla seems in no rush to leave. She stretches out on her back and holds Thea over her head, all the while singing a silly song about cows getting milked.

I figure this is a good time to get a little more info about my new babysitter's past. Despite her promise to pump Starla, Mary hasn't produced much intel. I sit on the sofa with Aiden in my lap to begin a chat. "Do you miss your family in West Virginia? How did they feel about you moving to New Jersey?"

Starla ends her song and sets Thea on her play mat. She answers me while focused on stacking blocks for Thea to knock over. "I miss my little brothers and sisters. My mama died a while back, and my daddy...well, he don't care about much except drinkin,' so he don't care where I go."

Poor kid! And yet she's so cheerful. "I'm so sorry about your mom—that must've been hard for you to lose her so young."

Starla squirms her whole body, whether in agreement or denial, I'm not sure. "She was sick for a long time. Mostly my older sister took care of me. She's got kids of her own now, so I needed to earn my way. There's not much jobs in the little town where I'm from, so gittin' out seemed like the best plan."

"What brought you to Palmyrton?" I can tell my questions are making Starla uncomfortable, but I can't restrain myself. It's only a five or six hour drive between rural West Virginia and suburban Palmyrton, New Jersey, but culturally, the distance is vast. How in the world did she end up here instead of Pittsburgh or Columbus?

"I went out to the truck stop to hitchhike. The first guy who said he'd give me a ride was kinda creepy, so I had to jump outta the truck. But the second man was real nice. He was driving to Elizabeth, New Jersey. I thought that sounded like a real pretty place, but he said it was where they unload the giant containers from ships, and it wouldn't be good for a young girl. So he dropped me off in Palmyrton." Starla smiles. "And he was right. I'm glad I'm here."

Before I can pump her more about this appalling story, Starla breaks into another verse of her cow song. Sean comes home during a refrain of riotous mooing. "Looks like everyone's having fun here."

"We surely are!" Starla hands Thea off to Sean and heads for the door. "I'll see y'all tomorrow."

After Starla leaves, I tell Sean about our conversation. "It sounds like she was forced to leave home. She hitch-hiked to get here, and the truck driver just dropped her off in Palmyrton. She didn't know a soul."

"Shows impressive resilience and initiative," Sean says as he alternates bouncing the babies on his knee. "A woman at work was telling us her kid called home from college asking how to mail a letter. I'd rather leave our kids with Starla than with a young adult like that."

"She's definitely competent. I just worry that we know so little about her." I begin setting the table for dinner. "Like how did she connect with that lady she lives with? You've never been able to talk with the old gal."

"Oh, I forgot to tell you. My mom found out that Starla met Mrs. Karpinski through her church. She's Methodist."

"That makes sense. Starla's always singing hymns and gospel tunes. She'd certainly head to a church for help if she found herself in an unfamiliar place." I pause with silverware in my hand. "Do you think it's a problem your mom left early today? Seems like she's phasing herself out of this job. Are you okay with that?"

"Let's turn the nannycam back on and see what goes on when they're together," Sean suggests.

"You're going to tell your mother we're watching her?"

"Nah—she'd be self-conscious and keep looking at the camera. We'll spy illegally for one day. Then if everything seems fine, we'll let Starla fly solo, but we'll tell her we're using the nannycam."

When I hesitate, Sean grins at me. "Aren't you dying to know what goes on between those two when we're not here?"

I have to admit, I am. "Okay, go for it."

"If the kids have already eaten and our dinner is ready, why don't we go out for a walk right now?" Sean suggests after he gets the nannycam set for tomorrow.

"I'm tired of walking the kids in the same two parks in Palmyrton. Let's go somewhere else for a change of scenery."

"Sure," Sean agrees. "We can go to Jockey Hollow, or...."

"I was thinking of Passaic River Park in Summit."

Sean eyes me suspiciously. "That's a twenty-minute drive. Is it an especially scenic park?"

"No, but it's a block away from where Emmeline Hartnett lives. I want to return her letters."

"Audrey, Audrey—don't you have enough to do? Put them in an envelope and mail them to her if you think it's so important that she gets them back."

"I want to talk to the old gal about St. Anselm's Academy. I want to ask her about that cage in the basement. And I want to know why all those suitcases were down there."

Sean grips my shoulders. "What difference does it make? You're at Villa Aurora to empty it out. Do your job and move on."

One thing that's essential to the success of any marriage is to be prepared when your spouse offers unwelcome advice. You must retain a mental spreadsheet of examples of times when he failed to do the very thing he's asking you to do. "Do your job and move on? What about the time your captain reassigned you and you kept working on the Colvanelli home invasion on your own time? And let's not forget the time the perp confessed, and the prosecutor made a plea deal, but you kept working on the case until you proved it was a false confession."

Before Sean can escalate with a counter-offensive, I throw my arms around his neck and whisper in his ear. "C'mon Sean—humor me. I really want to meet Emmeline Hartnett. I love librarians. They're just like me."

"How so?"

"They want to know stuff just for the sake of knowing."

Chapter 14

So we load the kids and the dog and the double stroller into my car, and set off for Summit. On the drive, I tell Sean about Constantine's death. "Alex was very upset, but he doesn't want to postpone the sale."

Sean's mouth twitches sideways. "That's the difference between rich entrepreneurs and people like us—they never let the death of a loved one get in the way of making money."

I slap my husband's arm. "It would've been hard to reschedule the sale when I've already sent out promotions for it. And Alex doesn't need to even participate in the sale. We can handle it."

I stop talking to point out the street we're looking for.

I haven't been able to find a phone number for Miss Hartnett, but I'm betting that we'll catch an 80-year-old at home right before dinnertime. And I'm betting a stranger who shows up with two babies, a rescue mutt, and a cop husband won't be perceived as a threat.

Sure enough, my entourage, along with the bundle of letters, brings Miss Hartnett out onto her front porch. She recognizes the letters before I even begin to explain.

"Where did you get these?" She has shrewd blue eyes that don't miss a trick reminding me of Joan Hixson playing Miss Marple on British TV.

I explain my connection to Villa Aurora and the things we've found. "I thought you might like to have these back, and I'd love to talk to you about St. Anselm's Academy if you can give me a few minutes of your time."

"These days, I've got nothing *but* free time. And there's plenty to say about St. Anselm's." She looks delighted at the prospect of talking to me, but her expression changes when she peers into the stroller where the twins energetically kick their feet. "I can't imagine those two would want to sit through it."

"Why don't you take them over to the park, honey?" I give my husband the sweetest smile I can muster.

Sean responds with his "you owe me, big time" look, but deciding I'm in no danger from the retired librarian, he takes the kids off for a roll around the park. "I won't be long," I call after him. "I'll meet you for the second lap."

After politely declining all offers of snacks and iced tea, I get down to the purpose of my visit. "Have you been following the news about Villa Aurora?"

"I read a few months ago that the building had been purchased by Agyros Property Group." Miss Hartnett purses her lips. "Ironic that they plan to turn it into a high-end wedding venue."

"Ironic? How so?"

"St. Anselm's Academy was designed to turn substandard girls into wife material. Now the most glamorous, successful young women will vie to get married there."

Substandard? Is that how poor little Emmeline saw herself? As the elderly Emmeline takes the letters from me, I suddenly feel embarrassed for having read her personal mail, even if it is over seventy years old.

She opens the unmailed letter that she had written as a child, her eyes scanning it so quickly that I'm sure she's not reading it word-for-word, but rather directly recalling the pain she felt all those years ago.

Miss Hartnett lets the paper fall into her lap. Eyes downcast, she takes a moment to compose herself. But when she looks at me again, she's as serene as when she greeted me at the door. "As you have correctly surmised, St. Anselm's was a terrible place, a school of last resort, a school that parents held over their daughters' heads when they misbehaved. 'You'd better be good, or we'll send you to St. Anselm's' was a common warning in the upper-class circles of Palmer County in the 1950s." The corners of her mouth pull down in a quick twitch. "Of course, in my case, it wasn't an idle threat."

"But you were only eight when your parents sent you there. What could you possibly have done wrong to make them punish you like that?" I'm even more outraged now that I've met this dear lady than I was when I read her childhood correspondence.

Miss Hartnett offers an unamused half-smile. "Prosperous people in the 1950s valued conformity, and none more so than my parents. My older brother Eliot was everything they wanted in a child: a good student, but not excessively intellectual; a respectable athlete, but not so talented that he'd attract the attention of recruiters; attractive, but not flashily handsome. Even as a child, Eliot had perfect manners and could carry on meaningless chit-chat with anyone."

A surprising jab of bitter sibling rivalry even after all these years.

Miss Hartnett tries to lighten her tone. "I was ten years younger than Eliot, and a te-r-r-ible disappointment. My mother hadn't planned on having any more children after she experienced a devastating stillbirth two years after Eliot. So imagine her surprise when she turned up pregnant at thirty-five, embarrassing evidence that she and my father still had marital relations." Miss Hartnett casts her gaze heavenward.

"I was thirty-five before I even got married," I confess.

"An old maid!" Miss Hartnett winks at me. "In my mother's rigid world-view, only Catholics had babies after the age of thirty. I started humiliating her even before I was born. And then, I had the audacity to enjoy playing outdoors and getting dirty instead of holding quiet tea parties with my dolls. By the time I was seven, I'd failed at both ballet and piano, and my first-grade teacher complained that my handwriting was deplorable and that I looked out the window during reading class." Miss Hartnett pinches a dead leaf from a nearby potted plant. "In short, I was difficult."

"You sound like you were a normal kid to me. So they sent you to boarding school at the age of eight?" I'm still incredulous. How is that even legal?

"Honestly, a nice boarding school probably would've been a welcome escape from my parents' constant criticism. But St. Anselm's wasn't nice." Miss Hartnett drops her lightly ironic tone. Now I can sense genuine anger beneath her calm façade. "The purpose of a St. Anselm's education was not to teach girls anything academic. The purpose was to break our spirits, thus making us socially acceptable young ladies."

Her eyes narrow as she stares back into the past. "We needed perfect penmanship to be able to write thank-you notes. We needed to be able to read well enough to follow a recipe or quote articles from *Good Housekeeping* or *Ladies Home Journal*. Most of all, we needed to be able to sit still and make small talk in order to snare a husband. And I couldn't do any of those things."

"What about the other girls?"

"Oh, we were all damaged goods, but each damaged in her own way." Miss Hartnett taps her foot. "In those days no one knew anything about learning disabilities like ADHD or dyslexia. Autism hadn't been named, but it certainly existed. Mental illnesses were regarded as deeply shameful, and intellectual impairment was even worse. Even having an artistic temperament or a free-spirited nature was evidence of deviancy." She leans forward. "We all had problems and not a single one of us received any treatment or counseling or therapy or understanding. Only punishment."

"Physical abuse?"

Miss Hartnett shakes her head. "No, they didn't want us to have bruises. Oh, the teachers would whack your hand with a ruler, but in those days, every public school teacher did the same. No, the punishments at St. Anselm's were crueler than paddlings would have been, I think." She lifts her letter. "We were denied food. We were denied recreation and locked alone in a dark room on the third floor. It was stifling in the warm months and freezing in the winter." Emmeline shudders. "The last room on the right. I'll never forget the dread I'd feel as they marched me toward it."

I reach out and squeeze her hand. Small comfort, seventy years after the abuse.

"Worst of all, in my opinion, we were encouraged to turn on one another," Emmeline continues. "Most of us were hungry all the time, so the girls would tattle to win some extra food. The girls whom the head mistress favored could lie with impunity, so the rest of us lived in fear of both them and the teachers. We were all victims, and yet we all preyed on one another to survive."

"My god! It sounds ghastly! And you were there from third grade through twelfth? How did you endure it?"

"When I was thirteen, a girl got very sick and nearly died. In hindsight, I suspect she must've had a mild form of cerebral palsy. She walked awkwardly and spoke with a stutter and struggled in every subject in school. The teachers and headmistress perceived her symptoms as signs of her willfully disobedient nature. Toward the end of one school year, she started to complain of exhaustion. She was pale and too tired even to walk downstairs to eat. Naturally, the headmistress attributed this to laziness and attention-seeking. Then one day, they found her unconscious in her bed, drenched in bloody vomit. I suspect she must've had some sort of internal bleeding that went untreated. She was taken away for treatment and the scandal was hushed up, but the

Diocese cautioned the headmistress, and they hired some younger teachers who weren't nuns. That year, Geneva Price arrived."

For the first time since Emmeline began telling the story, a happy smile lights her face. "Geneva was young and enthusiastic, with a genuine love for literature that she shared with her students. Best of all, she had struggled with reading as a young girl, but her parents worked with her to overcome her difficulties. She recognized that I wasn't stupid, but that I often transposed letters. She taught me strategies to make reading easier. Once I discovered the treasures that books contained, I was no longer restless in class. So my last three years at St. Anselm's weren't so bad."

"Did things get better for the other girls as well?"

Miss Harnett purses her lips and looks down at her tightly clenched hands. "Teenagers can be so self-centered," she whispers. "Geneva's arrival changed my life for the better. Finally, someone cared about me and valued my abilities." She lifts her gaze. "I didn't really notice how the others were coping with their problems, most of which were much more severe than mine. Geneva told me she focused her efforts on me because I was the one student she *could* help. The others—" Miss Hartnett lifts her hands in a gesture of helplessness.

Now I see my opportunity to ask more pointed questions. "Tell me, these girls with more serious problems—did you ever hear of any of them being punished in a cage in the basement of Villa Aurora?"

Miss Hartnett's eyes widen. "A cage? No, the room on the third floor was bad enough. I've never set foot in the basement, and I'm sure if other girls had been sent there, I would've heard about it."

So maybe the cage dates from the psychiatric clinic days. Or maybe, as Alex speculated, it really was just used to lock up supplies, so the staff (or starving students) didn't steal them. "I told you I found your letters inside a little blue and cream leather suitcase in the basement." I show her the pictures on my iPad. "Can you think why your suitcase and so many of the other girls' suitcases would be there? Why wouldn't they have packed them when they left the school?"

Miss Hartnett pauses to think. "Well, in my case, I think I must've forgotten about that small case. My mother gave it to me because she thought a lady needed a traveling vanity case." Emmeline scowls—at 80, she still shuns her mother's advice as a teenager would. "I honestly don't recall putting my letters in that case, but I suppose I must have. And then when I graduated, I left it behind?" Her sentence ends on the upnote of a question, as if she's trying out the logic of that theory.

"But that wouldn't explain why so many of the other girls' suitcases were still in the basement. They couldn't have all forgotten them—some were quite large."

The elderly librarian drums her fingers on the arm of her chair as she thinks. "You're certainly right. Did any of the other suitcases have name tags?"

"No. Some had monograms." I show her a picture of the big trunk with its chipped gold monogram. "Why would she have left such a big trunk behind?" I ask.

Miss Hartnett seems as puzzled as I am. Her blue eyes look into the past, keen with insight, not misty with nostalgia. "That's a very good question."

I feel my phone vibrate in my pocket. Sean is doubtless getting impatient for me to join him and the kids.

I tap Miss Hartnett's knee. "Want to help me find out?"

Chapter 15

"Miss Hartnett...is going to be...a great resource!" I'm a little out-of-breath from my brisk jog to catch up with Sean at the park. "She's sharp as a tack and looking for a challenge. And she has access to all the databases at the Summit Library."

"Resource for what?" Sean stoops to pick up a pacifier that Thea has tossed overboard. "What are you getting her involved in?"

"She's as baffled as I am about why so many of the students' suitcases were left behind in the basement."

And why someone would break into the house to look through them. I can't blame Sean for being impatient with me when he doesn't have all the facts. And I know he's nervous about leaving us alone while he's at his upcoming training class. I strive to make my project seem like some harmless historical research. "Miss Hartnett thought she might remember names of students as she thinks about it."

Sean stops pushing the stroller and faces me. "But Audrey, what's the point? What good can come of asking that nice old lady to recall painful memories of her past?"

I dig around in the diaper bag for a wipe to clean Aiden's drooly face. "She wants to do it. I suspect she feels a little guilty that her life turned in a positive direction, and she's wondering what happened to her other classmates."

"If she wanted to track down old school friends to reminisce, she could've done that on her own years ago."

The problem with my husband is he's too logical. "I don't think she considers the other former students her long-lost friends. The atmosphere of the school was too toxic to create friendships. I think she sees them as fellow victims. And she's interested in seeking justice, Sean. At least one of the St. Anselm's students nearly died of medical neglect. What if there were others? Someone should be made to take responsibility."

"But everyone involved must be dead by now. And there's a statute of limitations on most criminal and civil charges."

Not on murder. The thought pops into my mind, but I dare not speak it aloud. Sean will freak out if he thinks I'm looking for murders on the basis of a few old suitcases. So I continue on a different path. "The school stayed open for ten more years after Emmeline graduated. The students admitted then would only be in their sixties and seventies now—younger than my dad. They might remember even more than Miss Hartnett does." We pause by the playground so the twins can watch the big kids climbing and swinging. "Look Sean, maybe you're right. Maybe all that will come of this is that Emmeline connects with some former classmates, and they have a little St. Anselm's reunion."

Sean gives a gentle return kick to a child's ball rolling towards us. "Or maybe you'll succeed in stirring up a hornet's nest and getting yourself stung."

Chapter 16

The next morning when Ty, Donna and I enter Villa Aurora, we set off the pots and pans booby trap.

Ty gives a grunt of satisfaction. "Looks like we didn't have no visitors last night."

A knot of tension in my neck dissolves—I hope this means the nocturnal prowling isn't going to be a recurring problem. But I still wonder—did the prowler stay away because he already found what he came for? I wish I knew what it was.

I give myself a shake to clear my head and dive into pricing. Today, we're working in the formal front parlor. Although the oriental carpet is worn and moth-eaten in places and the upholstered chairs are saggy with wear, the tables and cabinets are all in good shape.

Donna is polishing a tall green vase painted with irises while I study the craftsmanship of an inlaid end table to establish when it was made when we hear a vehicle crunching the gravel of the driveway. Donna drops her dust cloth and runs to the window. I'm sure she's hoping it's Alex. I'd be glad to see him as well, so I can ask about who else has a key to the house.

But Donna turns away from the window with a downcast face. "It's the landscapers."

I join her at the window in time to see a short but muscular young man with dark hair jump out of a large truck with "Classic Views Landscape Design" painted on the side. A minute later, he's followed by a much older man in dusty overalls, who descends from the passenger seat with some difficulty. Together, they study the front of the house. The young man pulls out a scroll of drawings, pointing to spots on the ground and then to the papers. The old man sometimes nods in agreement, sometimes shakes his head vehemently and waves his hands. We hear raised voices but can't make out any words apart from an occasional "no!"

Donna laughs as she returns to the furniture. "An Italian grandpa and his grandson working together. You can expect a lot of yelling."

"How do you know they're Italian?" I ask. "Some sixth sense for spotting your ethnic group?"

Donna laughs. "No, silly! Remember Alex told us that the landscaper he hired is the great-grandson of the Italian stone mason who originally designed the stone walls and walkways here."

"And Donna remembers *e-e-everything* that Alex says," Ty mocks.

Donna aims her trusty spray bottle of white vinegar and water at Ty, and he runs off.

At 12:30, the pizza I ordered is delivered, and we break for lunch. "It's a beautiful day. Let's sit out on the veranda to eat."

By now, the landscapers are in the backyard with their drawings and a tape measure. They're still arguing. We arrange ourselves along the stone veranda wall to watch the show.

"The roots of this tree are pushing up the stonework in the fountain. Tree gotta go," Grandpa declares.

"It's a great shade tree, a perfectly healthy copper beech. I can trim the roots," his grandson objects.

"They just gonna grow back!"

"I can install a mesh barrier to protect the fountain. You fix the fountain; I'll fix the tree."

The old man shakes his head as the young man looks up and catches sight of us. I wave, and he crosses the overgrown lawn to greet us.

"Hi! I'm Nico and that's my grandfather, Arturo. Alex told me you guys would be working in the house."

We introduce ourselves, and I ask Nico if he has a key to the house.

"Me? No, I don't need anything from inside. We're just in the planning stages right now."

Arturo joins us. "That wall you're sittin' on..." he taps his chest..."my grandfather built it. Look at that—still straight and strong after a hundred years."

"It's beautiful stonework," I agree. "Did your grandfather teach you his craft?"

"He taught my father, and my father taught me." Arturo nods to his grandson. "His father didn't have a feel for the stones. He became an accountant."

Arturo says this as if that makes Nico's father the black sheep of the family.

Nico smiles fondly at the old man. "But I have a feel, right Grandpa?"

"Eh." Arturo makes a face as he points at his grandson. "He went to college to study landscape design. Learned how to make pretty pictures on the computer. I still gotta do all the hard work." Then his face softens. "Show them your drawings."

"We'd love to see them," Donna agrees.

So Nico unfurls the computer-aided vision of Villa Aurora's gardens, complete with a flowing fountain, blooming borders, and arbors dripping with flowering vines.

"Wow, that's gorgeous," Donna exclaims. "And you're going to build all these stone walls and walkways?" she asks Arturo.

"I'll be here every day to oversee the work," Arturo says. "You can't get real stonemasons from Naples nowadays. My best guys are from Honduras. They don't know nuthin' about design, but they're hard workers. They do what I tell them. Not like him." Arturo points to his grandson.

Nico's clearly unfazed by the abuse. "Without me, you wouldn't have this job."

"Pah!" Arturo looks up at the tower of Villa Aurora. "I'm not so sure I want this job. My grandfather always said this house is under the evil eye." He puts two fingers under his eyes and then waves the fingers at the house.

Nico laughs. "You weren't worried about the evil eye when you saw what we're getting paid for this project."

Donna and I immediately come to attention at the mention of the evil eye. Lamar also leans forward while Ty smirks and reaches for another slice of pizza.

"What did your grandfather tell you about working here?" Donna asks.

"Did he know Phineas Toliver?" I chime in, more interested in the link to the house's history than to this talk of curses.

Arturo beams, delighted to be the center of attention. Then he lowers his voice and widens his eyes. "The house was cursed from the time it was under construction. A wall that my grandfather built collapsed the next day."

"After a huge rainstorm," Nico reminds his grandfather. "The ground was unstable from digging the foundation."

Arturo dismisses this explanation. "Phineas Toliver made his money through other people's pain. That's why the house was cursed and his servants and his wife and his baby died."

"What business was he in?" Donna asks. She turns toward me. "Didn't you research that?"

"The article I read just said he was a manufacturing magnate."

He ran a silk mill in Paterson," Arturo said. "Lots of immigrants worked there. The factory was a dangerous place. Workers would get their hands and arms caught in the machinery."

Lamar shudders and hugs his arms to his side.

Arturo wags his finger. "If you got hurt like that, you would pray to die. Because you were a damaged man, couldn't work no more and a burden to your family. Back in those days, no disability insurance, no Social Security. You were in the poorhouse, your family out on the street. So in 1913, the workers in all the Paterson mills went on strike asking for better wages and safer conditions."

"Somehow I'm guessing this didn't end well," I say.

Arturo is enjoying giving his impromptu history lesson. "You guessed right. The strike lasted for months, but the mill owners came out ahead by switching to machines that didn't require skilled workers. Then they hired women and children to run them and paid them even less than the men. Then little children got their hands and arms torn off. "

"Phineas never helped the families of the injured men?" Donna asks. "And then he switched to child labor?"

"Why help?" Arturo demands. "Every day there was another boat bringing poor, desperate people from Italy, Poland, Hungary, Croatia. After you chew up the men, hire the wife and kids. But..." Arturo lifts his bushy gray eyebrows during a dramatic pause, "...the evil eye of a little girl named Aggie came for Toliver in this house."

"Grandpa, stop," Nico says, rolling his eyes. "You and your tall tales are going to scare these nice people."

Arturo shakes his head. "Ain't no tall tale. It's the God's honest truth. Aggie was a real girl who lost her arms. She's written up in a book."

Donna glances uneasily over her shoulder. "How do you know when the evil eye is finished with its work?"

Arturo fishes a gold chain out from his hairy chest and shows her a little gold horn charm dangling from it. "You need the *curnicello* to protect you."

"C'mon, Grandpa, you've done enough damage for today," Nico laughs and steers his grandfather back toward the fountain. "We got work to do figuring out how much tile to order." He waves to us. "See you around."

"Do you think Villa Aurora is cursed?" Donna asks once we're back at work pricing antiques. "Maybe it will be impossible for Alex to make a success of turning the house into an event venue. Nobody wants to get married under the evil eye."

"Of course, it's not cursed. But having a bad reputation can be a self-fulfilling prophesy. Phineas had a hard time selling the house because of the deaths associated with it. So I guess that attracted less desirable purchasers, like a school for wayward girls and a clinic for intractable patients, and the bad rap continued."

As I work, I think about what I've just said. Alex Agyros has spent millions to acquire this property and he'll spend millions more to refurbish it. I can't blame him for wanting to bury the sins of Villa Aurora's past—sins he had nothing to do with—to ensure the success of his new venture. I hate to admit it, but my husband is right. I'm pursuing my idle curiosity about the past for no viable reason in the present. I'm kidding myself if I think the girls harmed at St. Anselm's Academy will receive any kind of compensation now, sixty or seventy years later.

And my prying could hurt my client, a very nice man who's given me a lucrative job and deserves my support. And who's grappling with his own grief.

I resolve right here and now to forget about the suitcases, the cage, and any other dark secrets associated with Villa Aurora.

Well, maybe not forget...I just won't pursue anything I find.

And I won't encourage Miss Hartnett. Whatever she finds—if she finds anything at all—will stop with me.

Chapter 17

On Thursday after the kids have gone to sleep, Sean and I sit down to plan for the upcoming week. Tomorrow I'll be working from home with Starla helping while Ty and Donna set up our small house sale. Saturday, I'll work the sale with my staff while Sean watches the kids. Sunday is family day. And then we tackle our big week: the run up to the Villa Aurora sale combined with Sean's three-day trip to Austin for his anti-domestic terrorism training class. Sean's father has let it slip how disappointed Mary is to have to cancel their planned bus trip next week, so we're trying to decide if we can allow Starla to watch the kids solo.

Sean hands me a glass of white wine and sits beside me on the couch. "Let's watch the nannycam footage," he says as if we're settling in for an evening of Netflix.

Even without sound, it's crystal clear what's going on in every frame. Starla is in the middle of getting the kids dressed when Mary arrives. She reviews Starla's wardrobe choices for the kids, overrules them, and lays out different clothes.

Starla accepts the new selection without objection.

Mary makes tea and sits at the kitchen table while Starla bustles around cleaning the kitchen. Both their heads turn toward the back door, and a minute later, Mary admits Alma Bannerman to the kitchen.

Sean leans forward to study the action. "You know Alma had to come over to find out who this new person is. Look at the expression on Mom's face as she introduces them. She thinks Alma should butt out."

But Alma never notices when she's getting the cold shoulder. She sits right down and lets Mary pour her a cup of tea. Eventually, the twins start fussing and Alma leaves. Then Starla and Mary each take a twin and rock while giving them bottles of pumped breast milk. Only Starla's mouth moves—clearly, she's singing.

After the kids go down for their morning nap, Starla and Mary sit chatting at the table for a while, but before long, Starla is up doing laundry. When the kids wake up, Starla changes them and takes them out for a walk while Mary watches a soap opera.

Later, Mary pulls her phone from her purse, makes a face at the screen, then holds it to her ear.

I laugh and point. "Look—that must be when I called to see how they were doing!"

And it goes on like this all day—Starla doing ninety percent of the work while Mary offers advice from the sidelines.

Sean turns off the nananycam. "It's obvious Starla can handle the kids."

"Yes, but watching that reminded me of something. Starla doesn't have a cell phone." Because he's a safety freak, Sean has refused to disconnect our landline to rely solely on cell service. But we only have one phone connected, and it's upstairs in our home office so we can ignore all the spam calls that come in. "We need a way to keep in touch with Starla in case of an emergency."

"I'll go out tonight and buy her a cheap burner phone with one month of service. Starla's still less expensive than Roseline."

Sean and I look at each other. "That settles it—unless there's some catastrophe tomorrow, we're going with full-time Starla."

The next morning, Starla accepts her new, unsupervised position with complete confidence. Sean tells her about the nannycam while I observe, but she seems to find it amusing, not insulting.

"Y'all can see us through that thing?" she asks, squinting at the tiny camera eye peeking out from between some books on the family room shelf. She waves, then Sean plays the video back to her.

"I'm like a movie star!" she squeals.

Then Sean hands over the burner phone programmed with his and my numbers, plus every number of reliable friends he can think of. "Always keep it in your pocket," he instructs. "That way you can reach us in an emergency, and we can reach you. And you can always call my mom or Mrs. Bannerman if you need help with something during the day."

Starla nods solemnly, accepting the phone like it's a priceless diamond tiara. "Thank you so much. I'll take real good care of it."

It's hard not to love this girl—she's a throwback to a simpler era. Every middle-schooler in our neighborhood has a better phone than this one, but

Starla is delighted with it. So Sean heads off to work, leaving Starla singing, "Michael, Row the Boat Ashore" to her enthusiastic audience of two.

I'm working at home, consulting with Ty and Donna on the one-day set-up of our small house sale and taking care of some accounting tasks. Periodically, I pop my head out of our home office to see how Starla is managing with the kids, but I never catch her slacking. She's always actively engaged with the twins, and when they're napping she does little chores around the house.

She makes me feel guilty—I always put my feet up when the kids sleep.

At lunchtime, I sit down with her and the kids in the kitchen, prepared to get some information from Starla. She tells me that her grandmother taught her all the hymns that she sings, and her great-aunt taught her to cook.

Passing behind me as she bustles around the kitchen, Starla cranes her neck to look at my laptop, "Oh, lawd—look at all those charts! Do you really know what all those numbers mean?"

When I tell her I was a math major in college, she looks like I've admitted flying to the moon. "Wow! I wasn't ever too good with arithmetic...or history, or science either. I like to read storybooks, but I guess that's not too useful."

Then she asks me about how I started my business, and one question leads to another. Before I know it, I've spent an hour talking. When I catch sight of the clock, I jump up from the kitchen table to return to my home office.

On my way upstairs, I realize Starla has found out more about me than I've found out about her.

SATURDAY PASSES IN a whirl of work at our small house sale, and Sunday we all cocoon at home. That evening, after Sean and I have put the twins down for the night, I sit on our bed and watch Sean pack for his training trip. "Are you excited about the class?"

"I'm looking forward to learning the techniques. But I'm worried about leaving you and the kids. Are you sure you'll be okay?"

"Yes, dear." We've been over this multiple times. I've learned not to reason, just reassure.

"You'll be tired after a long day at work and there won't be anyone to help you."

"I can ask Starla to stay through dinner if I need her help."

"Why not have her sleep over while I'm gone?"

"Sean, please—I'll be fine."

"But Starla—"

I take my husband's hands in mine. "You know I'm an introvert. I need some alone time at the end of the day to recharge. That's why I've never wanted an au pair or any kind of live-in nanny. I don't want outsiders in our house twenty-four/seven."

I bring my face inches from his. "Listen. To. Me. I can ask my dad and Natalie for help. I can ask your parents for help. I can ask Deirdre for help. Or Ty, or Donna or Grandma Betty. Stop acting like I'm a pioneer woman alone in a sod house on the prairie. I'm surrounded by friends and family in Palmyrton."

"I know, but there will be times during this training class when I'm totally out of reach." He drops a pair of rolled socks. "Maybe I should postpone this until the twins are older."

Now I'm getting annoyed. This feels less like thoughtful concern and more like lack of trust. "I am competent to care for our children, Sean."

My husband hears the frost in my tone. "I know you are. I'm just—"

My glare stops the words on his lips. He picks up more socks and tucks them into the corners of his suitcase. "Fine. Fine. I'm going."

While Sean finishes packing, I slip out of our bedroom, glad to have the task of walking Ethel before bedtime. I figure a walk around the block in the cool evening air will calm me down. I don't want my husband to leave tomorrow with a veil of irritation between us.

I clip the leash on the dog's collar. "You'll help me take care of Thea and Aiden, won't you, girl?" Ethel's tail beats against the floor.

We set off on our journey around the block. The peaceful chirp of crickets and the intermittent flash of fireflies calm my anxious mind. If I'm honest with myself, I must admit I'm a little daunted by the prospect of solo parenting for three days. But I can't admit my fears to Sean, or he'll cancel his trip for sure. And I want him to have this opportunity. I'll call my sister-in-law Deirdre tomorrow—she's a great source of reassurance, and she never offers unsolicited advice.

Ethel sniffs busily, investigating then rejecting several spots where she might do her business. "Come on, now," I urge her. "We're not walking clear down to Sycamore tonight."

Three-quarters of the way around the block, Ethel does her duty, and we head for home. I'm lost in thought about the price I assigned to an armoire at Villa Aurora when the leash pulls tight, and Ethel lunges into the darkness barking like a maniac.

I fumble for my flashlight, hoping Ethel has surprised a raccoon, not a skunk.

Ethel pulls me toward a clump of tall trees in our neighbor's front yard. "Ethel, no!"

Then a dark figure separates from the trees and lopes down the block.

A person, not an animal.

Chapter 18

Sean and I wake before dawn and turn toward each other without speaking. He had been asleep last night when I came back from walking the dog, or maybe he just pretended to be. Time and rest has healed our rift. We make love in the darkness as the twins sleep, all irritation and worry banished from our minds.

Of course, there's no lounging in bed afterwards. Thea wakes with a howl at six, claiming the first nursing slot while Aiden patiently waits his turn. Sean changes and dresses the kids, pausing to hug and kiss them so often that Thea finally pushes him away in irritation. Then we all go out on the front porch to wave good-bye to Daddy as he departs on his trip.

WHEN I ARRIVE AT THE Villa, the Classic Visions Landscaping truck is already parked out front. I go around to the back door, where I find Nico taking measurements in front of the veranda. He waves cheerfully and returns to making notations in his tablet computer.

"Where's your grandfather today?"

"Too hot for him. I told him to stay home and take it easy. If he's with me, he always overdoes it." Nico drops to his knees to examine something along the foundation but keeps talking. "Thanks for being so patient and listening to all Pop-Pop's crazy stories last week. Evil eye!" Nico shakes his head.

I unlock the back door but return to the edge of the veranda to continue our conversation. "I thought it was interesting he knows so much about the Paterson Silk mills. I went home and looked it up. He was right about the strike and the child labor."

"My cousin has been researching our family tree. She's tracked down all these second cousins and first cousins twice removed." He laughs. "Those are different, but don't ask me how. Anyway, she's got us on Ancestry.com and found all these relatives we never knew we had. She's been asking all the old-timers questions about their childhoods and if they remember stories their parents and grandparents told to them." Nico shakes his wafer-thin computer. "And she's writing it all down. Pretty cool, actually. But now Pop-Pop and these other old guys who never even knew about each other until last year get together and tell family stories. It's crazy."

"Sounds like a wonderful project. I'm an only child and so were both of my parents. So I really don't have any relatives that I know about except for my dad."

Nico laughs as he heads out into the overgrown lawn. "Get my cousin on the case. She'll find you some."

I enter Villa Aurora feeling wistful. My longing for an extended family has been a continuing lament in my life even now that I've married into a big Irish clan and can see the downside of too much family togetherness. Maybe I should do a DNA test and put it on Ancestry. After all, everyone has ancestors, even me. I didn't spring up from a rock.

But I know what my relentlessly logical father will say if I discuss it with him. *Why do you want to track down strangers you don't even know? Why do you think you'd enjoy spending time with them more than with the wonderful friends you've chosen to surround you?*

I'm still mulling this when Ty and Donna walk in bickering.

"Why you wanna bring down more work on our heads today?" Ty drops a load of yard signs with a clatter. "Can't you see she's trying to mooch off your good nature?"

"I don't think that's it," Donna objects. "She has a legitimate reason—"

"Ask Audge." Ty points at me. "She'll back me up."

"Ask me what?"

"Audrey, there's an email in the office account from a woman who saw the suitcases on Instagram and wants to come here today to see them," Donna explains. "I told her no early birds, but she's really persistent. She emailed two more times, tagged me on Instagram, and left two messages on the office voicemail."

"I told her to ignore the lady," Ty says before I can answer. "But you know Donna can't never say no to nobody."

I'm still stuck inside that triple negative when Donna jumps to her own defense. "She's not just the standard early bird who wants to beat out all the other shoppers. She says one of the suitcases belongs to her great-aunt, who was a student at St. Anselm's."

"Pah—she handin' you a line, and you all set to take it." Ty stomps off to the foyer, where's he's been arranging some of the antiques from the attic.

But the woman's claim strikes a nerve with me. "Show me the emails."

I saw your Instagram post and showed it to my great-aunt because I knew she had gone to school in that house when it used to be St. Anselm's Academy. She got very emotional and said the dark red suitcase in the middle of the stack was hers. She begged me to get it back for her. I have to work the weekend of the sale, and my aunt is in poor health and can't drive. Can we please come today or tomorrow to buy the suitcase? My aunt is very eager to get it back. She will pay any amount (even though really, it's hers).

Melinda Forsyth (on behalf of Constance Forsyth)

Donna and I lock gazes.

"We have to let her come, right?" Donna says.

"I think so. Let's go look at the red suitcase." We head to the dining room and Donna stops cold in front of me.

"Uh-oh—look." She points to the stack of suitcases which, after the visit of our nighttime intruder, is no longer in the same order as it was in her photo.

The red suitcase is now on the top of the stack.

Chapter 19

Donna scratches her head. "Does this mean the person who broke in was after Constance Forsyth's suitcase?"

"Possibly. Or maybe he...or she...just restacked the suitcases randomly after searching them." I take the small suitcase off the top of the stack and open it. A musty lavender scent rises from the faded pink satin lining.

It's empty.

"Damn," Donna whispers, tracing the monogram CEF. "Constance must've wanted something that was inside here. She wouldn't be that desperate just to get the suitcase itself, right?"

"I'm afraid you're right. She's a few days too late." I close the suitcase. "But I'll still let her niece come and get it. It's the least we can do. I'll explain to her what happened. Maybe she'll have some idea why so many suitcases were left behind. And who might have broken in here."

Donna calls Melinda Forsyth and tells her she's welcome to come any time today before five. "She and her aunt will be here at eleven," Donna announces when she hangs up. "I told her to come around back and text me when she's here."

We return to our work, but now the suitcases and the break-in loom larger in my imagination. This luggage seems to be old baggage in both senses of the term.

Shortly before eleven, Donna's phone pings with a text message, and both of us go to the back door to greet our visitors. A woman in her seventies clings to the arm of a sturdy woman in her forties. Although clearly younger than Emmeline Hartnett, Constance Forsyth lacks the older woman's vitality. She's not only unsteady on her feet, but she also seems drained by life.

"Thanks for letting us come," Melinda says, stepping into the back hallway and looking around with open curiosity. "What do you think, Aunt Connie? Does it look familiar?"

Constance clutches her niece's arm so tightly, I'm sure she must be leaving fingerprints. Constance shakes her head. "No. No, all this is different." She points to the metal shelving, which probably dates from the eighties.

"Come on into the main part of the house," I say. "The suitcases are in the dining room now, but we found them down in the basement."

I lead the way silently, not wanting to distract Constance who needs her full concentration to put one foot safely in front of the other. As we emerge into the foyer, Constance gasps and staggers.

Donna quickly grabs her other arm to prevent her from sinking to the floor, while I grab an armchair and slide it under her. "Do you need a drink of water?"

Constance lifts her right hand limply. "No. I'm fine. It was just the shock of seeing the front door and the staircase."

Donna and I exchange a glance. Everyone else has been impressed by the beauty of the foyer. Constance seems stunned by anxiety.

Melinda crouches before her aunt. "Are you sure you want to be in here? I can take you out to the car and come back for the suitcase."

Constance shakes her head. "No. I want to see it. I want to see it before I die."

"You're not dying anytime soon." I notice an eye roll as Melinda stands to face me. "St. Anselm's Academy really did a number on my poor aunt. She's never been able to put it behind her, even after all these years. I told her I'd get the suitcase, but she insisted on coming along."

"It's in here." I point to the door leading to the dining room. Shall I bring it out, or—"

Constance pushes against the arms of the chair, struggling to stand. "I want to go in there. I want to see the dining room."

So Melinda and I pull her up from the chair, while Donna leads the way into the dining room. Ty observes the proceedings, less suspicious now that he sees Constance truly is in poor health.

Constance Forsyth pauses on the threshold of the dining room, and again sways on her feet. Melinda and I tighten our grip. But Constance regains her bearing and shakes free of my hand. She points to the center of the room. "There used to be two long tables, one for the older girls and one for the younger." She turns and points to the back corner. "And there was a round table over there for the girls being punished. We had to sit and watch the others eat, while we got nothing but water."

I cringe. This is verification that Emmeline wasn't exaggerating the punishments at St. Anselm's.

Melinda hugs her aunt. "Oh, Aunt Connie—I wish I'd never shown you that picture. This is too upsetting."

Constance doesn't answer; her gaze has fallen on the red suitcase. With Melinda holding her elbow, she shuffles toward it. Donna fetches a chair, and I place the suitcase in her lap. I've decided I won't mention the night prowler until after she opens the case.

Constance runs her bony, spotted fingers over the cracked red leather.

"Is it definitely yours?" Melinda asks.

Constance nods. With trembling hands, she opens the case and shows us the monogram. "Caroline Elizabeth Forsyth."

"Caroline?" I ask.

"Caroline was my older sister. She was sent here first." Constance's voice cracks. "Then our parents sent me."

Man, parents wanted to get rid of *all* their daughters here? Emmeline explained why she was banished: the learning disability, the tomboyish behavior, the feistiness. But Constance seems so meek and delicate. Was she ever rebellious? Why would her parents have sent her to a school for troublesome girls?

Melinda looks at me over her aunt's head and mouths, *Caroline died.*

Here? Now I'm really intrigued, but Constance seems so close to the breaking point that I dare not ask questions.

Constance begins to pluck at the satin lining of the case.

"Careful, Aunt Connie—you'll tear the lining," Melinda cautions.

"I need to lift it up, get behind it." For the first time since we've met her, Constance seems strong and determined.

Melinda holds her back. "It's not ours. We haven't bought it yet."

"I'd give it to you for free, but it's not mine to give," I say. "The terms of my contract say I can only give away things that don't sell after the sale. But I'll give you a bargain—five dollars."

From the corner of my eye, I catch Ty's scowl at the discount. As soon as the money changes hands, Constance goes back to pulling at the pink satin lining, her lips pressed in a hard line "Do you have scissors?" she asks me when she can't get the lining to separate from the case.

"I thought you wanted to keep this as a memento," Melinda protests. "Why do you want to ruin the lining?"

"I don't care about this dusty old suitcase. I want to find the diary my sister left."

Ty and I stiffen. Donna gasps.

Melinda notices our reaction. "What's going on?"

I explain the break-in to the Forsyths. "Maybe whoever broke in and went through the suitcases was looking for the same thing as you. Would anyone else know about Caroline's diary?"

Melinda looks at me like I'm ranting about space aliens. "Why would anyone break in here to steal a schoolgirl's diary from fifty years ago?"

Exactly. Why?

"Because they know Caroline was murdered," Constance says with surprising vehemence.

Melinda massages her temples. "Let's not start with that again, Aunt Connie. You promised me you wouldn't bring up your theories. They only make you upset."

Of course, I want to ask her why she thinks her sister was murdered, but Melinda clearly won't approve. But Constance doesn't need any prodding from me. "My sister fell to her death. Her body was found in that foyer." She points over her shoulder. "The school tried to pass it off as an accident...said she tripped and fell down the steps. But I peeked through the balusters from above. I saw the nuns and the headmistress moving her body before the police came. They arranged her to make it look like she fell."

Melinda looks pained. "It was an accident, Aunt Connie."

Constance opens her mouth to respond, but she's distracted by Ty.

While we've been talking, Ty has gone into the kitchen. Soon he returns with the thin metal spatula Lamar used to pry open the basement door lock. "Here, let's see if we can spring that top lining out with this." He takes the suitcase from Constance and runs the thin metal tool between the lining and the hard upper lid. A piece of stiff particle board, to which the pink satin is glued, pops out.

"Ah!" Constance's eyes light up and she snatches the suitcase back from Ty.

But the space behind the lining contains no diary. Constance's face falls.

"What's this?" Donna leans over Constance's shoulder and picks up some tiny shreds of yellowed paper. "It looks like the little scraps of paper that are left if you rip a page out of a notebook."

Constance looks up at us, her faded blue eyes watery with tears. "Caroline's diary wasn't a real book, just a tiny spiral notebook where she wrote her thoughts and her prayers that God would deliver her from her trials." Her jaw juts defiantly. "Which he clearly didn't do."

"It looks like the diary really was hidden in here." I touch the empty upper lid. "The thief got to it before you did. I'm so sorry."

Constance slumps back in her chair and shuts her eyes. "Caroline always tried to protect me. She said she'd take care of me here. But she couldn't. The nuns separated us. We rarely got a chance to talk." She straightens up and speaks more forcefully. "Caroline wrote in that diary nearly every day, but she'd never let me read it. She said a diary was supposed to be a place for a girl's most private thoughts, thoughts she couldn't even share with her sister. But after she died, I looked through her things trying to find it, and I never did. I thought the teachers found it first."

Melinda shifts her weight from one foot to the other. "Lots of teenage girls keep diaries...boys they have a crush on, that sort of thing. If it was just a little notebook, it probably got thrown out. I'm sure it didn't contain anything about why she com—"

Constance turns to glare at her niece. "Caroline did *not* trip and fall. She was pushed. She knew things, and they wanted to keep her quiet."

Melinda doesn't respond. She's taking deep breaths to steady her nerves. Finally, she says. "We'd better get going Aunt Connie. We've taken up enough of these people's time."

"We were happy to take a little break from our work," I assure them. Now is my chance to ask Constance who she thinks could have been after her sister's diary. "Constance, who do you think entered Villa Aurora to search the suitcases? There was no sign of forced entry. It had to be someone with a key."

Constance shakes her head. "You don't need a key to get in and out of this place. The older girls knew a way to slip out. I never did it. Too scared of getting caught and punished."

"The older girls would come and go?" I'm surprised, given how strict the school seemed.

"Some of them," Constance confirms. "One ran away and never looked back."

"Wow!" Donna gushes. "A secret entrance? Do you know where it was?"

"Somewhere through the tower."

Chapter 20

As soon as Constance and Melinda leave, Ty grabs the spatula. "I suppose you want to break into the tower now."

"Definitely," Donna agrees. "I'll go get the skewer."

But try as we might using the same tools Lamar used, the tower door does not pop open as the basement door did. Either Lamar has a more skillful touch, or the lock on this door is sturdier. I shut my eyes and try to remember what the door looks like from the other side. "I think there's a deadbolt that opens from the other side. I can picture it from when Alex gave us the tour."

"Let's go outside and look at the tower from there," Donna suggests.

So we troop outside, and as Donna and I watch, Ty climbs up a trellis onto the porch roof and squints up at the base of the tower. "Huh. I never noticed that." He points to a wide decorative ledge running around the base of the tower.

"Don't even think of pulling yourself up onto that," I warn. "The stonework could be crumbling."

Ty walks along the side of the veranda roof so he can see where the tower connects to the house. He disappears behind an overhanging tree, but his voice carries down to us. "Oh, yeah. Now we're talkin.'"

"What? What?" Donna and I follow Ty's progress from the ground, but we can't see what he sees.

"There's a little access door at the base of the tower, looks like the Keebler elf door. Maybe they put it in after the house was built to get electrical wiring up there. There were some vines growing over it, but they've been pulled away. Looks like recently, because the leaves are still green, but they're wilted." Ty swings down from the veranda roof. Once he's back on the ground, he demonstrates the size of the door with his hands. "It'd be a tight fit for me to get through there, but teenage girls could do it easy."

"So our intruder was a teenage girl?" Donna looks skeptical.

"No, I'm just sayin' Miss Forsyth must be right—girls from the school could've gotten in and out through there back in the day," Ty clarifies.

"And whoever got into Villa Aurora two days ago knew about the door," I continue Ty's line of reasoning. "But to get in there, they'd have to be agile enough to get up on the veranda and climb to the ledge. And small enough to get through the door. And then they could unlock the tower door from the inside and get into the main house."

"I don't see one of Miss Forsyth's classmates being willing to risk breaking a leg up there. I'm guessing a young, wiry, woman or man," Ty concludes.

"It's still possible the intruder came in through the back door with a key, but now it seems more likely that someone from the school's past saw Donna's post about the suitcases, remembered how to get into the Villa, and got a younger, more nimble friend or relative to break in," I say.

"That explains how they got in. We still don't know why." Ty makes a face. "I'm not sure I buy Miss Forsyth's theory that her sister was murdered here. She seemed a little"—Ty rocks his hand—"unstable."

Donna gives him a little kick with her sneaker. "That's so typical. Men don't believe women. And no one takes old people seriously. So naturally you're not going to believe an old woman."

Ty is offended. "Hey! I like old folks. You two are always tellin' me I'm good with them. But Miss Forsyth's own niece seemed to think she was carryin' on about nuthin.' Maybe she built up this whole story that someone killed her sister in her head because she didn't want to accept that Caroline committed suicide." Ty rubs his fingers together. "You ask me, it makes more sense that someone broke in to steal something worth cold, hard cash."

I'm enamored of the stolen diary theory, but Ty does have a point. The students at St. Anselm's were all from well-to-do families. There could've been a long-lost piece of jewelry in one of those suitcases, and the original owner saw an opportunity to get it back.

"I don't see how we can ever know for sure." Donna drags her toe through the gravel of the driveway. "It all happened so long ago."

"W-e-ell, there's one person who might be able to shed some light on this." I gaze up at the leafy branches swaying above me. "Emmeline Hartnett."

DONNA, TY, AND I REACH a good breaking point in our work at four, which leaves me a little time for a visit with Emmeline before I need to be home. I call her, and as I expected, she's delighted that I want to visit. "I have a little news to report, and I'm eager to hear your news," she says. That sounds promising.

Within half an hour of leaving Villa Aurora, I'm sitting in Emmeline's cozy living room enjoying a cup of tea and some Mint Milano cookies. Behind us on the dining room table, Emmeline's laptop is open, her papers spread around it. "You go first, she says," beaming like a child with a secret.

Before I spring the tower door on her, I ask if she knows anything more about the suitcases we discovered. "Did you happen to see the photographs of the other vintage suitcases we found in the basement? My assistant posted it on Instagram and Facebook."

Miss Hartnett shakes her head. "I only check in on Facebook occasionally to find news of old colleagues and college friends."

"So as far as you know, there are no St. Anselm's reunions or social media alumnae groups?"

Emmeline snorts. "No one wants to reminisce about the most painful years of their life."

So if there's a circle of St. Anselm's alumnae buzzing about what's happening at Villa Aurora, Emmeline doesn't know about it. I continue. "While you were a student, do you remember girls sneaking out of the Villa?"

"There was some talk among the older girls." Emmeline pauses to sip her tea. "But by the time I was in the upper grades, Geneva had arrived, and I was much happier. I didn't want to risk getting in trouble because of some lark that was bound to be uncovered."

"Do you remember how the girls got out?"

She looks up at the ceiling. "Supposedly there was some secret door in the tower. It sounded like nonsense to me."

"What would you say if I told you we discovered that door today?"

Emmeline startles and some tea sloshes over the rim of her cup as she replaces in it the saucer. "Really? The secret door isn't a myth?"

"It's at the base of the tower and leads out onto the roof of the veranda. We saw it from the outside. It's partly covered by vines." I lean forward in my chair. "Were there girls who ran away from the school? Could the suitcases left behind in the basement have belonged to them?"

Emmeline pauses to consider this. "One night shortly after I was enrolled at the school, there was a terrible commotion. All the adults were up in the middle of the night running around...doors opening and closing, people shouting. All of us little girls were told to stay completely silent in our beds. I was scared enough just being away from home, so of course I stayed quiet." She falls silent, lost in thought.

Finally, I get impatient. "You think a girl ran away? Did they find her?"

"No one told me anything. But I remember for the next few days, girls were called into the headmistress's office and would emerge crying. It makes sense that a girl might have run away, and the administration was trying to find out how it happened and who helped her."

"But you don't know who it was?"

Emmeline shakes her head. "I was only eight, just trying to keep my head above water. All the activity swirled around me but didn't touch me." She stirs her tea. "But a few years later when I was more clued-in to the workings of St. Anselm's, I recall girls talking about someone. No one had actually met her, but her story got passed down. She was like a legend, a mythical creature. The girl who got away. Honestly, I never paid much attention. The idea that someone could have escaped from St. Anselm's seemed absurd to me." She lifts her hands in dismay. "Even if a girl managed to get out of the building at night, where would she go?"

"Hitchhike to Palmyrton?" I suggest. "Take a train to the city?"

"None of us girls were allowed to keep any cash." Emmeline takes a big swallow of tea. "If there really was a girl who escaped, she had to have had help."

The escapee could account for one or two of the pieces of abandoned luggage. And then there was the girl who was rushed away in medical crisis—some might belong to her. Now it's time to ask about the student who died at St. Anselm's.

"Do you remember two sisters named Caroline and Constance Forsyth?"

Emmeline jolts to attention. "Yes, the only sibling pair I can remember at St. Anselm's. They were younger than I." She peers at me through her glasses. "How did you hear about Caroline and Constance?"

"I met Constance today. She came to claim her sister's suitcase. She was hoping to find Caroline's diary hidden inside. But it was gone." I tap the table between me and Emmeline. "The school said that Caroline died in a fall down the grand staircase, but Constance thinks her sister didn't fall. She claims the girl was murdered."

Emmeline twists her lips in doubt. "Constance must have been devastated by her sister's death. They were very close." She bites her bottom lip. "I remember Caroline as a lovely girl. She had no enemies at the school."

"No enemies among the students. Could a teacher or an administrator have—" I make a pushing gesture.

"Oh, no—my dear! That's a little hard to imagine even for someone like me, who despised the school. Neglect and cruelty, yes. Outright murder? I don't think so." She squints at me. "What would be the motivation?"

I lift my shoulders. I haven't been able to come up with one, and if Emmeline can't either, then Ty's suspicion that Constance Forsyth was over-reacting may be correct. I decide to hold off telling Emmeline about the break-in and the diary Constance was hoping to find. "Now, what did you have to share with me, Emmeline?"

"I decided to do some research into the history of St. Anselm's Academy. I wanted to know how and why it was founded, and if it was always intended to be a school for troubled girls or if that reputation settled on it later for some reason."

"That sounds like a good line of inquiry."

"Digging around at the library I discovered a monograph written by a sociology professor at Drew University, "A Cultural Assessment of Class and Religion in Mid- Twentieth Century Palmer County," Emmeline continues.

I make a face. "That sounds like a pretty narrow topic, not to mention dry."

"Indeed it is, dear. But people love to talk about their specialties. This fellow has agreed to meet me in his office tomorrow, and he assures me he knows all about the founding of St. Anselm's."

She throws back her shoulders and arches her eyebrows, barely restraining herself from saying, "how do you like that?"

Clearly, she expects praise and I'm happy to oblige. "Very impressive, Emmeline. I'll be eager to hear what he has to say. How did you connect the title of that monograph with St. Anselm's?"

She presses her hand against her chest. "That's what librarians do. Make connections."

"That's what estate sale organizers do, too. Tell me, what made you decide to get a degree in library science?"

Emmeline settles herself in her chair, prepared to tell a long story, and I worry I'll be late getting home. But unlike Alma, who rambles endlessly, Emmeline knows how to narrate a good tale.

"The idea of spending every working day in a library seemed like heaven to me. My parents had no intention of sending me to college, but Geneva helped me apply and find scholarships. Much to the chagrin of Mother and Father, Rutgers accepted me into their library science program. College was a revelation to me. For all my life, my circle had been so small. The students and staff at St. Anselm's totaled fewer than 100 people. Add to that my family and my neighbors—that's all I knew. Suddenly, on campus I met people from across the country and around the world. Some of the young women were just like my mother—prim and proper with their bouffant hairdos and strands of pearls. But I managed to find the counterculture. The beatniks and the early feminists and the artists—oh, how I loved college!"

"But after you graduated, you returned to Summit. Didn't you want to move to New York or San Francisco?"

"I toyed with the idea. But I knew how my parents would react. They'd tell themselves I was a fallen woman, and they were well rid of me. They'd tell their friends that I'd married a boy I met in college and moved away. I didn't want to give them the satisfaction of writing my life story the way they saw fit."

Emmeline lifts her chin in defiance. "I accepted a position as a librarian at the Summit Public Library so I could live as an unmarried, independent career woman right under their noses, smack in front of their friends." Miss Harnett's eyes twinkle like she's a mischievous kid who's pulled off an epic prank. "Not that my parents ever darkened the door of a library—my mother didn't read for pleasure, and my father subscribed to Readers Digest Condensed Books. Libraries were for intellectuals and the poor, two classes of people my parents abhorred."

She's hooked me. "How did they react?"

Emmeline claps her hands. "They were appalled! Even though I rarely saw them, I made my presence felt. As I spent more time in my position, I ran special programs and applied for grants to improve the library—my picture was in the local paper all the time." Emmeline is overtaken with giggles. "And Mother's charity-minded lady friends would report back to her how lovely it was to work with me to plan benefits for the library, but what a pity I'd never married. Working at the Summit Library provided me with thirty years of very enjoyable revenge for the ten years of suffering my parents put me through."

Emmeline pauses and scrutinizes me with her bright eyes. "I suppose you think that's petty."

I smile. "Not at all. You did great work at the Summit library even while you were getting under your parents' skin."

Emmeline nods, glad that I understand. "You know the old saying, 'revenge is a dish best served cold.'"

Chapter 21

It's 5:45 by the time I make it home. I burst into the kitchen full of apologies but find Starla calmly feeding the twins mashed avocado while singing, "Will the Circle be Unbroken" in her clear, true soprano.

I'm about to tell her that only Aiden likes squash when Thea opens her mouth obediently to the spoon, never taking her eyes off Starla's dreamy, music-transported face.

"I know you like to nurse them as soon as you get home, but they were getting a little persnickety, so I thought I'd give them a snack," Starla says.

"That's fine," I assure her. "I'm so sorry I'm late."

"You go ahead and work as long as you need to." Starla puts the kids' dishes in the dishwasher. "I got no place I need to be."

When she turns to face me, I notice she's wearing a pale pink tee shirt imprinted with a rainbow unicorn that says, "Unicorns are Real" in glitter type. It's stretched tight over her very flat chest, which makes me suspect she got it from the children's table at the clothing bank. This poor kid! What kind of life is this for a twenty-one-year-old? She should be buying trendy clothes at the mall and going out to bars with her friends, not singing gospel tunes to babies and wearing cast-offs from a middle-schooler while living with an elderly woman

"Have you made any friends your own age since you arrived in Palmyrton?" I ask her.

She startles, and I realize my question came out of the blue. "I mean, you said you had no place you needed to be. I just wondered if you ever get a chance to go out in the evening with friends."

She smiles shyly. "Oh, sure—sometimes. But not, like, during the week, ya know?" She turns away to say the next words. "In fact, if y'all ever need to work real late or want to go out by yourselves, I could even sleep over here. I wouldn't mind."

I'm not sure why this suggestion bothers me, but it does. I've never wanted a live-in nanny. I don't know how rich people cope with having live-in servants, even in a very large house. I couldn't bear having an employee always present in my home, not even an employee I love, like Ty.

And I don't love Starla. I like the kid, but she's a stranger to me. "Thanks for the offer. But Sean and I enjoy spending our evenings with the kids."

"Of course, you do." Starla strokes Aiden's curls. "They're so precious." She sits down with Aiden in her lap at the kitchen table as I pick up Thea to nurse. Clearly, she's in no rush to leave. "But you have such an interesting job. Last week Sean's mother told me you're working at a big mansion. I've never seen so many big houses as I have since I moved to Palmyrton."

With Sean away on his training class, I have a long evening ahead of managing both kids. I might as well accept Starla's help for a little longer. "Yes, the mansion is called Villa Aurora. It's got seven big bedrooms on the second floor and a bunch of tiny rooms on the third floor. It's even got a tower."

"A tower! Like in Rapunzel?" Starla hangs on my every word.

It's hard not to enjoy such a rapt audience. So I tell her about the history of the house, and the trap door we discovered. Then we swap twins, and while I nurse Aiden, I tell her about how Alex plans to turn it into a wedding venue.

"Wow! That's amazing." Starla gazes into space. "Where I come from, everyone lives in little houses and trailers and such. The principal of my high school lived in a brick house with three bedrooms on the second floor, but I never did get to go up there. And if people get married, they just have the party at the VFW hall."

With that one remark, Starla's presence begins to grate on my nerves. Can a person born in the 21st century truly be that unworldly? I guess Starla makes me feel guilty for my comfortable middle-class life. If I were a better person, I'd let her move into our guest room.

But I'm not that good. I'm a working mother who wants a little alone time to relax from a long day. I stand up. "Well, I'm expecting a call from Sean when he's done with his class for the day. So let me pay you now."

I thank Starla again for staying late and watch her wobble off on her bike.

When Sean calls at eight-thirty, I snatch up the phone with delight. He wants to FaceTime so he can see the twins, but they're already asleep. Despite my eagerness to prove I can manage on my own, I do miss him. As soon as I see his face on the screen, I start chattering about the twins...Thea tried mashed avocado and liked it...Aiden figured out how to press the button to make his toy dog bark, which he did repeatedly once he realized it startled Ethel.

Sean laughs and asks questions, but as our conversation continues, I sense he's holding something back.

"What's wrong? Is your class not what you expected?"

"No, the class is great. I'm learning a lot." Long pause. "Audrey, I don't want to upset you, but I feel you need a heads-up before the news hits the papers tomorrow."

My stomach tightens. "What news?"

"Constantine Agyros was murdered."

"What?! They found something in the autopsy?"

"Poison," Sean says. "Tetrahydrozoline—the active ingredient in eye drops that get rid of redness."

"No way! You can poison someone with Visine?"

"Yep. It constricts your blood vessels. You feel groggy and dizzy. Eventually you pass out, and with no medical assistance, you can die. There were several high-profile murder cases in other parts of the country where one spouse killed the other with eye drops."

"So that's why it seemed Constantine died in his sleep."

"The pathologist thinks he ingested it in the late afternoon—there were cheese and hummus and crackers and wine in his stomach, but no sign of dinner. The theory is, he felt unwell in the evening, went to bed early, and never woke up."

"Are they sure it's murder? Maybe he accidentally swallowed some eye-drops as he was using them"

"Unlikely. A grown man would need to drink a couple ounces for it to be fatal. It doesn't have a strong taste, so the wine would cover it. His death has been ruled a homicide. Rob Porter is leading the murder investigation."

"How horrible! Someone poisoned Constantine over wine and hors d'oeuvres?"

"His wife's in the clear—she hadn't seen him since breakfast and can account for her whereabouts all day," Sean explains. "She didn't think her husband was expecting any guests. Your client Alex is having a harder time coming up with witnesses to prove where he was. He seems to spend a lot of time driving around alone."

"That's not suspicious. He's a real estate developer—they're always on the road. Ask Isabelle," I add, offering up my realtor friend as an example.

Sean takes a deep breath. "I suppose it's pointless to ask you to drop this job."

"Drop the job! After all the work we've already put into it? No way!" I pace around the family room holding the phone out in front of me. This is so typical of Sean—overreacting, perceiving danger everywhere. Rather than argue about my work, I deflect his attention back to the investigation. "Rob Porter must have other suspects. Constantine has been in a cut-throat business for decades."

"The team will certainly look at any business associates he might have screwed over. But the family are always prime suspects until they prove they couldn't have done it."

"There was no bad blood between Alex and his father," I insist. But as the words leave my mouth, I recall the little squabble they had in front of me. But that was just normal parent-child irritation. I've seen Sean snap at his own father worse than that when Joe tries to offer police career advice.

Sean laughs at me. "How would you know? You've only met the guy a few times!"

Of course, Sean is right. But still, I feel I have a good sense of people's natures, and Alex struck me as an outgoing guy proud of his family business.

"You need to be careful, Audrey." Sean kneads his eyes. "Don't spend any time alone with this guy."

"Alex isn't the murderer," I insist. "He was shocked and devastated by his father's death. I could hear it in his voice when he told me about it."

"Maybe what you heard was shock at his own success."

Chapter 22

The next morning, Starla arrives on her bike fifteen minutes early. She takes over changing Thea's poopy diaper, singing "Michael, Row the Boat Ashore" the entire time. It's hard to find fault with a babysitter who's punctual, cheerful, and musical. Still, I can't resist giving her a long list of reminders about food and naps and sun hats in case they take a walk. Starla accepts all the instructions with good grace.

"Okay." I pick up Aiden and Thea in turn to give them hugs, then check my tote bag to make sure I have everything essential for my day. "I'll be home by five-fifteen, I promise. But don't hesitate to call me if you need anything. And Alma Bannerman is right across the street if you need short-term help."

"Oh, we always stop by to visit with Mrs. Bannerman when we go out for our walk, don't we?" Starla turns to the twins for verification. "You just go on to work. We'll be fine here."

Reluctantly, I edge toward the door, waving to my children. But they don't even notice me leave because they're bouncing and clapping to one of Starla's songs.

On the way to Villa Aurora, I listen to the news on the radio, but there's no mention of Constantine's murder. When I arrive at the mansion, I park beside Donna's car and check the PalmyrtonNow website to see if there's any news on Constantine there. But the biggest headline belongs to the local Little League play-offs. Since the news hasn't broken to the general public, I decide I won't mention it to Ty and Donna. Donna will go into another round of worrying how to offer support to Alex, and Ty will probably say something insensitive like "people get murdered for a reason" that will upset Donna further. In the interest of fostering a productive workday, I keep Sean's inside information to myself.

By mid-afternoon, we've priced so many items that all our markers have dried out, and I offer to run to Staples to get more. My phone rings as I'm driving back to Villa Aurora.

Alma. Decline call.

It rings again five minutes later. Alma. Decline call.

And again in two minutes.

Finally, I cave in and answer.

"Hi, Alma. I'm driving. Can this wait?"

"Audrey?" Alma's querulous voice comes through the ether. "I know you're busy, but I'm awfully worried. Starla didn't walk the babies today at eleven like she always does."

I grip the steering wheel. Now poor Starla is under surveillance from Alma as well as Sean. "She's not required to walk them at precisely the same time every day, Alma." I don't care that my voice is sharp. This has to stop.

"No, of course not but...."

"But what?"

"The FedEx man left one of your packages at my house, so I went over to deliver it and I rang the bell, and no one answered."

Smart Starla. I guess even she has reached her limit with Alma's visits.

"But Ethel barked and barked and barked."

Well, yeah. Have you ever met a dog who doesn't bark when someone's at the door?

Alma continues, undeterred by my silence. "I heard the babies crying."

Because the dog and the doorbell woke them up.

"So I left the package on the front porch and went home. But it's been two hours and Starla still hasn't brought the package in. So I went back over and I heard the dog barking and the babies crying even before I rang the bell."

Now Alma has my attention. It couldn't hurt to check with Starla. As I listen to Alma on speakerphone, I command Siri to text the nanny. *Everything ok there?*

No answer.

"You see, I saw a car in the driveway earlier in the morning," Alma continues.

"No one I recognized. And Starla has never had friends over while she's working."

Now a niggling grain of anxiety has settled in my chest. "I'm putting you on hold while I call Starla," I tell Alma.

Starla's phone immediately rolls to voicemail—either it's turned off or out of juice. That's never happened before.

I pull into a parking lot and turn the car around toward home as I get Alma back on the line. "Thank you for calling, Alma. I'll be there in ten minutes."

BY THE TIME I'M HEADING down my street, I've worked myself into a panic. I called Donna to let her know I wasn't coming back to Villa Aurora, and her agitated reaction to my story got me even more worked up. My heart pounds and my hands slip on the steering wheel. I keep telling myself, if they're crying, they're alive. My sister-in-law Dierdre, nurse and unflappable mother of four, lives by that mantra.

I pull into my driveway to find Alma pacing on the front porch. For once, I wish I had a key hidden under a flowerpot that would have given her access. As soon as I reach the door, I can hear a cry.

One cry.

Thea.

My hands tremble so much, I drop the key trying to unlock the door. Finally, I'm in and running toward my daughter. I round the corner into the kitchen and see both kids strapped into their highchairs, with Ethel pacing and whining between them. Thea is bright red, screaming her head off, snot and tears and drool streaming down her face.

Aiden slumps in his chair, his head lolling on his chest.

I scream and fumble to unstrap him.

Immediately, he wakes up, his face breaking into a gummy smile.

Alive.

Lightheaded with relief, I clutch him to my chest. Meanwhile, Thea delivers a furious kick to the tray of her highchair. Clearly, she's been awake and screaming throughout their ordeal, while her brother must have collapsed from exhaustion.

Alma stands in the doorway of the kitchen, eyes agog. I hand her Aiden, sodden from a leaky diaper and hours of tears, while I unstrap Thea.

As soon as she's in my arms, she quiets down and lays her head on my shoulder with one last, outraged hiccup.

Both kids are fine, but they both cling to me. Alma tries to hold each one in turn as I work to get them cleaned up, but they squirm away from her, desperate for my comfort. Ethel surveys the scene, her eyebrows knotted in worry.

"You're a good dog, Ethel," I assure her. "You did your best to warn us something was wrong."

"Do you want me to go upstairs and see if Starla fell asleep?" Alma offers.

I'm quite sure no one could sleep through all the noise these three were making. What if Starla fell and hit her head, or collapsed despite her youth and apparent good health? Something bad had to have happened to her—she wouldn't have abandoned the kids in their highchairs.

What if... my head pivots to check the back door—no sign of forced entry. But Alma said there'd been a car in the driveway earlier in the day. My mind returns to the night before Sean left on his trip, the night I saw someone hiding in the neighbors' trees, then running away.

Why didn't I tell Sean about it?

With the children nursing in my arms, my panic recedes and I'm able to think more clearly. If there's something terrible to be discovered upstairs, I don't want poor Alma to be the one to do it. All the people I'd normally rely on—Sean, Ty, Donna, Deirdre—are too far away to help me here and now.

Should I dial 911?

Thea's eyelids flutter and she dozes off, exhausted by her effort to alert the world to her and her brother's plight. Aiden raises one hand toward my face, checking to make sure I'm really here.

The last thing I need is three police cars, lights flashing and sirens wailing, to thunder into my driveway.

I've got to go upstairs myself and look for Starla.

I slide the sleeping Thea onto Alma's lap and carry Aiden upstairs with me. With his head nestled into the crook of my neck, he won't see anything before I do.

At the top of the stairs, I head directly for the nursery. The stuffed animals lined up on the shelf smile at the empty cribs. The twins' clean laundry has been folded and put away. I move to the hall bathroom—no signs of trouble. Then I poke my head into our bedroom and bath, even checking the closets. Nothing. By the time I reach the vacant guest room, I'm forced to accept the truth: Starla has walked out of this house and abandoned my children.

Guilt surges through me. Guilt, not anger. How could I have misjudged Starla so completely? How could I have chosen her to watch our children? How could I have agreed with Sean that we should give her a chance?

And then there's my guilt over Alma.

I regret every eye roll, every complaint I've ever made against the poor soul. Thank God for her nosiness! The twins could have been strapped into those highchairs all alone until 5:30 if Alma hadn't called me.

I return to the family room a humbled woman. Alma looks up expectantly, and I shake my head. "Starla's not upstairs." I sit beside her on the couch and squeeze her hand as Thea continues to nap in the old gal's lap. "Thank you, Alma. Thank you for keeping an eye out for my children. Thank you for calling me when you knew something was wrong."

She smiles. "My Ernie always said I had a sixth sense for trouble. When Starla didn't walk the twins at 11:00 and stop to see me on my porch, I knew something was wrong. I could set my clock by that girl."

"You never got the impression she was irresponsible?"

"Starla? Oh my, no. She has a gift with children even though she isn't a mother herself. Some women do."

"I felt that way, too. But—" I brush my lips against Aiden's fine, red-gold hair. "How could she...?"

"I think she must've gone off with whomever was in that car I saw in the driveway," Alma says. "I wish I'd been watching when it left. I must've been in my laundry room, switching the clothes from the washer to the dryer."

I can't help smiling at Alma's tacit admission that she watches my house all day like it's the latest binge-worthy series on Netflix. Ethel comes over and lays her head on Alma's knee, and my neighbor strokes the dog's ears. "You saw what happened. I wish you could talk and tell us."

Ethel's brown eyes shift from Alma to me, and I get the sense the dog definitely witnessed something. And then I remember how Sean joked that the nannycam was back-up protection to help Ethel with her guard dog duties. My gaze moves to the tiny camera nestled between two books on the top shelf. Its beady eye points directly toward the kitchen, recording every movement the caregiver makes as she feeds the twins.

I jump up and grab my laptop. "We do have a witness, Alma. The nanny-cam."

Alma's brow furrows as she watches me log into the system and pull up the live feed. Then I scroll backward until the screen fills with me kissing the twins good-bye this morning. I speed up the playback, and Starla races through the morning routine of changing the twins and cleaning up after breakfast, her mouth moving silently as she sings and talks to them in their playpen, and the twins giggle and wave in response.

All normal and happy.

Then the camera shows Ethel charging out of the room at 9:45.

Alma points to the screen. "I bet whoever arrived in that car is at the door."

Starla disappears from view and a few moments later returns, followed by a tall, wiry man wearing a hoodie with the hood up.

I slow down the playback and Alma and I lean toward the screen. "I can't see his face," Alma complains.

The man stands with his right shoulder toward the camera, only his chin periodically visible from behind the hoodie.

Starla faces him, all the good cheer gone from her face.

"La!" Aiden points to the screen.

"Yes, sweetie—it's La La."

Frustration wells up in me as I try to discern what's happening between Starla and her visitor solely by watching the expression on her face. At first, she listens intently, then she drops her gaze like a scolded child. She edges backward, trying to put some distance between them.

Alma's bony fingers dig into my arm. "I think he's threatening her!"

Aiden begins to whimper. Does he understand what's coming, getting scared all over again? I pause the video to walk him around the family room, torn between my desire to keep my son happy and my need to know what happened to Starla. Finally, Aiden settles down in the swing with his favorite toy, and I return to the video.

Now Starla is putting the twins in the highchairs and preparing their bottles. She sprinkles some Cheerios on their trays, and the effort of trying to pick them up and get them in their mouths keeps both babies occupied while the discussion continues.

Starla keeps her back to the man as she works on the bottles, but he comes up behind her and looms over her. She edges past him and hands a bottle to each twin.

The man grabs Starla by the forearm and starts dragging her toward the back door. She struggles, pointing toward the babies. I can't read lips, but I'm sure her open mouth is screaming, "no!"

She reaches for the phone we gave her. He snatches it from her hand and pockets it.

Then the man raises his left hand and slaps Starla across the face.

Alma screams as we watch the girl stagger backward, saved from falling only by the man's grip on her arm. Ethel jumps up, doing her best to protect Starla, but the man kicks her away.

"Oh, no! Oh, no—he's hurting her," Alma wails at the screen as if she can change the inevitable outcome.

The tall, hooded man drags Starla out the back door.

Aiden and Thea finish their bottles and look around the kitchen.

Ethel sits between them, her doggy brow furrowed.

Minutes tick by. Thea tosses her bottle to the floor.

Then the crying begins.

Chapter 23

The end of the video makes me feel simultaneously better and worse.

I was right about Starla. She didn't recklessly abandon our children.

But something bad has happened to her.

I glance over at Alma—she's pale and trembling with shock. I fumble with my phone to call Sean but see his last text: *At the gate. Plane on time. Home by midnight.*

He's in the air, somewhere between Texas and New Jersey.

I have to call the police. Of course, I'm not going to call 9-1-1 and try to explain to a dispatcher that I have videotape of my nanny being abducted. Instead, I call Sean's partner, Pete Holzer, and explain the situation. Within minutes, two patrol cars and an unmarked car, all without sirens and lights, roll up. I'm so relieved to see Holzer that I throw my arms around him. He's shorter and older than Sean, but such a rock of stability.

I'm in good hands. We'll find Starla. We have to.

I play the video again, and it's more shocking because I know what's coming. Alma covers her eyes.

Holzer watches impassively, giving only a grunt at the moment the assailant slaps Starla.

"She clearly knows the guy. She ever talk about a boyfriend?"

"No, she doesn't talk about herself much. All we know is that she grew up in a small town in West Virginia and came to New Jersey for better work opportunities. But with only a high school diploma and no local references, she was having a hard time finding a job with a day care center or a nanny agency. We told her the job with us would be temporary until our regular nanny returns, but she wanted to do it as a way to get a local reference. At first, she was helping Sean's mother, but when Mary had another engagement, we let Starla work alone." I run my hands through my hair. "Oh God, what were we thinking? We never should have left her alone with the kids."

Holzer pats my hand. "Don't blame yourself. The kids are fine. They won't remember this. Let's focus on Starla. Give me everything you've got on her: Social Security number, address, phone. "

"We were paying her cash. I don't even have her Social Security number." This is technically a violation of the tax code, but Holzer doesn't work for the IRS. And I'm sure we're not the only law enforcement family to pay a babysitter off the books. "The phone the attacker took from her is a burner phone Sean just bought for her so we could stay in touch. Before that, she didn't have a phone of her own." I lean back and close my eyes, trying to picture where I put the scrap of paper with the landline number Starla gave me when we first met. Finally, I find it in a stack of unopened mail on the kitchen counter. The original post-it note is stuck to an envelope where Sean has written the name and address of the old lady Starla lives with. "Sean tried to visit the woman, but she never answered the door. Starla says she's hard of hearing. Apparently, Starla got matched up with her through church—my mother-in-law says it's the Methodist Church."

"This is all good. We'll follow up on all these leads. Now tell me again—how did you first meet Starla Douglas?"

"She showed up at one of my estate sales. She overheard me tell my assistant, Donna, about our childcare problems, and she said she could help." Repeating this story makes me cringe. It's as random as if I'd met her at a bus stop or in line at Walmart.

But Holzer doesn't display a trace of disapproval.

At least, not openly.

"And where was the sale?"

He frowns when I give him the Corrigans' address.

"That's pretty far out from downtown Palmyrton. How would she have gotten out there with no car?"

"I didn't ask that day. But then she came back on the second day to follow up with me. She said a friend had given her a ride." I gnaw my lower lip. "I never saw any friend with her either day. But I wasn't really looking. And the friend could have been wandering around in the house." I throw my hands up. "I'm no help at all."

Holzer turns to Alma. "Can you describe the car you saw in the driveway?"

My neighbor sits up straight and pulls her cardigan close around her. "Old and beat up. Faded navy blue or gray with rust patches and a droopy bumper."

"Make and model?" he asks hopefully when Alma is able to provide such a detailed description.

"I'm not so good with that." Alma squeezes her eyes shut to summon a clearer picture. "It was a four-door sedan, that much I know. Nothing fancy. Maybe a Ford or Chevy."

"License plate?" Holzer asks, aware he's pushing his luck.

"I don't know the number, but it must've been a New Jersey plate because I'm sure I would've noticed if it was from another state. My husband and I used to love to play the license plate game whenever we traveled. We once spotted plates from forty-seven states at a parking lot in Colonial Williamsburg."

"You're doing great ma'am. This is very helpful. Did the car have any bumper stickers or other decals?"

"You mean like those stick figures that show how many people are in the family? I think those are silly."

Holzer smiles. "Yes, or a windshields sticker that mentions a college or high school. Or a political sticker. Anything would help."

Alma's eyebrows scrunch with effort. "Yes. Yes, now that you mention it, there was a sticker on the back bumper." She takes off her glasses and polishes them on the hem of her blouse. "But I can't read a bumper sticker from clear across the street. I just noticed a bright green blob against the dark car."

Holzer writes this down. "You're very observant ma'am."

You can say that again.

Holzer continues. "So you live right across the street, Mrs. Bannerman? Any chance you have a video doorbell that might have recorded what was happening over here?"

Alma waves this thought away. "Too new-fangled for me." Then her face brightens. "But Lucy and Carlos who live next door to me have one. Such a nice young couple. They're hardly ever home, so I have to collect their packages and mail all the time."

Props to Alma! Sean and I trade Alma stories with Lucy and Carlos all the time. We've even been to their house for dinner, but I wouldn't have been able to tell you what kind of doorbell they have.

"Okay, Mrs. Bannerman, thank you very much. I'm going to have Officer Conway here walk you home." Holzer makes eye contact with me. He clearly has more to tell me.

Alma pushes herself out of our squishy sofa. "Are you sure you'll be all right on your own, dear?"

"I'll be fine, Alma. Sean will be home soon." I stand and give her a hug. "Thank you so much for all you've done."

"That's what neighbors are for!"

Once the door closes behind her, Holzer draws his chair closer to mine. "Here's what's going to happen next, Audrey. Sean won't be permitted to work on this case since the crime happened in your home and you two know the victim. I'm going to need to interview Mary—"

I groan and massage my temples. My mother-in-law will flip out.

"—but she and Joe will think Sean died if they see his partner show up on their doorstep at night. You'd better call them but tell them as little as possible. I'll be over there in fifteen minutes."

As Holzer turns to go, I grab his arm. "You'll find her, won't you? You don't think she's—" I can't bring myself to speak the word.

"She clearly knew her attacker, so it's not a random home invasion or abduction. Probably some jealous, controlling jerk who doesn't want his girlfriend to have her own life. Or maybe someone from West Virginia came to take her back."

Pete Holzer moves towards the door. "We have a lot of leads. We'll track her down."

Chapter 24

The next morning, we all sleep late, exhausted by our ordeal. When Sean arrived home at midnight, he found me dozing in the rocker in the twins' room. I'd been unwilling to let them out of my sight for even a minute. When I tell him what happened and show him the video, he's furious, ready to run directly to the Palmyrton police department to find out what progress is being made to capture the man who took Starla, and by extension, put our children at risk.

But I succeed in holding him back. I want my husband home with us, and I remind him that he won't be able to help with the case. Sean contents himself with texting Holzer, who has nothing new to report yet.

Sean lies rigid beside me in bed. "We should never have left the kids home alone with Starla. We know practically nothing about her. Who is this guy?"

"I've been beating myself up with the same thoughts." I lay my head on Sean's broad chest. "But what if he had come when your mother was here with Starla? That could've been even worse. Mary could've had a heart attack."

"True. What did my mom say when you called her?"

"Luckily, your dad answered, and I broke the news to him. Before I could tell him all the details, Holzer showed up at their house. So Pete did the heavy lifting."

Sean pulls me into his arms. "I'll call her in the morning."

"Good. I'll be working from home."

WHEN I CALL TY AND Donna in the morning, they assure me they can manage fine at Villa Aurora without me.

Today.

Then what am I going to do?

I push my worries to the back of my mind and spend the morning enjoying my time with the kids. They seem utterly unfazed by what happened yesterday. I wish I could say the same for myself. We walk to the park and stop to visit Alma on the way home. Only after I put them down to their naps do I allow myself to fret over Starla and my new childcare crisis.

I sit in the rocking chair in the twins' room reviewing my calendar. The sale opens in two days, and runs Friday, Saturday and Sunday. I have to be on-site all of those days. Sean was on-call two weekends ago, so he should be home to watch the kids on the Saturday and Sunday of the Villa Aurora sale. But I need childcare for tomorrow through Friday.

As I look at my daughter sleeping peacefully, it dawns on me that I haven't checked in with Roseline to see how her daughter is doing with her cancer treatment. The least I could do is show a little concern for another mother who's suffering.

Before I type the text, I say a little prayer. *Please let the news be good.*

Roseline answers promptly. *She had the first treatment and handled it well. She is strong!*

Whew! That's a relief. I reply with wishes for continued improvement, careful not to ask when Roseline might be thinking of returning.

While I'm answering Roseline, another text comes in.

It's Alex saying he needs to talk to me and asking what time I'll be at Villa Aurora. My hands clench the phone. I'm not about to tell him I'm working from home today—he might suggest coming here to talk to me. Two days ago, I would've been fine with that. But after what happened yesterday, I'm taking Sean's warning seriously. There's no way I'm letting a man who's a suspect in the murder of his father—even if I think he's an unlikely suspect—anywhere near my kids.

I close my eyes thinking of a plausible excuse to stall him. Finally, I text, *Can't talk now. At doctor's appointment with my twins.*

I expect him to reply "call me when you're free" or "I'll catch you later," but there's nothing more from Alex. Before long, the twins wake up and my mommy routine resumes. Alex slips from my mind.

Sean returns home at six and I feel like a 1950s housewife as I run to greet him at the door. "What happened at work today? Any news on Starla?"

Sean heads for the kids, taking them both in his lap as he talks to me. "Here's what we've got so far. They reviewed Lucy and Carlos's doorbell video, and it does show the car in our driveway. The guys in the lab were able to enhance the video enough to make out the license plate."

My eyes light up. This is progress! "Fantastic!"

"Not really. The plates are stolen." Sean builds a tower of blocks for Aiden to knock over, a game that never gets old. "They belong to a twenty-year-old Caddy that was donated to charity by its owner's heirs. Those cars get junked, and somehow the plates never got returned to the DMV." Thea howls when she misses her chance to knock over the blocks, and Sean distracts her by loading more blocks into a dump truck. "If there's a connection between the original owner, the heirs, the charity and our abductor, we're not likely to untangle it anytime soon."

I stamp my foot in frustration. "Are they even trying? Or is this a back-burner case because Starla is poor and has no local family to pressure the police?"

Thea pushes Sean's hand aside and works on filling the truck herself. Then she spies a red block she wants at the edge of the blanket and gets on her hands and knees, rocking back and forth. She's dying to crawl so she can get whatever she needs, but she hasn't figured out the alternating hand/knee motion yet.

"Starla's case has me applying pressure." Sean's voice gets agitated, and he thumbs his chest. "You don't think I want to find that poor kid?"

"Of course, I know you do. I know it's frustrating you're not allowed to work on the case." A thought pops into my mind. "Hey, if they were able to read the license plate, were they able to make out what the bumper sticker said?"

"It said, 'Consume a Cleaner Vitality.' Does that mean anything to you?"

I shrug. "It sounds like a health food slogan."

"They googled it. Couldn't come up with anything much. Doesn't seem to be for sale anywhere. Another dead end."

Thea dumps the blocks from the truck, and she and Aiden explode in giggles. Then they work together to refill it.

"What about the old woman she lives with?"

"I don't know how to tell you this. Starla doesn't live there." Sean pushes more blocks towards the twins to keep them engrossed in their game.

I can't process this. "What do you mean, she doesn't live there?"

"The house is owned by a Thelma Karpinski, but she's been in the hospital and then a rehab facility for months. Her family's trying to convince her to sell the house, but they haven't succeeded yet. None of them know Starla."

I feel my allegiances shift slightly. "So Starla lied to us about where she lived? Or if the house was empty, could she have been squatting there?"

"We've looked around the outside. No sign of forcible entry; neighbors haven't noticed anything suspicious. But it's possible Starla got in somehow. We've asked Mrs. Karpinski's kids to come and let us in so we can check."

I'm still struggling to reconcile this deceit with the Starla I knew—so open and guileless. "But Starla told your mom she met Mrs. Karpinski through the Methodist church. Was that a lie too?"

Sean pinches the bridge of his nose. "I went over and talked to my mom at lunchtime. Turns out Starla didn't actually volunteer that information. Seems Mom made some assumptions and Starla simply agreed."

"Or didn't deny." I'm familiar with Mary's MO. She develops an explanation that agrees with the way she sees the world, and very quickly her theory becomes her hard truth. And everyone around her agrees simply to avoid an argument. Mary asks people if they're Catholic within ten minutes of meeting them. When Starla said no, Mary probably rolled through Protestant denominations until Starla agreed to one. From there, it was a quick leap to assume she found her housing via her church. Because if Mary were ever stranded in an unfamiliar town, she'd head right to the local Catholic church for help.

"Mrs. K. isn't a churchgoer," Sean explains. "And no one at the Methodist church has heard of Starla."

Thea dumps the load of blocks on top of her brother's foot, unleashing a howl of protest.

An equal load of outrage settles in the pit of my stomach. How could we have been duped like this? I pick up Aiden to soothe his tears. "Have you found her family?"

Sean shakes his head. "Starla Douglas may not be her real name. We're not finding a birth certificate in West Virginia with that name anywhere close to her age."

I rock back in the sofa, holding my son close to my heart. "She even lied about her name? Who *is* this kid?"

Chapter 25

Day Two of working at home begins with my phone ringing off the hook with offers of babysitting assistance. I guess when your friends and family learn that your babysitter has been abducted, they're more eager to help than if she'd just up and quit. First, my friend Madalyn calls and says her son and daughter-in-law are trying to get pregnant and the three of them want to get some real-life baby experience. I'd be doing them a favor by letting them babysit. Given that Madalyn is a nurse who's raised four kids and that the prospective new parents might be years away from a baby, the favor angle seems like a gross exaggeration. But I won't argue. That's one day taken care of. Then Sean's sister Deirdre calls and says our niece and her friend need supervised childcare opportunities to qualify for their Red Cross baby-sitting certificate. Could I please bring the twins to her house so the girls can practice while she hovers over them. Another day covered.

Soon Ty calls me to review some pricing decisions. He sends me photos of the items in question, and we get involved in a long debate about the likelihood that one of our regular customers will be interested in a particular chest of drawers. Only after he hangs up do I realize that I never asked him if Alex showed up at Villa Aurora yesterday. Sean offered to come home early today if I want to meet with Alex here, but my client hasn't called me, and I'm tempted to leave well enough alone.

Then the doorbell rings.

My heart skips a beat. Could that be Alex stopping by unannounced? A glance at the monitor reveals Ty's grandmother on my front porch. I run to the door. "Betty! What are you doing here?"

She elbows past me, dropping her large purse and reusable shopping bag on the hall floor. "What kind of hello is that? What happened to, 'Betty, I'm so glad to see you?' "

I hug her tight. "I'm very glad to see you."

Especially since you're not who I expected.

"Ty told me all about what happened with that Starla girl. I'm here to watch those beautiful babies until your real nanny comes back from Texas."

Grandma Betty barges past me to scoop Aiden up from his bouncy seat. "Hello, handsome! Give your Grandma Betty some lovin'."

Aiden immediately obliges by snuggling his head into Betty's neck. Not to be left out, Thea waves her hands from her seat, begging to be picked up. I spend the next ten minutes insisting that the twins are too much work for Betty. Meanwhile, she tickles them, bounces them, examines their gums for new teeth, opens my fridge and cupboards checking for supplies, and unpacks her shopping bag.

"Okay—I'm all set." Betty plops down on the family room sofa. "You better get yourself over to that Villa place. Ty is waitin' on you."

————————◆————————

LEAVING THE TWINS IN Betty's care makes me anxious. But it's my only option since Ty's grandmother has no intention of departing my house, and it will be hard for me to work at home with her talking to me nonstop. As soon as I arrive at Villa Aurora, I begin scolding Ty. "Why did you tell your grandmother to come to my house to babysit? Are you really not able to manage here without me?"

Ty fixes me with the prison death stare. "I didn't tell her to go over. I just told her what happened with Starla, and she took it from there. Now that Lo is in nursery school, Grams feels like no one needs her anymore."

"But your sister thinks Lo is too much work for Betty. How can I stick her with the twins?"

"Charmaine is right. Lo is four, and he never stops runnin'. The twins can't even crawl yet. Grams can manage them fine." Ty squeezes my shoulder. "You just freakin' because of what happened with that guy comin' to your house. You better believe Grams not about to let in any abductors."

This is true. Grandma Betty is every bit as street smart as Ty. So I decide to get to work. Ty shows me some items he priced yesterday, and we discuss how to handle a pretty dresser with a deep scratch across the top. Only after we settle on a price do I notice that Donna isn't around even though her car is out front.

"Where's Donna?"

"Alex showed up lookin' for you, and we thought you weren't coming in today. So he asked Donna if he could talk to her...*privately*." Ty rolls his eyes. "You know she was all over that."

I feel a twitch of alarm in my gut. Sean's warning not to be alone with Alex applies to Donna as well as me. The fact that Constantine appears to have been poisoned has finally made it to the local news, but the coverage hasn't been that prominent. It's possible that Donna totally missed it—she's not a news junkie like I am. And I've been so preoccupied with the Starla incident that I never mentioned to Ty or Donna what's going on with Constantine.

"Where did they go?" I ask Ty.

He shrugs as he lifts a small end table.

I reach out and grab his shirt as he passes. "Ty, this is important. Why did you let Donna go off with Alex?"

Ty sets down the table and puts his hands on his hips. "I'm not the boss of her. She tells me that all the time. If Donna says she's goin' out, why would I stop her?"

It's true that Ty and Donna's only disagreements come when one tries to wield authority over the other. Although Ty has been with me longer, I consider them both equally competent, just with different skills. And threat perception is definitely not part of Donna's skill set. "I'm sorry. I didn't mean to blame you. It's just...have you heard the news about Alex's father's death? Constantine was poisoned. Sean says Alex is considered a possible suspect."

"Poisoned!" Ty takes a step backward as if I shoved him with my words. "Alex didn't mention anything about that when he showed up here."

"What exactly did he say? Why did he want to talk to me?"

"He wasn't specific. I figured he wanted to talk to you about how the job was going. He hasn't been here since his dad passed, and I assumed he was just getting back into the work groove. Of course, Donna was fussin' all over him...hugging him, offering condolences, asking if he needed anything. I said 'sorry for your loss' and left it at that." Ty extends his hands palms-up. "I guess that's why he asked to talk to Donna. He can tell I don't really like him."

I pull out my phone and text Donna. *Where are you? Are you OK?*

While waiting for her answer, I continue my conversation with Ty. "Why don't you like Alex?" Ty is usually a good judge of character, but I thought his aversion to Alex had to do with Alex's flirtatious behavior toward Donna. Is there more to it?

Ty's lip curls in distaste. "I don't like big talkers like him. He keeps jivin' about all his plans for Villa Aurora. Me personally—I don't go countin' my chickens before they're hatched."

I suppose Ty is right about that although I put it down to Alex's boundless enthusiasm for his project, not to bragging. But Ty doesn't seem to be uneasy about the man's danger to others.

Donna's answer comes through. *Sure, I'm OK. I'm having lunch with Alex. Do you need me?*

I look up from my phone to report to Ty. "They're having lunch. Do you think she'll be okay? Should I ask where they're eating?"

Ty tilts his head and looks at me like I've lost my marbles. "You think Alex is going to poison Donna at lunch? I mean, he might have a reason to kill his old man, but he doesn't have a motive to get rid of Donna."

"I suppose. It's just...Sean warned me not to be alone with Alex. He would've been happy if I walked away from this job."

Ty raises his eyebrows. "Not for nuthin' Audge, but Sean has a way of over-reacting when it comes to you getting mixed up with crimes."

"Given my track record, his worry isn't entirely unjustified." I look back to my phone, still trying to decide how to respond to Donna.

The tone of Ty's voice softens. He can tell I'm worried whether it's rational or not. "Just act like you're curious about their date. Ask how it's going...where they're eating. Girl stuff. Then you'll know."

I nod acknowledgement of this inspired idea as I type. *Oooo! Lunch with Alex! Where did he take you?*

The Black Horse Tavern in Mendham. We're almost done. I'll be back at the Villa soon.

The Black Horse is a busy, popular place. Nothing could happen to Donna there. But what if Alex puts date rape drugs in her drink? My imagination revs into overdrive.

Tell him your boss is checking up on you. LOL!

I pace around Villa Aurora for the next half hour, unable to concentrate on anything until I'm sure Donna is safe. How long should I wait before I drive over to the restaurant to check on her? What if nothing's wrong? How would I explain myself?

Finally, I hear a noise at the back door and run to greet my assistant.

Donna jumps when I appear in the back hallway just as she walks through the door.

"Hi!" She removes her oversized sunglasses. "I didn't realize you were texting me from here. I thought you were working from home. Who's watching the kids?"

"Grandma Betty came over and insisted she could watch them while I'm here." I peer over her shoulder. "Where's Alex? Yesterday he texted me that he wanted to talk to me."

"He dropped me off and left. He has another appointment to get to."

Donna slips past me and heads for the dining room. I trail behind her. "So was lunch business or pleasure?" I ask her back.

"Mmmm—A little of both, I guess."

"Did Alex say what he wanted to talk to me about?"

"Just wanted to know how we were getting on with our preparations for the sale." Donna busies herself dusting and arranging some vases she found in the attic. "I filled him in. Said we'd be totally ready by Friday."

Donna continues to fuss and fiddle, not meeting my eye. If all Alex wanted was a simple update, why didn't he ask for that in his text to me? I get the distinct impression Donna is keeping something from me.

"That's it?" I don't hide the doubt in my voice. "Ty said Alex wanted to discuss something privately. Surely, Alex could've asked you about our progress right here."

Donna lets out a loud huff. "Ty should mind his own business."

I plant myself in front of Donna, forcing her to make eye contact. "Ty's business is watching over my business, and I want to know everything that's going on with our client."

Donna sets down a large cloisonné vase so hard it rocks on the table. Both of us are surprised by the harshness in my voice. I never speak to Donna and Ty with an "I'm the boss" tone.

"I'm sorry," I say. "I'm really on edge after what happened to Starla, and, and..." Surely, Donna knows about the cause of Constantine's death by now. "Did Alex mention his father? I suppose you've heard the news that Constantine was poisoned."

"Yes, but Alex doesn't believe that's true. His family is hiring their own forensic scientist to do a second autopsy." Donna tosses her hair back. "Alex is devastated by his dad's death, but he knows his father really wanted the Villa Aurora project to succeed. That's why he's pushing to have the sale as scheduled."

I notice Donna has taken out her usual clip, so her hair was loose for her lunch date. I had considered the flirtation between Donna and our client to be harmless, especially since Alex said he'd wait until after the job was complete to ask her out. Now he seems to have accelerated his courtship schedule. I can't help but wonder why. "We're absolutely moving forward with the sale. But Donna, we need to be careful. Constantine was murdered for a reason. Maybe it has something to do with Villa Aurora, or maybe it's totally unrelated. Hopefully, the police will figure it out soon, but it might not be before this weekend. Until we know what's really going on here, we have to proceed with caution."

Donna's eyes narrow. "What's that supposed to mean? We can't trust our client?" Her voice grows louder. "We have to treat Alex like he's a murderer?"

I try to continue in a reassuring manner. "We don't know who killed the old man. But the police always consider family members suspects in a murder investigation. After all, Alex must be a beneficiary of his father's estate."

Donna flings down her cleaning cloth. "Sean told you the police think Alex killed his father for money, and you automatically believe that? He loved his dad. He's heartbroken."

This isn't going well. "Donna, I just don't want you to get hurt. You still haven't explained why Alex wanted to talk to you privately if all he wanted to know was if we were on schedule. Are you keeping something back?"

"I'm a grown woman, Audrey, as you're always reminding me." Donna spins on her heel and heads for the foyer. "I don't have to ask your permission to go out with a man for lunch."

I stare at the empty doorway through which Donna has just disappeared. This behavior is so unlike her. True, she's always empathetic to other people's pain and always sees the best in people. So I'm not surprised she doesn't want to suspect Alex of any wrongdoing. I didn't either when Sean first warned me. But her snappishness towards me is totally out of character. Donna's a lousy liar, so I'm left with the conclusion that Alex told her something he doesn't want her repeating to me. Lashing out is her only strategy for keeping the secret.

I fully intend to get to the bottom of this. Pulling out my phone, I call Alex. Not surprisingly, it rolls to voicemail as Donna said he was on his way to another meeting. I leave a message in the sternest voice I can muster.

If he doesn't call me back....well, I can be persistent.

Chapter 26

In a house as big as Villa Aurora, it isn't that hard for Donna and me to avoid each other for the rest of the afternoon. The sale prep really is shaping up well. All the important pieces of furniture and art acquired by Phineas Toliver for his family home have been priced and notices sent to our best customers. For the rest of today and tomorrow, we're focusing on pricing the utilitarian items left from the eras of the school and the clinic: desks, tables, books, kitchenware.

We've decided on our layout strategy: the tower, basement, attics and third floor servants' bedrooms will be closed off from shoppers. Certain large bedrooms on the second floor will be open, with all the saleable furniture moved into those spaces. Anything destined for the dumpster, like mattresses and bedding, will be moved into the smallest bedrooms, and those will be blocked off for the sale. Charmaine and Ty will work up here on the first day of the sale, with Donna and I handling the main floor. Lamar will be our runner.

I decide to go upstairs to check that nothing left in the small bedrooms needs to come out. As I reach the top of the grand, curving staircase, I stumble slightly and grab the solid chestnut banister for support. I was never in any danger of falling, but the sensation of unsteadiness makes me think of poor Caroline Forsyth. I look down at the black and white terrazzo tile of the foyer, and my stomach flip-flops. What a long way down and what an unforgiving surface for a fragile teenage girl to encounter! My gaze travels along the loggia as I try to imagine the spot where she went over. I grip the baluster and shake it, wondering how sturdy it is. Near the top of the stairs, it feels very solid indeed. I walk along, running my toe against the spindles. Midway down the hallway, my sneaker encounters a wobble in the wood, and I drop to my knees to look more closely. There's a vertical split in this spindle that's been mended. A shiver runs down my spine. Was this damage caused by a furious kick from Caroline as she was forced over the railing?

"Whatcha lookin' at?" Ty asks, emerging from one of the bedrooms.

I point. "That spindle is damaged."

"Yeah, the baseboards and door and window trim in this house all have a lot of dings and gouges," Ty says. "I guess the clinic patients and staff were pretty hard on Villa Aurora's woodwork. Lotta refinishing ahead."

Of course, that's it—simple wear and tear. This broken spindle is another example of my imagination running wild. I'm glad I didn't say more than I did to Ty.

Together, Ty and I tour the second-floor bedrooms. The four smallest rooms are filled with unsellable junk. Stacks of thin, stained mattresses straight out of "The Princess and the Pea." Iron bedframes with rusted springs. Mounds of frayed, yellowed sheets and ratty gray blankets. Could anyone ever have gotten a good night's sleep on these?

My sensitive nose catches a whiff of an old smell. "Does it smell smoky in here?" I ask Ty.

"Yeah, kinda." He steps toward the fireplace and shoves a stack of mattresses away from the hearth. "Look, the floor is black here. Looks like the fire spread outside the fireplace."

I inspect the damage. "Surely they didn't have fires in the patients' rooms." There's no more singed wood, but now that I'm paying attention, I can see the walls in this room are stained with soot. A bead of sweat trickles down my chest as I imagine some mentally ill patient trapped in here.

I nudge Ty toward the door. "Let's get out of here."

Since the rooms can't be locked, we seal them with painter's tape and hang "do not enter" signs.

"That should keep most people out," Ty says. "'Course there's always gotta be that one person who thinks the sign doesn't apply to them."

"Well, if they snoop in these rooms, they'll certainly be disappointed."

The larger bedrooms contain the less valuable furniture from the attics, all nicely displayed and accurately priced. "You and Donna have done a great job up here, Ty."

"Toldja we'd get it all done on time."

One part of me wants to confide in Ty about my spat with Donna, but I resist the impulse. I don't want to play them off against each other.

As we reach the end of the hall, Ty notices me looking at the narrow stairway to the third floor. "Totally empty up there," he reports. "Let's string some tape across the stairs to keep the snoopers out."

"Okay, but I want to go up there first." When Ty looks offended, I quickly reassure him. "Not to check up on you. I want to look at the room where Emmeline Hartnett told me the girls were locked up for punishment."

The last room on the right.

I climb the narrow, dark stairs to the third floor with Ty trailing behind me. It's suffocatingly hot up here, and I detect the telltale aroma of a dead mouse. Six tiny bedrooms line this narrow hallway. At first glance, the last room on the right seems identical to the others, but darker.

I realize there's no window in here. The only light comes from the hallway.

I enter cautiously although I'm not sure why I'm hesitating. Certainly, there's no place to hide in here, not even a small closet. Ty stands in the doorway watching me.

The walls are painted a putrid goldish brown. Unlike the smooth oak floors downstairs, the floors in these bedrooms are rough, unfinished pine. I imagine an eight-year-old girl alone in the dark, sitting on that floor with splinters scraping her legs below her plaid uniform skirt, listening to the skittering of mice and the creaking of the old building. How long the hours of her punishment must've seemed!

"Huh. Look at this," Ty says from behind me.

I turn to see Ty shining his phone's flashlight down at the baseboard. The extremes of temperature on the third floor have caused the baseboards to warp, and there is a space between the wood and the plaster wall. Out of the space, the corner of a folded piece of paper is just visible.

Ty leans down to pull it out.

"Don't rip it," I warn.

"It's stuck." He looks up at me. "Is it okay if I pull the baseboard back some more?"

What the heck—if Alex plans to use these third-floor rooms, they'll have to be completely redone. "Go ahead."

With a creak, Ty pulls the dry wood away from the wall and fishes out the yellowed paper. He unfolds it and we read:

I am banished for merely existing.
I am blamed for a sin that is not my own.
I am punished for daring to tell the truth.
I am fading away.

Chapter 27

A shiver passes over me as I study the frayed paper. The penmanship is careful, but the note wasn't written on a smooth desk, but on the rough surface of this room's floor, so the letters are bumpy and uneven. I imagine a young girl struggling to scratch out this plea in the dim sliver of light coming in under her prison's door.

"Why was she sent here?" I wonder aloud. "What was the sin she was blamed for?"

Ty exhales deeply. "I never shoulda pulled that paper out. Now you're gonna worry about a girl who was up here sixty, seventy years ago. Ain't nuthin' you can do about her problems."

Ever practical, that's Ty. But his remark has not reassured me. "I'm stunned that young women were treated like this in the 1950s and 60s. It's not that long ago."

Ty puts his hand on my shoulder and gently but firmly guides me out of the room. "Human nature never changes," he says. "Maybe she was mistreated, but then again, maybe she was just a teenage drama queen. You shoulda heard some of the fits my sister pitched when she was fifteen."

I'd like to believe this note was written by a teenager feeling sorry for herself as the victim of adult injustice. I remember casting my father as the villain in my life story when he wouldn't let me go to the Jersey Shore for a weekend of partying after the prom. But he didn't lock me in a dark, windowless room.

At the bottom of the third-floor stairs, Ty strings up the Do Not Enter sign. I wish I'd skipped going up there. The satisfaction I was feeling at the end of a productive workday is tarnished by the discovery of the note. I slide it into my pocket, unwilling to throw it away.

"Tomorrow, we'll price the last of the small stuff, put up the signs, and organize the check-out area. Then we're good to open the sale on Friday," Ty says.

"And you've got Lamar lined up to help during the sale, right?"

"He'll be here."

By the time we go downstairs, it's five o'clock and Donna's car is gone. If Ty thinks it's odd she left without saying good-bye, he doesn't mention it. He and I lock up, and I follow him down the long driveway.

On the drive home, my Spotify playlist is interrupted by an in-coming phone call. I glance at the dashboard screen, hoping it's Alex finally returning my call. Instead, the name on the screen is Emmeline Hartnett.

"Hi, Emmeline. How are you?"

The elderly librarian's voice brims with excitement. "I met with the sociology professor from Drew, and he provided some very interesting information. It's too complicated to explain on the phone. I need to show you the documents. Can you come over tonight?"

I'm bone-tired from my long day at work compounded by worry over Donna and Alex and Starla. But I do want to show her that note. "I can't get away from home tonight, Emmeline, but you're welcome to come to our house."

"I don't drive at night, dear. But I can come tomorrow during the day."

"I'll be working at Villa Aurora. Would you be willing to meet me there?"

"Oh, my yes!" she sounds like a teenager who just won tickets to see her favorite band. "I want to see the place again."

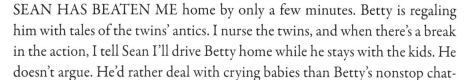

SEAN HAS BEATEN ME home by only a few minutes. Betty is regaling him with tales of the twins' antics. I nurse the twins, and when there's a break in the action, I tell Sean I'll drive Betty home while he stays with the kids. He doesn't argue. He'd rather deal with crying babies than Betty's nonstop chatter.

On the way through the middle of Palmyrton, while we're stopped at a light, we see a large, bearded man in a dirty trench coat digging through a trash can. He finds a discarded soda can, shakes it, and tips it up to his lips to drink the dregs.

"Ugh—poor soul." Betty searches through her voluminous purse and produces two crumpled dollar bills. "Pull up to the curb there, Audrey."

"But, Betty—"

"It's okay. I know him." She powers down her window. "Charlie! Hey, Charlie!"

The man looks up, his face a mix of fear and confusion. I signal and slide up to the curb. Betty hands him the money. "Now you go down to Dunkin' and get yourself a hot coffee, you hear me?"

Charlie takes the cash and shuffles away.

"So sad," Betty says. "He's not right in the head, but they let him live out on the street like this."

"How do you know him?" I ask as I catch a last glimpse of Charlie in my rear-view mirror.

"He's a regular at the soup kitchen. When my church group volunteers there, we see him every time. My friend Berenice knew him when he was a patient at the Center for Mindful Living. Then the place closed down, and Charlie is out on the street."

My spine stiffens to attention. "Ty told me you have a friend who used to work there."

"Oh, yes—Berenice has some stories to tell, for sure."

"Did Ty tell you about the big cage we found in the basement of Villa Aurora?"

"Yes, he did. I asked Berenice about it—she said it was just to keep supplies locked up. Stuff was always disappearing. The staff walked off with food and toilet paper and any other useful thing they could get their hands on. I'm not sayin' it's right to steal, but that guy who owned the place paid the aides so poorly that they took what they could to survive. And he made Berenice cook on a budget of eight dollars a day for each patient." Betty shakes her head. "What can you get for that?"

A knot in my gut loosens. "We were worried that patients got locked in there. It's a relief to hear the cage was just for supplies."

"Oh, the clinic was bad, but not that bad. Poor old Charlie, he's harmless. But Berenice says some of the other patients had violent tendencies." Betty clicks her tongue in disapproval. "They kept those poor souls all drugged up with pills. But sometimes the drugs would wear off or stop working or whatever, and then fights would break out. It was not only dangerous for the patients, but also for the staff. Berenice was safe back in the kitchen, but aides got hurt all the time. That's another reason the owner had a hard time keeping workers."

"Was he a psychiatrist?' I ask.

"No siree. He was a money man." Betty gestures with her fingers as if pounding an imaginary calculator. "Accountant or something. Always lookin' at the bottom line."

"But Berenice stayed there?" I ask.

"The fellow paid her a little better than the others. People gotta eat, you know, and there was no one else who could cover for her if she walked out."

"But then the clinic closed. What happened?"

"What caused the end was this." Betty shakes her finger. "One of the patients took it in his head to start a fire in the fireplace in his bedroom. Except all those fireplaces have been sealed up for years. So the house filled with smoke and all the alarms went off and the police and the fire trucks and the ambulances all came runnin'."

"A fire! Ty and I saw the traces of it in one of the bedrooms. Did anyone die?"

"Nah. Nobody got hurt bad—a couple had to go to the hospital for smoke inhalation. But that episode brought the state inspectors out. They said there wasn't enough staff for that many patients, and the fire doors weren't right, and the medications weren't stored properly. And the result of all that was The Center for Mindful Living had to close down. The owner said he couldn't afford to run it the way they said it had to be run."

I shake my head. "Cutting corners to turn a profit and putting vulnerable people at risk. That's despicable."

"Well, girl—you might say that. But you know there's always two sides to every story. The Center wasn't a great place, but it was better than nothing. The families couldn't afford the fancy clinics, and most couldn't manage the sick person at home. Imagine if I had to take in a grown son with mental illness and try to make him take his pills and keep him outta trouble. Can't be done. And Palmyrton Memorial Hospital won't keep these folks for more than a day or two. They pump 'em full of drugs and send them right back home. That's why poor Charlie is out here on the streets. His family won't keep him and there's no place else for him to go. And he's not the only one. Not by a long shot."

Betty is right. My first reaction was outrage, but the problem of how to help severely mentally ill people is complicated. We learned that lesson when we worked to clear out Harold the Hoarder's house so he wouldn't become homeless.

"So what happened to the man who ran the clinic?" I ask as we pull into the parking lot of Betty's apartment complex.

"That I couldn't tell you." Betty gets out of the car. "Goodnight, Audrey. I'll see you and those babies next week."

Chapter 28

On my way home, I think about the third phase of Villa Aurora's life. A patient setting a fire in one of the old, unused fireplaces could have ended in a catastrophic loss of life. Instead, it was just enough danger to bring about the end of the Center for Mindful Living. I wonder if there was a similar event that ended the St. Anselm's Academy era at Villa Aurora. Maybe Emmeline's visit tomorrow will provide an answer.

When I get back to my neighborhood, I notice lots of houses have junk piled at the curb—plastic playhouses, broken wheelbarrows, unwanted treadmills and rowers. Ah! Large item pick-up for our quadrant of Palmyrton must be tomorrow, and once again, Sean and I are caught unprepared. Maybe Sean will have the kids put down by the time I get home, and we can hustle a few items out to the curb.

A car in front of me slows then pulls to the curb without signaling. A man jumps out and assesses the viability of a small two-wheeler with training wheels. The poachers are out!

It occurs to me that with two soon-to-be mobile toddlers, I should keep an eye peeled for baby gates and push toys. I turn the corner onto Sycamore and it's as if the Garbage Gods have read my mind. There's a perfectly good plastic baby gate leaning against a mailbox. I pull up and grab it, and as I'm getting back in my car, I notice a familiar figure digging through the piles of stuff at the next house on the block.

Of course, Man Bun the Freegan would be here. Large Item Pick-Up Day must be like a national holiday to freegans. As I watch, he hauls a small love seat toward his dilapidated van. He lifts one end up onto the back of the van and attempts to push the small sofa in, but it won't budge. Taking pity, I go over to lend a hand.

"Need some help?"

He startles but relaxes when he recognizes me. "I'd appreciate that. The legs are stuck on something. Would you mind getting in the van and lifting while I push from below?"

I do as he instructs, and the love seat is quickly loaded into his already crowded van. When I jump down, I notice some of the bumper stickers on the rear doors: They're so worn and peeling, I assume they've been stuck there since the van's original owner. But they make me think of the bumper sticker on Starla's abductor's car. It sounded kind of tree-huggerish. Maybe Man Bun would know what it means.

I follow him to the curb, where he's returned to excavating the piles of junk. "Say, does the phrase, 'Consume a Cleaner Vitality,' mean anything to you?"

He stops in his tracks and slowly turns. "Yeah. Why?"

A flutter of excitement pulses in my gut. "A car that came to my house had a bumper sticker on it that said that, and I wondered what it meant."

He scratches under that mangy manbun. "It's a phrase associated with the biodiesel movement. But there are no manufactured bumper stickers. Making worthless junk like bumper stickers just feeds the waste stream. And no one is converted to the wisdom of biodiesel by reading a sign on someone else's car."

"I agree. But bumper stickers are usually more about signaling your own virtue than about making converts. Maybe this biodiesel user made his own little sign."

"Why didn't you ask the driver when he was at your house?" He goes back to picking through the selection of glass canning jars at the curb.

I hand him one of the better Mason jars. "Do you know someone who drives a gray sedan powered by biodiesel?"

He hesitates. "Possibly. Why?"

"The man driving that car forcefully abducted a young woman and left the two babies in her care abandoned for hours."

"Why would you think I know anything about a violent crime?" Now Man Bun is outraged. "Just because I don't fit with your idea of convention-ally acceptable society, does that mean I'm in touch with criminals?"

"No, of course not. I'm trying to help the police track this man down because the girl taken was my babysitter. I'm really worried about her. That bumper sticker is one of the few clues to his identity. I thought you might know him."

He staggers under the weight of his two canvas tote bags, rattling with stacked glass jars. "Look, there's not one big freegan organization. There's no Pope of the freegans. There're just individual small communities trying to live a life that doesn't further degrade the planet. We don't gather together for conventions."

"But you do share and trade with other groups. You know one another, or know of one another," I prompt him. "You must have some means of communicating with other groups."

He bends his long neck. "Yes. When I discovered your estate sale just by driving by on the day you were setting up, I circulated the information in an on-line freegan forum. I thought others could benefit from the excess of resources there."

"So if Starla, my babysitter, had been living in a freegan community, that could explain how she showed up on both days of the sale."

He drags his worn boot through the dust. "Possibly."

"Did you notice anyone at the Corrigan sale that you're...er...acquainted with through freegan circles?"

Long pause.

I know I should keep quiet and wait for Man Bun to talk. But I feel every second is wasted if naïve little Starla has fallen in with people who want to control her. "Okay, I get it. This guy is not your friend. But do you know who he is?"

"I am unwilling to bring the forces of the authoritarian state against a fellow traveler whose personal relationships are not connected to my own."

Lord, give me strength.

"Can I show you the video of him attacking Starla? His face isn't visible. But maybe you'll recognize his build, or his mannerisms."

I pull him over to my car where I grab my iPad from my tote bag and show him the nannycam video that I've downloaded and saved. He leans forward, his nose nearly touching the screen when Starla's attacker appears. He watches intently, and when the slap comes, he recoils.

Seeing the violence with his own eyes has changed his attitude. "I know who it is. You see that bracelet visible when he grabs her arm?" He replays the video, stopping it at the critical moment. A braided leather bracelet with a silver clasp encircles the man's wrist. I hadn't paid attention to it before.

"I know a guy who wears a bracelet like that. His name is Josh. I don't know his last name. His group is small."

Now we're getting somewhere! A first name...a connection to the freegan community. But I need more. "Where does his group live?"

Man Bun shakes his head. "No idea." He places his bags in the van and slams the rear door.

"Wait." I grab his arm. "Can you tell me your name and phone number? The police will want to follow up with you."

He shakes me off and jumps into the driver's seat. "Sorry. I don't want to get involved with the oppressive injustice system."

I let him go. But I snap a picture of his license plate as he departs.

Chapter 29

Sean stares at me with one hand suspended over a pile of baby clothes he's folding. "I send you off to drive Ty's grandmother home and you return with a lead to Starla's abductor? How is that even possible?"

I join in folding and stacking little overalls. "What can I say? I know a lot of people." The moment I walked in the house, I started with the punchline: I met a guy who recognizes the man who took Starla. Now I fill in the back-story.

Sean continues to shake his head as the details spill from me. But when I hand him my phone with the crisp photo of Man Bun's license plate, he starts to laugh. "Excellent work, Audrey."

"So you'll pass it along to Holzer, right? Oh, and tell him the freegans all like garage sales and they get their biodiesel from fast food restaurants so if they hang around those places, I bet they'll run into this guy."

Sean leaves the room to call his partner, patting my shoulder on the way out. "Relax, Audrey. We'll take it from here."

THE FOLLOWING MORNING, I set off for work in high spirits know-ing the twins are in great hands with Madalyn. Her son and daughter-in-law plan to work from my home so they can experience first-hand what it's like to juggle work and childcare. Good luck with that!

I'm also feeling lighthearted knowing I've given the police a solid lead on Starla's abductor. Despite her deceptions, I'm still worried about the kid. Maybe by the end of the day, we'll know what happened to her.

I arrive at Villa Aurora before either Ty or Donna. But the driveway isn't empty. Alex's BMW sits gleaming in the sun.

I consider turning around and leaving so I don't have to be alone with him in that house.

Too late. Alex appears from around back, waving. But it's not his usual cheerful greeting. More like a testy restaurant patron flagging down a neglectful waiter.

Alex strides toward my car. "Audrey! I'm glad I caught you. We need to talk."

That's for sure. But I'd prefer to be doing it with Ty in shouting distance. I get out of my car, but keep my keys firmly grasped in my right fist.

I go on the offensive. "I understand you took Donna out to lunch yesterday to talk about the job. I'd really prefer you have those discussions with me."

"Yes—well, here we are." The affable salesman has disappeared, replaced by a steely-eyed entrepreneur. "Donna tells me there was a break-in at the Villa. Why didn't you notify me immediately?"

"It happened the night your father died. We discovered it right after you called to tell me he had passed away. Since nothing valuable was taken and nothing was damaged, I decided not to bother you when you were grieving." I take a breath. "I'm sorry if that was the wrong decision, but that was my reasoning."

Alex frowns. "That was last week. You could have told me since then."

He's got me there. But the break-in was pushed to the back of my mind by the news that Constantine had been murdered and the police regarded Alex as a suspect. Before I can offer an excuse, Alex continues, his voice rising in agitation. "And what's this about some crazy old woman coming here and claiming her sister was murdered in the foyer?"

Clearly, Donna spilled her guts about everything that's happened in Villa Aurora since we started organizing the sale. No wonder she was defensive when I asked what they talked about. Did she also tell Alex how the landscapers think the house is under the evil eye? "A woman saw our social media post about the luggage in the basement. One of the suitcases once belonged to her sister."

"Why are you selling stuff from the basement?" Alex runs his hands through his perfectly styled hair. "I thought we agreed there was nothing worth bothering with down there?"

I draw myself up to my full height and speak in my calmest voice. "I believe we agreed that I should sell everything that has value. And those suitcases and the tools in the basement are attractive vintage items."

Alex paces across the width of the driveway. "I should never have used this sale as a way to attract publicity to our project. My partner is right—the house's past needs to be obliterated." He waves a folded section of newspaper pulled from his inner blazer pocket. "Did you see this BS article in the Palmyrton *Daily Record*?"

I take it from him and read the front-page headline: **Is Agyros Murder Part of the Villa Aurora Curse?** "The Daily Wretched is notorious for whipping up controversy to sell a few papers. No one takes it seriously," I say even though the question posed in the headline has crossed my mind, too.

"I can't have this talk of curses circulating around Villa Aurora. No one will want to start their marriage in a cursed venue." Alex folds his arms across his chest. "I'm calling off the sale."

Whoa! Whoa! This is not the outcome I want, but I keep my voice steady. "If you cancel the sale, not only will you lose the $200,000 I estimate it will generate, but you'll have to pay me a cancellation fee and pay us for the time we've spent setting up, as stipulated in our contract."

Alex and I glare at each other. I'm not about to back down, but I do want to talk him off the ledge. I soften my tone. "Look, Alex, obviously there are no such thing as curses." I say this with more confidence than I feel. "The best way to prove that is to let the public come and check the place out. If you cancel at the last minute, people will be suspicious. And lots of them won't get the word and will show up here anyway." I gesture to the grand façade of Villa Aurora. "The weather this weekend is supposed to be gorgeous. The house will look lovely. And if any troublemakers show up, Ty and Lamar will escort them out, no worries."

Alex continues to stare at me. But after a moment he drops his gaze. "Fine. But stop encouraging these people from the St. Anselm's School era."

I think about Emmeline Hartnett's plan to come here today. I'll have to waylay her, especially now that I know Donna will report on me to Alex. "I don't think we'll hear any more from them," I assure him. Then I add cautiously, "Do you anticipate the investigation into your father's murder will affect the sale in any way?"

Alex clenches his fists. "He was not murdered! Our family has hired our own pathologist to conduct another autopsy. We'll prove he died of natural causes."

I study Alex's handsome face, now mottled red with anger. Surely, the only reason to insist that the death wasn't murder is because Alex or someone else in the family is the primary suspect. If not, wouldn't he want the police to find the person who ended his father's life?

"I see. Well, I hope you get the desired outcome. In the meantime, I'm just wondering how you want me to handle questions from the public." I point to the newspaper he still clutches in his hand. "You know, in case they ask if the mur—" I catch myself. "—the death has anything to do with Villa Aurora."

"Tell them to mind their own—" Alex stops and takes a deep breath. "Tell them it is your understanding that Constantine Agyros had no involvement with the redevelopment of Villa Aurora."

"Okay, sounds good. But just between us, wasn't it your father who recommended Another Man's Treasure for this job? I remember seeing him at our last big sale, observing our work."

Alex flinches. Clearly, I've surprised him. "My father is, was, retired from the business. Occasionally, he handled small tasks for me. Researching an estate sale agent was one of them."

I nod. "And your partner—you keep saying he disapproves of the sale. Who is he?"

Alex turns toward his car. "No concern of yours. I'm the public face of this venture."

Chapter 30

As soon as Alex's car heads down the driveway, I pull out my phone to call Emmeline Hartnett. She answers immediately, and when I tell her I'm not going to be able to meet with her today after all, I hear the disappointment in her voice.

"I understand you're busy, dear. But I think you'll be very interested in what I've discovered about the origins of St. Anselm's Academy."

"I am interested, Emmeline. It's just..."

It's just I'm a day away from a sale that's going to bring in a ton of money and I have a prickly client and can't afford to screw up this job. But somehow, I don't think Emmeline will approve of that excuse. So I dig for a better one, even though it's not true today. "You see, I've been having childcare problems, which caused me to have to work from home a few days when I should have been here at Villa Aurora. So today, I have to work nonstop—I didn't realize how far behind I am. There's no time for even a short break."

Emmeline sighs. "All right. I'll type up my notes so that when you do have time to meet, I'll be able to show you all I've learned very efficiently."

"Great idea! I'll come and visit you on Monday morning when the sale is over."

"I'll see you before that, Audrey." Emmeline's voice brooks no disagreement. "I fully intend to come shopping at the sale on Friday."

Hmmm. The sale is open to the public. I can't very well forbid her to attend. "Okay. I'll see you then. But I'll be too busy to talk." And that's the absolute truth.

"I'm sure you will, dear. I'll keep myself amused, I assure you."

<hr />

BY THE TIME I HANG up with Emmeline, Ty has arrived. "How come you're standing around out here?" he asks.

I tell him an abbreviated version of my run-in with Alex. "We need to keep our heads down and forget about the past eras of the Villa. Let's not mention the note we found yesterday to Donna."

Ty gives me a puzzled look as if to remind me he's not the one obsessed with the traumatized schoolgirls of St. Anselm's. "Fine with me."

Ty and I are discussing placement of the check-out table when Donna arrives with an armful of signs. She jumps right into the conversation as if nothing happened between us yesterday. Even though I'm still annoyed that she spilled her guts about our business to Alex, I'm not angling for an apology. I need everyone working efficiently for the next four days. We can take up the breech of confidence later.

Ty and I go outside to place the signs while Donna finishes the pricing inside. Soon, the Classic Visions landscaping truck rumbles up the driveway, and Nico and his grandfather Arturo start pacing around the front yard. By the time Ty and I return from placing directional signs along the road, the two men are discussing—or perhaps I should say arguing about—the stone retaining wall that separates the overgrown flowerbeds from the front lawn.

There's a lot of hand-waving and head-shaking going on, and then Nico calls out to me to solicit my opinion. "Don't you think a curved wall is more pleasing to the eye than a straight one?"

"Uh...I—"

"What's it matter what she thinks?" Arturo butts in before I can answer. "I give you one long curve, not two short ones. The wall will stand longer that way. You wanna be back here in two years making repairs?" He stomps over to the wall and picks up a large rock that's come loose from the wall. "My grandfather built that one hundred years ago, and there's only a few loose stones. He gave his best to every job." Arturo looks up at the villa. "Not that Toliver appreciated craftsmanship. He treated my grandfather like slave labor. Men broke their backs building this place, and what did they get for it?" He spits on the ground. "Pennies!"

The old man teeters, and Nico rushes to steady him. "Grandpa, that stone is too heavy for you. And you're getting worked up. You know your doctor said to take it easy."

"Pah!" Arturo shakes off his grandson's hand and drops the rock. "What? I'm supposed to just sit around and wait to die?" He hobbles off to examine a distant section of the crumbling stone wall.

Nico adjusts his baseball cap against the glare of the sun. "I thought my grandfather would enjoy working on this job because his grandfather built the original walls and walkways. But he gets so agitated over every design choice I make. On other projects, he's happy to make just a few suggestions."

"I guess he really cares about this place," I say. "It's good for him to take an interest."

"Yeah, but I don't want him to keel over while he's here."

I pat Nico's shoulder. "My father's friend recently died on the tennis court at age ninety-two. My father was delighted. He said that's the best way to go."

"I can see his point. Unfortunately, the rest of my family will blame me if Grandpa dies on my watch." A flash of pain crosses Nico's face. "I guess at my age, you're supposed to be prepared to lose your grandparents, but I'm not ready. He's stubborn as a mule, but I love him."

"I think its great you two work together. You'll always have those memories."

Nico forces a smile. "Yeah. Yeah, that's true."

Chapter 31

On my way home after a full day of work, I pass the supermarket. I should run in and get something for dinner tonight, but one look at the teeming parking lot tells me there will be no "running" at ShopRite at five-thirty. I've already left the twins with Madalyn longer than I intended, so I head straight home.

When I arrive, Madalyn's son and daughter-in-law look shell-shocked and beat a hasty retreat.

"I think this experience may have set back the timeline for my becoming a grandmother," Madalyn says. "Which is fine. I'm enjoying having no one dependent on me."

While I nurse the twins, Madalyn stays to chat, filling me in on the latest gossip in our circle of friends. Roz has finished the first draft of her book, so she's less stressed. Lydia and Dave just got back from their first vacation together, and they're still a couple. And Madalyn's daughter Ginny has had some of her paintings accepted into the Palmyrton Art Fair. Madalyn takes Thea onto her lap while I nurse Aiden. "We're all coming to your sale tomorrow. Even Isabelle. She says the real estate market is so slow right now, she can take time off on Friday afternoon. Will all the good stuff go in the morning?"

"No, there's plenty to sell. And even if you don't buy anything, it's worth coming to see the house." I feel a little wistful that my friends will be enjoying the sale as an outing while I'll be working. "When's our next girls' night out?"

"Do you think everyone would enjoy going to the art fair next week?" Madalyn asks. "Then we could all come back to my place for drinks and snacks."

"That sounds like a perfect plan. Sean would do anything to avoid the art show—he'll happily go on duty with the kids so he can stay home and watch baseball."

Madalyn and I finalize our plans, and I encourage the twins to wave good-bye as she leaves. Then I turn my attention to dinner.

I open the fridge. Can I make a meal from olives, half a package of butternut squash ravioli (one square suspiciously furry) and a jar of applesauce?

"We've got nothing for dinner," I tell Sean as he arrives home a moment later.

"There must be something in the freezer." He opens it and we stare at a wall of frozen cubes of mashed organic carrots, beans, and squash. Plenty for the kids; nothing for us.

"What's that?" I point at a frost-encrusted package.

"Those weird-tasting chicken sausages we bought when we were trying to eat less red meat," Sean says. "And that," he points to a frozen bowling-ball-shaped object, "is the rump roast we bought before we gave up red meat. It'll take about three days to thaw and cook." He slams the freezer door. "I'll call out for pizza."

I clutch my stomach. "I had pizza for lunch. I can't eat more carbs."

"I'm too hungry for sushi," Sean complains. "And the Mexican place that delivers sucks."

I glance over at the twins, who are chipper and alert. "Think we could take them to the Apollo Greek diner? I could go for a Greek salad and a slab of spanakopita."

Sean's eyes light up. "And some pastitsio!" He scoops up Thea. "Can you behave yourself in a fine dining establishment?"

"Bah!"

"I'll take that as a yes."

Before we have time to talk ourselves out of the trip, we load up the kids and take off.

On the way to the diner, I ask Sean if there have been any new developments in the investigation into Constantine's murder. He takes his eyes off the road long enough to give me his "don't go there" look.

"Yeah, yeah—I know you can't talk about the case with me. But I saw Alex today and he keeps insisting that his father wasn't murdered and that his family has hired their own pathologist to prove it. Has that ever happened before on a case you've worked on?"

Sean shakes his head. "You hear in the news about high-profile police brutality cases where the family hires their own pathologist, but that's because the family thinks the police are hiding something. They want to prove that the death *is* murder, not prove it isn't. I don't understand what the Agy-ros family is up to."

"What about Alex's partner in the Villa Aurora re-development? When Constantine was at the house, he seemed to disapprove of the guy. And Alex is so cagey about admitting who the partner is. Could he have killed the old man?"

Sean signals to make the turn into the diner parking lot. "I've got an idea, Audrey. Why don't you sell Another Man's Treasure—"

"What?!"

"—and enroll in the police academy. It's not too late for you to start your official career in law enforcement."

"Ha, ha, ha." I get out of the parked car and begin grappling with the twins' car seat buckles.

Sean takes Aiden from my arms. "Seriously, I'm sure the team investi-gating Constantine's murder is looking at all business associates the firm has ever worked with. Most murders are spontaneous, violent outbursts with a lot of forensic evidence, which leads to a quick arrest. This one was carefully planned, so they may well have identified their suspect, but it will take a while to build a solid case. Making an arrest too soon can jeopardize a successful prosecution."

"So in the meantime, a murderer is walking around among us."

Sean holds open the diner door. "That's precisely why I told you to be careful around Alex Agyros."

<hr />

WE ENTER THE DINER and walk straight into a giant revolving glass dis-play case. Wedges of lemon pie with mile-high meringue, bricks of baklava, and teetering triangles of coconut layer cake spin before our eyes as we wait to be seated. The waitresses at the Apollo Diner look like they've collectively raised twenty kids. They put us in an out-of-the-way corner booth and line up two highchairs for Thea and Aiden. We order without even looking at the menu, and soon the kids are gnawing on wedges of pita bread, and Sean and I are enjoying our salads.

Some teenagers laugh and horse around in another booth, and a couple with school-age kids eat while mediating squabbles. A long table of elderly men tell tales and shout over one another. "This was an inspired choice if I do say so myself. No one cares that our kids are noisy and messy." I use a wad of napkins to pick up a gummy blob of bread that Aiden has dropped and hand him another wedge of pita, which he accepts with a delighted shriek.

"What's the latest with Starla's case?" I have to assume that the police haven't found Josh, the man in the video, or Sean would have told me as soon as he came home.

"Holzer talked to your customer, who wasn't too happy about cooperating, but he got some good leads to follow up."

"Is he staking out garage sales like I suggested?"

Sean looks at me from under his sandy brows. "No, honey. The Palmyrton police don't have time to watch every garage sale in town." He bites into a hot pepperoncino and severs the stem. "Are you eager to find Starla so you can give her a piece of your mind, or are you genuinely concerned about her?"

I kick him under the table. "Of course, I'm concerned. I mean, she did lie to us, and I definitely will never entrust our kids to her again, but I liked Starla and I'm worried about her. Someone is taking advantage of a vulnerable young woman. Can you blame me for wanting to stop that?"

Sean moves all his kalamata olives into my salad as a peace gesture. "I'm worried about her, too. But I trust Holzer, and so should you."

"What if Starla refuses to testify against her abuser? What can you charge him with? She let him into our house, so it's not a home invasion."

"Often, domestic violence cases have no witnesses—it's he said/she said, so if the woman changes her mind and won't cooperate, the DA has no choice but to drop the charges. However, in our case, we've got the video, so we can get him for assault and possibly even unlawful detainment."

Our main courses arrive with impressive speed, which is good because Thea is showing signs of impatience at being confined to the highchair. A girl from the loud teenager table waves at her, and when Thea smiles, the girl plays peek-a-boo with her menu. That's good for five more peaceful minutes. I stop chatting and dive into my spanakopita.

"How come that guy over there keeps looking at us?" Sean angles his head toward the long table of old men. "Do you know him?"

I look up in time to catch the eye of a short old man with thick gray hair. We study each other for a second until my mind makes the connection, and I wave. "It's Arturo, the grandfather of Nico, the landscaper designing the grounds at Villa Aurora. He comes with his grandson to offer advice about rebuilding the stone walls and walkways. I didn't recognize him out of context without his overalls and tools."

Arturo has placed me as well because he smiles and nods. The teenagers who have been carrying on behind us choose this moment to get up and leave. Suddenly, our back corner of the restaurant is quieter, and I can hear the conversation going on at Arturo's table in the background while in the foreground, Sean tells me about the latest financial disaster to befall his brother Terry.

"So the guy stiffs Terry for the work he's already done..."

I'm embarrassed to say, I tune my husband out. I've heard Terry's tales of woe so many times, I can predict every twist and turn and the inevitable tragic ending. For greater entertainment value, my ear tunes in to Arturo's table. I bet the group is the second cousins reunited through genealogy research that Nico told us about.

"I explained this already," one old man says crossly. "My grandmother is your second cousin once removed."

"Yeah, yeah—whatever." The guy across the table taps his knife for attention. "How is she connected to the little girl who lost her arm in the factory?"

"The little girl, Aggie, was my grandmother's older sister," an old man explains. "By the time my grandmother was ten, little kids weren't allowed to work in the factory no more. But she always remembered having to take care of her older sister." He gestures broadly, nearly knocking over his water glass. "Aggie wasn't ever right after the accident. She couldn't work. No one would marry her."

I lean forward as if this will help me eavesdrop better with my left ear while Sean fills my right with more dismal details of his brother's struggles. The story the old men are telling is related to the one Arturo told us about why Phineas Toliver was cursed by the evil eye.

A low-pitched side conversation develops at the other end of the table. They seem to be seeking clarification on something.

Overhearing the convo, Arturo responds. "My grandfather married his grandmother," he puts his hand on his own chest, then points to Aggie's relative before interlacing his fingers. "That's how the two sides of the family came together."

"Yeah—two poor families came together to make a third poor family," the man related to the injured child proclaims.

Another guy at the foot of the table dismisses this with a wave. "You did all right." He turns to the man beside him. "He's still got the first dollar he ever made."

I smile because their squabbling teeters on the edge of good-natured and aggrieved. As with any big, extended family, there are factions and disputes and jealousies.

"So now, Terry has hit up Mom and Dad for a loan...again." Sean's agitated voice brings my attention back to him. He wraps up his story at the same point where the Terry tales always end.

I lay a reassuring hand on my husband's arm. "Your parents are perfectly capable of handling it. They've been through this drill before."

This is Sean's cue to launch into a diatribe about how unfair Terry's behavior is to everyone else in the family. I switch my attention back to the big table, where the old guys are arguing about the check. "You had salad and soup. I just had salad." A skinny teenager has appeared and stands behind Arturo's chair tossing car keys from one hand to the other.

Arturo stands, pulls out his wallet, and tosses several bills on the table. He waves the young man with the keys toward the door as he speaks to the men at the table. "Life's too short to argue about pennies. I'll see you next month, God be willing."

Chapter 32

I t's show time!

The first day of the Villa Aurora sale has finally arrived. All our preparations are about to pay off, big time.

As I drive toward Ty's apartment early Friday morning, my heart is light. Sean is taking the twins to his sister's house, so I know they're in good hands. Ty and I have agreed to drive to the sale together because we think parking will be an issue. All the antique dealers eager to get the best selection will come today, and they will all demand my attention. Of course, there will be curiosity-seekers every day, but I'm guessing Saturday will be a bigger day for them. And then the bargain hunters will turn out in force on Sunday.

Today is my day to get top-dollar for the most impressive items in the sale. I'll have to sow the seed of doubt in my customers' minds: act now, or forever regret the one that got away.

I pull up in front of Ty's apartment building, where he and Lamar are waiting in the parking lot. The AMT van sags as Lamar settles in the front seat and Ty climbs into the back. "Ready for your first big sale, Lamar?" I ask the big man.

He smiles and lifts his hands palm-up. "Can't be worse than gettin' tackled by a 350-pound linebacker."

"Don't count on it, man. Wait'll you meet our most demanding customers."

I glance over my shoulder at Ty. "Are Donna and Charmaine ready?"

"Yep. Charmaine just texted that she's at Donna's place waiting for us."

I stop at Donna's condo and the two women pile in. "Move your big butt," Charmaine demands, pushing her brother affectionately.

"Watch your step, girl—we got three days of togetherness comin' up here."

The van rolls on, all of us in high spirits.

When I signal to make a left onto the winding road that leads to the Villa, three cars ahead of me wait to make the turn. After we pull onto the smaller road, we pass a man who lives in one of the smaller houses at the bottom of the hill angrily waving off cars trying to park in front of his home. "Oh, geez—look at all these people. And it's only 7:30."

The van crawls around the last bend in the road and the Villa looms ahead of us.

"Holeee Canoli!" Donna squeals from the back seat. "This has to be the biggest opening day crowd we've ever had."

"Looks like all your social media promotions and special email alerts have paid off, Donna."

Cars are parked up and down the street, the driveway, and on the flat parts of the overgrown lawn. I carefully navigate the van through the narrow strip of driveway and pull it around to the back, while our regular customers, recognizing us, jump out of their cars and start forming a line at the front door.

"I've got the numbers," Donna says as she exits the van. "Lamar, come with me while I pass them out. If anyone argues about their place, just give them a dirty look. You don't have to say a word."

Lamar rolls his shoulders and paints his best game-day scowl on his normally genial face. Donna claps her hands. "Perfect!"

While those two deal with the crowd, Ty, Charmaine and I enter through the back door. Charmaine hasn't been here yet, so Ty takes her on a quick tour and shows her where she'll be stationed. Meanwhile, I do a quick walk-through of the downstairs rooms.

The parlor and dining room look perfectly arranged for the opening bell. But when I get back to the library, I notice the books we have categorized so carefully look like they've been gone through...as if someone's already been shopping here. I step closer—there's fiction mixed in with nonfiction and valuable hardcovers mixed in with old junk.

Someone went through all these books and then hastily put them back without knowing, or caring, what went where.

Who?

Did our night-time visitor return? Did Alex ever do anything about the tower trap door after Donna told him about the break-in? Certainly, no one came to seal up the door while we were here working.

I do what I can to straighten the books, keeping an eye on the time.

Five more minutes. I head for the foyer, where Donna is now stationed behind the check-out table. I consider telling her about what I discovered in the library but decide to hold my tongue. I want to be the one who informs Alex this time.

I prepare to fling open the grand front door as soon as the clock strikes eight. As I stand with my hand on the massive brass doorknob, I feel a presence behind me. Expecting Ty, I pivot and find myself eyeball-to-eyeball with Alex Agyros.

"Good morning. I didn't hear you come in. As you can see, we've got quite a crowd."

"I thought I'd help out by welcoming the initial customers." Alex produces a stack of glossy tri-fold brochures with an artist's rendering of the remodeled Villa Aurora and a headline that reads, "Make your dreams come true with a Villa Aurora wedding."

I smile with all the sweetness I can muster and step aside. With the horde of people pressing against the front door, this is not the time to tell him about the library. I'll wait until after the initial rush. "Great. I'll be in the parlor. Don't let the crowd trample you."

From my spot in the grand front room, I can hear Alex begin his spiel. "Welcome to Villa Aurora. This Italianate mansion was –"

A man's voice cuts off Alex. "Where's the oil landscape painting by Emilio Lasconi? Audrey sent me an email."

"And the art deco etagere?" a shrill woman's voice adds.

Ah, my regulars—gotta love 'em! And they want no part of Alex's sales pitch.

Seconds later, buyers enter the parlor and I sell relentlessly, not backing down on any of my prices. Again and again, Lamar and Ty carry out large paintings and antiques.

I'm in the middle of a sales pitch for a rococo revival desk when Alex enters the parlor accompanied by a man with a camera slung around his neck. Immediately, I recognize him as a reporter for PalmyrtonNow.com, our local news website. The two men listen to me extolling the virtues of the antique, and the reporter snaps my picture.

Spooked by the attention, my customer says he needs to think about the desk. But Alex doesn't seem to mind that he botched my sale. "Action shot!"

he exclaims. "A story about the sale at Villa Aurora will be up on Palmyrton-Now within the hour. Great publicity!" Alex grabs the reporter by the elbow. "Let me show you the library and the back veranda."

The reporter resists, choosing to ask me a few questions about what items have sold. I make sure he gets my name and the name of Another Man's Treasure spelled correctly before Alex succeeds in whisking him off. I want my fair share of the publicity, too!

It's nearly lunch time before I can take a quick bathroom break. "What happened to Alex?" I ask Donna as I pass through the foyer.

"He couldn't stay any longer. He had a meeting to get to. But he's pleased with the way the sale is going." Donna makes change for a customer and includes one of Alex's brochures. She waits for the lady to leave the check-out area before continuing. "Alex is relieved that reporter didn't ask about the curse."

Lamar returns from carrying out some furniture and joins our conversation. "I had a lady ask me if this place is haunted. I told her ghosts take one look at me and they head for the hills!" He slaps his knee at his own hilarity.

"Lamar, that's not funny," Donna scolds. "We have a duty to present Villa Aurora in the best possible light."

My gaze meets Lamar's over Donna's head and I wink. She sure is a devoted evangelist for Alex's project.

Customers continue to surge through the house. Some buy small items, but many of the late afternoon customers leave empty-handed except for Alex's brochure. These curious tourists seem satisfied by their glimpse inside this legendary mansion.

"Imagine living here!" one lady says.

"Imagine washing all these windows," her friend responds. "But maybe my daughter will want to have her reception here if her boyfriend ever pops the question."

Now that most of the best items in the parlor have been sold, I wander back to the library, where ten or twelve people leaf through the books. "Look at this penmanship primer, Rose," one old lady says to another. "Remember how we used to have to write these sentences over and over again?"

"Total waste of time," Rose replies. "My handwriting is chicken scratch."

I sidle up to them, wondering if I've found more St. Anselm's alumnae. "Did you ladies attend St. Anselm's Academy here in the Villa?"

"No, we went to the public school in Palmyrton, but we used this same primer," Rose explains. "St. Anselm's was for rich girls."

"Weird rich girls," her friend clarifies. "I'm glad my parents didn't have the money to send me away."

More anecdotal evidence that St. Anselm's was the school you didn't want to get into. I take a quick tour of the tables in the library to see which books have sold. All the valuable ones have been snapped up by collectors as have some of the oddball textbooks from the fifties and sixties. Then my gaze falls upon a bin of old mass market paperbacks left behind by the patients at The Center for Mindful Living. We hadn't really sorted them—just stuck a fifty cents each sign on the bin. Now that some of the books have been sold, I see what lies beneath them: a stack of spiral bound notebooks belonging to St. Anselm's students. Somehow, items from two different eras have been mixed together.

I pull them out and flip through the pages: sentence diagrams, algebra problems, definitions of major events of the Civil War. As I continue to leaf through the notebooks, a sample of handwriting catches my eye. It's the same careful, precise handwriting as on the note Ty and I found in the attic room used for punishment. This notebook must belong to the same girl.

I flip to the cover looking for the student's name.

Caroline Forsyth.

With no time to read, I put the stack of notebooks on a shelf keeping only the one with Caroline's handwriting.

I'll show it to Emmeline when she gets here. In fact, I'm surprised she hasn't shown up yet.

My phone buzzes with a text from Donna. *Where R U? Ur friends R here.* Is that her?

I head back to the foyer where Isabelle, Lydia, Roz and Madalyn are looking around. "This place is amazing," Lydia gushes. "I hope someone I know throws a party here one day, so I can come back and see it all spruced up."

"Where's the library?" Roz asks. "I only came to check out the books."

Stashing the notebook in my tote bag, I quickly show them around the first floor. As we walk, I ask Isabelle if she's sold the Corrigan house yet.

She lifts her hand to indicate the topic is painful. "Ugh! I haven't had one showing since the open house. Those huge houses are albatrosses these days. Gen Z buyers don't want to live far away from the center of town with three acres of grass to mow and six thousand square feet of floors to vacuum." Isabelle looks at an ornate mirror carried by a stylish woman. "Is that real Art Deco?"

"Yep. So the Corrigans are in Singapore and their house is unsold?" I ask.

Isabelle grimaces. "Ethan Corrigan refused to let me list it at a reasonable price. It'll have to sit on the market until he comes to his senses."

The Corrigan house is empty.... An idea pops into my head, but a customer approaches with questions about a walnut inlaid armoire. I'll have to set my theory aside for now.

———◦———

THE FIRST DAY OF THE Villa Aurora sale is an unqualified success. Revenue is higher than my most optimistic estimate, and I haven't heard any commentary about curses. But that reminds me—I really do need to tell Alex my suspicion that someone again entered the Villa through the tower door. I don't want to be accused again of withholding information. While Ty and Donna straighten up for tomorrow, I send Alex an email with a preliminary revenue report and add a few sentences about the disturbance in the library.

Then we all pile into the van to make the trip back to Palmyrton. After dropping off my staff, I come to an intersection. To the right, the road to my house: Sean, cuddles with the kids, dinner with my family. To the left, the road to the Corrigans': possible answers to my persistent concern about Starla and her well-being.

I could tell Sean my theory, but face it—he's not going to be any more impressed with this one than with my advice to stake out garage sales. I can hear him saying that the police don't have time to check out every unsold house sitting empty in the stalled real estate market.

I put on my turn signal.

What harm could it do to drive by the Corrigan house?

Chapter 33

The Corrigans' neighborhood continues to exist in its picture-perfect stupor: no kids playing, no gardeners digging, no chefs barbequeing. Just huge, silent homes sitting in the middle of acres of smooth grass, separated by hedges of tall spruces or impenetrable rhododendrons.

Who would notice if someone infiltrated the Corrigan home? Who would care? Here, no kindly Alma Bannermans keep watch.

The Corrigan house perches alone and aloof on its hill, a Royal Realty sign with Isabelle's face and number planted by the curb. A new thought springs to mind. Maybe I'm wasting my time—how would squatters enter this house without setting off the state-of-the art alarm system? As I guide my car up the long curving driveway, I flash back to how I entered the Corrigan house every day that we worked here: through the garage with a code for the keypad. It was an easy code to remember: 1379, the numerals in the four corners of the keypad. Could Starla or the "friend" who brought her to the sale have observed one of us punching in that code?

But surely, the Corrigans would have changed the code after giving it to me?

Then I think about frazzled, distressed Everly Corrigan trying to wind down her life in New Jersey and prepare for her big move abroad, and I'm quite certain that code hasn't been changed.

I exit my car and take a slow walk around the house. In the unlikely event that anyone's watching, I hope they'll take me for an interested buyer. The house is being sold with all its window treatments, and the curtains and shades are all drawn. But the big French doors off the breakfast nook have no curtains. I shade my eyes and peer in. The kitchen is clean and empty, waiting to be shown to potential buyers. I feel a tug of disappointment. Did I expect a pile of beer cans and pizza boxes? No—freegans wouldn't eat that. Maybe a pile of apple cores and tomatoes seeds from produce scavenged at the farmers market.

I complete my circle of the house. Should I punch in the code and check out the garage? Well, I've come all this way—my mind won't rest unless I turn over this last stone.

1-3-7-9-enter. The big double garage door hums to life and begins its slow ascent.

The garage is not empty.

Chapter 34

I step inside the huge space which Ty had swept clean at the end of the sale. In the far back corner, away from the windows, two sleeping bags are spread out. I approach cautiously, but there's no place to hide in here now that all the shelving and junk has been removed. Next to the bed rolls, I see a large but worn-out backpack and a small canvas tote bag. Peeking out from the top of the bag is a pink tee-shirt with sparkly script that spells Unicorns are Real.

Starla's tee shirt.

My heart accelerates. I've found her hiding place. But her abductor must be here with her. What's my next step?

My overheated brain rolls through options. Definitely can't call 9-1-1. How can I explain my illegal entry here to patrolmen? And if they arrive with sirens and lights and Starla is nearby, we'll have lost her and Josh again.

Sean.

But he'll be *so* angry that I came here alone.

Holzer? He won't be too mad at me, but he sure as hell won't keep my interference a secret from Sean.

Finally, I settle on Isabelle. I close the garage door and retreat to my car, calling her as I walk. She picks up as I start my car, and I begin talking before she can even say hello. "I came to the Corrigans' house because I had this wild idea that Starla might be squatting here."

"Wha—?"

"Don't ask questions till I finish. I was right. I found her stuff in the Corrigans' garage."

"How did you—"

Isabelle follows commands about as well as I do, which is not at all. I talk right over her. "I opened the garage door with the code. The Corrigans hadn't changed it. Listen, Isabelle—Starla's stuff is here, and there's another backpack that must belong to her abductor, boyfriend, whatever. I don't want them to slip away. This is what I need you to do."

"Have they trashed the house?" Isabelle's voice has changed from confused to indignant.

Ever the real estate agent! "I don't think so. Listen—I need you to call the non-emergency number of the police department and ask to speak to the detective handling the Starla Douglas case. His name is Pete Holzer. When you get to Pete, tell him you were showing the house and discovered some stuff that shouldn't be there, and you think it belongs to Starla. Tell him you know about Starla because you're friends with me and Sean."

"I'm coming right over to make sure the house is all right."

Isabelle is very protective of her clients, and that's going to come in handy here. "Wait and come with Detective Holzer. You don't want to be here alone in case Starla and the creep come back." Now I know Isabelle will be very motivated to connect with Holzer and get him over here. Pete Holzer doesn't stand a chance against a determined Isabelle Trent.

"Fine. I'm going to call right now."

"Call me back and tell me what he says." By this time, I'm at the end of the driveway. I don't want to leave the neighborhood until Holzer gets here just in case Starla and Josh return and decide to pack up and leave. I look for a place to park my car where no one will notice it. The streets in this development of executive homes twist and turn, leading from one cul-de-sac to another. I park at the end of the adjacent cul-de-sac and walk back toward the Corrigans' house. I check my phone—six minutes have passed since I hung up with Isabelle. She's probably still explaining the situation to Holzer.

I wonder if Josh is still driving the "Consume a Cleaner Vitality" car. A smart criminal would have ditched it, but good freegan biodiesel vehicles are probably hard to come by, so I'm betting he's still driving it.

When I get to the bottom of the Corrigans' driveway, a text from Isabelle arrives.

Detective Holzer is checking out the house first. He wants me to wait at home until he calls me.

I walk up the driveway looking for a hiding spot where I can keep an eye on the place until Holzer gets here, then slip away. The garage doors face the side yard, but directly behind in the backyard, the Corrigan kids have a large tree house—professionally built with a safety railing all around, of course. From up there, I'll have a view of the garage and driveway.

I cross in front of the garage doors, and that's when I smell it.

A faint whiff of stale fried chicken.

Biodiesel.

I think Starla and Josh have returned in the brief time I was away parking my car. I dart into the back yard and climb the ladder into the tree house. Should I forget trying to conceal my involvement? As I pull out my phone to call Holzer directly and warn him, I hear a car in the driveway. Peeking through the branches, I see the familiar shape of a Palmyrton PD unmarked sedan. Holzer jumps out holding a large flashlight in one hand.

Too late to call him now.

I watch him enter the code into the garage keypad. Something makes Holzer hesitate. Does he smell the biodiesel, too? Or does he hear something from within?

As the garage door rises, Holzer flattens himself against the side of the house.

Moments later, a car backs out at full speed.

It turns to head down the driveway, but Holzer's car blocks the way. Hedges on one side and a retaining wall on the other make driving down the lawn impossible.

"Stop! Police!" Holzer holds his gun out in front of him. "Get out of the car with your hands up!"

My heart lurches. I know Holzer to be a good cop, a calm and steady presence. Still, this moment feels fraught with danger for everyone.

The passenger door opens first. A slender figure emerges with her trembling hands raised straight up. "Don't shoot me," Starla whimpers.

Holzer commands her to lie flat on the ground with her hands over her head. Then he shouts again for the driver to get out.

I hold my breath. What if the driver won't come out? Does Holzer have a plan for a stand-off? Has he called for backup? Should I call 9-1-1 now?

Slowly, the driver's side door opens. A tall, rangy man emerges with his hands lifted parallel to his ears, technically in compliance with Holzer's command. He has his back to me, so I can't see his face. Not that I'd recognize it.

"Get your hands all the way up where I can see them," Holzer barks.

As the man extends his arms, the stretched-out sleeves of his hoody slide down. Encircling his left wrist is a dark bracelet.

This is Starla's abductor.

In the distance, I hear the wail of sirens. The cavalry is on the way. When the first patrol car zooms up the driveway, I see my opportunity.

I climb down from my perch and slip through the hedges to the yard behind the Corrigans'.

By the time I arrive home, Sean is full of news. "Guess what! Holzer found Starla and arrested Josh ."

I busy myself with the twins and hope that my husband won't notice that I'm not bowled over with shock and amazement as I ask questions to which I already know the answers. Finally, I get to fresh territory. "Has he questioned Starla yet? Does he know what went on between her and Josh here at our house?"

"He's in with her now. He said he'd call as soon as he knows more."

The evening passes in a blur as we eat dinner and get the kids put to bed. As I attempt to unwind with a book and a glass of wine, we still haven't heard from Holzer. And then another concern pops into my head. Emmeline never came to the sale today. That's odd, given how determined she was to explore Villa Aurora.

I check my email one last time and see a message from Alex. *Thanks for reminding me about the access door in the tower. I sent someone to nail it up after all the customers were gone. Since things went so well yesterday, I probably won't drop by the Villa until later in the afternoon.*

Nothing from Emmeline.

I consider calling her, but hesitate when I see the time—nearly nine pm. She might already be in bed, or if she's not, she'll want to talk to me about her discoveries with the sociology professor, which could take a while.

I'm too tired for that right now. I'll call her tomorrow.

Fifteen more minutes of reading and the book slips from my hands.

Chapter 35

It's Saturday morning and the line-up of cars in front of Villa Aurora is just as long as on Day One of the sale. There will be more Looky-Lous today and fewer high-ticket sales, but I'm still expecting a good day. We're all more relaxed today since yesterday went so well. And with Sean in charge of the twins, I can work without worrying.

Once again, Donna hands out numbers to the waiting crowd while the rest of us take our battle stations. We've moved some of the second-tier antiques into the magnificent parlor space because everything looks more appealing in here. But the walls now have pale spaces where paintings have been sold and carried off. One large one remains—a dark portrait of some nameless Italian prince. He looks down at me scornfully.

I return the stare. "I bet you've seen a lot over the years, haven't you, buddy? Too bad you can't talk."

I turn away from the painting as the first customers of the day pour in. Among them is a short old man and a tall, skinny teenager. "Hi, Arturo!" I greet the landscaper. "You've come to shop?"

"Pah! I don't want no part of Toliver's stuff. I came to show my other grandson a little bit of history." He turns to the teenager shuffling restlessly beside him. "This is Nico's kid brother, Petey."

"Pete," the teenager corrects sulkily.

"He's my driver today. The family won't let me behind the wheel of a car no more." Arturo looks around the parlor, opening drawers in a side table and peering inside a curio cabinet. "You find any records from the old Toliver factory in this furniture?"

"No, if he left any of that behind, it must've been discarded over the years." My attention moves to a woman studying a bureau, who I judge to be a serious buyer. As I cross the room to her, Arturo directs his grandson's attention to the ornate plaster medallion on the ceiling. "You see that? Days of backbreaking work to make that one fancy little detail, and the guy who did it didn't get paid enough to feed his family."

Still griping about Toliver, but at least today there's no talk of the evil eye.

Soon I'm called into the dining room to answer a question, and on my return trip through the foyer to the parlor, I come upon an unfolding drama. A woman with a platinum blond bouffant hairdo and leopard print wrap dress stands in the middle of the marble-tiled floor staring up at the grand staircase. As I enter the space, she lifts her ornate walking stick and shakes it. "Ah, you old crones! You thought you'd crush me, but I won. I won!"

Her voice reverberates off the hard surfaces. Other customers turn and stare as Donna shoots me a "you handle this" look from the check-out table.

I glide up to her. "Hi. Can I help you with something?"

She turns and smiles brightly as if she hadn't just been shouting at the top of her voice. Her bright red lipstick bleeds into the wrinkles surrounding her mouth, and I realize she's older than she looks from a distance. "Hello, I'm Diane Gold, and I escaped from this place in 1953. I thought I'd come back to show the ghosts I'm still kickin'. Are you the boss lady here?"

I take her elbow and guide her toward the dining room, where there are fewer customers to overhear her talk of supernatural entities. "I'm Audrey Nealon. I'm running the estate sale." I offer her a seat in a throne-like chair that's unlikely to sell unless my favorite theater props manager shows up. "Did you say you escaped from St. Anselm's?"

"Yep, went right through the trap door in the tower," she points her stick above her head in the general direction of the tower. "My grandfather sent me here. Thought those dried up old nuns could teach me to be a lady. Ha!" She leans back in the velvet-covered chair and looks at me from under her long fake eyelashes. "They said I was sexually vor-aye-shuss."

She draws out "voracious" as if the word were a juicy peach she's bitten into. I have to laugh.

"They were right," she continues. "I've always enjoyed the company of men. Been married four times." She displays her left ring finger which is stacked with diamonds up to her knuckle. "My last husband was the best. He left me sitting pretty with a house in Palm Springs. But I follow the news in every place I've ever lived, which is quite a few. When I saw that they were turning this place into a wedding venue, I just had to come back to see it." She cackles. "Talk about coming full circle! I eloped from here to marry my first husband, Antonio."

"We've had other St. Anselm's students visit Villa Aurora, and they shared rumors of a girl who ran off," I tell her. "We discovered the trap door, but we wondered how you got away—the house is so remote."

"Antonio met me at the bottom of the drive. He was my grandfather's handyman—did all sorts of odd jobs for him. Antonio was teaching me how to drive grandaddy's old Buick when our lessons veered in a different direction." Diane delivers a broad wink. "Anyhoo, Antonio was friends with a fella who did gardening and odd jobs here at the Villa, and we hatched a plan for my escape."

"That was brave. You were awfully young to get married."

Diane waves a bejewelled hand. "Antonio was a lot of fun, but he wasn't husband material. He got me to Manhattan, though, where I met my second husband. He was in the theatre." She gazes off into a fond memory of the past, then snaps to attention. "I came here because I want to set the record straight."

"Uhm, what record is that?"

"There was a story in the *Daily Record* that mentioned a curse on this house." She leans forward, her coral-painted nails gripping the carved lion's head on her stick. "There was evil done here, but it was done by real flesh and blood people. No curse involved." She folds her hands on top of her walking stick, pleased with the startled reaction she gets from me.

"And how do you plan to set the record straight?" I suspect Alex will like this even less than talk of the evil eye.

She arches her penciled brows and smiles, revealing a smudge of lipstick on her front tooth. The V-neck of her leopard-print dress exposes a wrinkly bosom and an inch of sturdy, white bra.

I'm not sure what to make of this slightly preposterous old gal. Does she really know something, or is she just an attention-seeker looking to inject some excitement into her life? I'd be happy to listen to what she has to say, but not when I can feel my phone vibrating in my pocket with text messages. I pull it out—three from Charmaine, one from Lamar and one from Ty, all needing me to settle issues with customers. "I'd love to talk to you more, but I've got a sale to run. You're welcome to look around, but could you keep the talk about evil on the downlow?"

"Bad for business. I get it." She winks, making her fake eyelash droop. "I'll just mosey around a bit. I promise to be good."

She toddles off leaning on her stick, and I have no choice but to take her at her word as I move to solve all the problems my staff has bombarded me with. About an hour later, when I'm zooming through the foyer again, I catch sight of a flash of leopard print. Mrs. Gold struggles with the heavy front door. As I hold it open for her, I ask, "You traveled here all the way from California just to shout that message in the foyer?"

Diane giggles like the naughty teenager she once was. "I've always enjoyed a dramatic gesture. But no, I didn't come to New Jersey just to visit Villa Aurora. My son and some other distant relatives live here, so I thought I'd combine fun with family commitments."

"Did someone drive you here?" We're both out on the porch, and I shudder to think of this elderly lady maneuvering her vehicle around all these crookedly parked cars.

Diane digs through her designer purse and produces a phone. "Nope, I took an Uber. I'll call another to get back to my son's place." She taps away. "Too bad they didn't have Uber when I was a kid. I wouldn't have had to elope with Antonio to get away from here."

Chapter 36

At the end of the day, Alex arrives, and we all sit down for a wrap-up. "Maybe we should move everything that's left upstairs down here and seal off the second floor," Ty suggests. "Charmaine had a few people today giving her a hard time about wanting to go up to the third floor or into the closed bedrooms."

Lamar stretches his muscular arms over his head. "Move it down now. Move it down once it's sold—all the same to me."

But Alex shakes his head. "No, I don't want to prevent people from going upstairs. They want to see all of Villa Aurora. The article on the Palmyrton-Now website yesterday was very positive." He looks at Charmaine. "Who wanted to go up to the third floor?"

She makes a face. "Some kids. I caught them trying to unstick the tape we put across the staircase. I told 'em, 'What? You think that sign only applies to other people and not to you?' They took off after that." Charmaine shoots a look at her brother. "I can handle the second floor just fine."

Alex smiles. "Good, good. We'll keep it open."

While this debate is going on, I wrestle with whether to tell Alex about Diane Gold's visit. Is she a serious troublemaker or just a cute crackpot?

Donna makes the decision for me. "Alex, there was a weird lady here today. She kinda caused a scene, but Audrey shut her up."

Alex turns to me for further information, eyes wide open with concern.

"Her name is Diane Gold," I say. "She was a student at St. Anselm's."

Alex frowns. "I hope she wasn't talking about curses and the evil eye."

"No, in fact, she said there was no curse, but that evil had been done here by real people and that she'd come to set the record straight."

Alex leans forward, his voice more agitated. "What? Set the record straight how?"

"I asked her that and she just smiled and arched her eyebrows. She was shouting about how the nuns hadn't succeeded in repressing her." I waggle my hand. "Sort of clownish—I didn't take her seriously. She said she eloped with her boyfriend by escaping through the tower trap door."

"Eloped." Alex repeats the word like he's trying to master new vocabulary. "Okay. Right." He jumps up and glances at the check-out desk as he turns to leave. "I see you've distributed quite a few of my brochures."

"I offer one to every customer." Donna beams. "Quite a few people have said they've got weddings coming up or they're going to pass them along to friends and family who are planning events."

Alex's gaze meets Donna's. "Thank you so much for your support. I feel this sale really has done so much to promote Villa Aurora."

Ty keeps his eyes firmly focused on his size 12 Adidas until Alex finally says good-bye and departs.

As we straighten up, I realize the second day of the sale is over and again, no Emmeline.

A worm of worry squirms in my gut, so I step away from Donna and Ty to call her cell. The phone rings a few times, then is answered by a young, brisk voice that is most definitely not Emmeline.

"Hello. Miss Hartnett's line."

"Uhm...hello. This is Audrey Nealon. May I speak to Emmeline please?"

"Are you a relative?" the voice demands.

"No, a friend. Who's this?"

"I'm a nurse at Palmyrton Memorial Hospital. We've been trying to reach Miss Hartnett's next-of-kin. Do you know who that would be?"

"Next of kin?" My stomach lurches. "No...wait, why is she in the hospital? Is she okay?"

"Privacy laws forbid me from sharing her health details." The nurse's voice is cool and impassive. "That's why it's important we contact her next of kin. If you could reach out to them—"

"She doesn't have children." Now I'm getting flustered. Emmeline's parents are long dead. She had a brother whom she didn't seem to care for much. Would he be alive? Does she have nieces and nephews? What was the brother's name? I wrack my brain but come up empty. If the nurse is asking me all this, Emmeline must be unconscious. Did she have a stroke? A heart attack?

"Can I come and visit her?" I ask.

"Only relatives may visit patients in the ICU," the nurse says. "Let us know if you are able to contact her family." And the line goes dead.

"What's the matter?" Ty asks as he enters the foyer to find me blankly staring at my phone.

"Emmeline Hartnett is in the ICU. That's why she didn't come to the sale."

Ty busies himself arranging some unsold items. "That's sad. What happened to her?"

"I don't know. The nurse wouldn't tell me anything. But apparently she's unconscious."

Ty eyes me sharply. "Why are you so upset? I mean, she's a nice old gal, but you barely know her."

"She was eager to tell me something she'd discovered about the origins of St. Anselm's Academy. And now she can't talk, and I'm not allowed to visit her. The timing seems strange."

Ty plants his hands on his hips. "Timing of what? She's like a hundred years old—"

"Eighty-one," I correct. "And not at all frail."

"Still, at that age, anything could happen. Her heart probably gave out."

I nod, not wanting to share the horrible and possibly outrageous thought that's worming into my mind. Constantine Agyros was a healthy older person associated with Villa Aurora who was murdered. What if a similar fate has befallen Emmeline Hartnett?"

I wait until Ty has moved into the front parlor to straighten up in there before I call Madalyn. She works at the hospital. Maybe she can find out something about Emmeline's condition. When she doesn't answer, I leave her a long voicemail. Then I get back to work.

<hr />

I ARRIVE AT HOME TO find the twins both crying lustily.

"I think they got over-stimulated getting so much attention from their cousins. Brendan's kids came over with him to watch the baseball game," Sean explains as Thea furiously flings a handful of mashed bananas onto the floor.

"Come here, my love. Let's rock and nurse for a while, shall we?" I feel my own tension ebb as my daughter and I glide in the rocker. Watching her long lashes flutter against her rosy cheek as she consoles herself with mother's milk makes me forget about the cares of the day. Finally, drunk on milk, Thea lets her head loll back and she drifts off to sleep. I put her in her crib and find that Sean has succeeded in settling Aiden with a bottle of pumped milk.

"Whew!" Sean pulls me close for a hug. "How was your day?"

"Strange. Tell me about your day first."

Sean and I cuddle on the sofa, both too tired to contemplate meal preparation. "I finally got a chance to talk to Holzer about Starla," Sean begins. "What she told us about herself was a mix of truth and lies, but I think the lies weren't malicious."

"Start at the beginning. Is Starla Douglas her real name?"

Sean gives a short, unamused laugh. "Yes and no. Apparently her parents have a common law marriage. Starla's mother's last name appears on her birth certificate and her school records, but she's always referred to herself by her father's name, Douglas. She left her family in West Virginia because of a combination of abusive male relatives and lack of employment. She really did hitchhike from a truck stop and got dropped off in Palmyrton by a driver who thought it was a good town for a girl in her situation."

"Is there a good town anywhere for young women who are homeless and broke?"

Sean pulls me closer, and I know we're both imagining the unimaginable—our own kids in such a terrible situation. "A bum in the park told her about the soup kitchen, and she happened to arrive there on one of the days they do free distribution of produce rescued from the supermarkets. And that's where she met Josh."

"There aren't many young people who go to that grocery distribution," I say. "It's easy to imagine them gravitating to each other."

"He gave her some line of BS about his freegan community and invited her to join. She had no place else to go, so she accepted."

I sigh. "Poor Starla. She's such a babe in the woods."

Again, Sean chuckles without humor. "The girl is sharper than you give her credit for. Josh heard about your sale at the Corrigans' on the freegan chat group, but Starla approached you for the babysitting job without him knowing. Josh's little freegan cell was making her uneasy, and she wanted to find a job and get away from them. She had enough experience with abusive men in West Virginia that she could spot trouble brewing."

"That's why she asked me about whether I wanted her to sleep over here."

"Yes, she was very disappointed when you shot that down. Meanwhile, she was hoarding the cash we paid her, telling Josh she earned less and hiding the rest."

"Ugh. Let me guess. He found the money she was hiding and that's why he came here to get her."

"Yep. He didn't want her getting too independent."

"What's she going to do now? Is she in trouble for squatting in the Corrigans' garage?"

"No. The DA says he can only make a good case against Josh, so he's not pursuing charges against Starla. And this whole episode has connected her with social services. She's been admitted to the battered women's shelter, and they'll help her find employment. But she asked if she could come and talk to us, to apologize for what happened. Holzer said she broke down when she saw the nannycam video of the twins left all alone, crying."

I pull back so I can look my husband straight in the eye. "I'm willing to talk to her, but we're not taking her back to watch the kids, Sean. I don't blame her for what happened—not really—but I'd never rest easy leaving them alone with her again. I don't know what we'll do for childcare until Roseline comes back, but it won't be Starla."

"I totally agree. But I'd like to hear what she has to say. I told Holzer she could come here after you finish with the sale tomorrow."

I nod in agreement just as a text comes in from Madalyn. *Got your message. Emmeline Hartnett was admitted with a head injury. I was here in the ER yesterday when the EMTs brought her in. They said she was the victim of a home invasion.*

Chapter 37

The phone slips from my fingers and clatters to the floor.

"What's the matter?" Sean asks.

"Emmeline Hartnett was the victim of a home invasion. She's unconscious in the ICU." I clutch Sean's arm. "Can you call the Summit police and find out what happened?"

He makes the call, and I watch his face for clues as he listens to what his counterpart in Summit tells him. I don't get much from his stoic expression, but a slight wince five minutes into the conversation makes my heart drop. What's happened to that bright, feisty librarian?

Finally, Sean hangs up. "What happened?" I demand.

"A neighbor noticed Miss Hartnett's front door was ajar and called the police. The patrolmen found her crumpled on the dining room floor. Blunt force trauma to the head."

My hand rises to my mouth. "Oh, no!"

"She lost a lot of blood—they're not sure how long she lay there before the neighbor called."

My imagination kicks into overdrive picturing her cozy little house as a gory, blood-drenched crime scene. "What was stolen? Emmeline's not poor, but she's certainly doesn't have the electronics and jewelry and cash most home invaders are after."

"The house wasn't ransacked," Sean says. "The crime scene guys think the invader didn't even go upstairs. But since they can't talk to the victim and haven't found any family members, they're not sure what's missing."

I have a sinking feeling I know what Emmeline's attacker was after. "Emmeline has a laptop computer. She uses her dining room table as a desk. Did they find any file folders or notes? She was doing some research."

Sean narrows his eyes. "For you?"

"Not *for* me."

But because of me. My idle curiosity has exposed this dear woman to danger.

"I'm the one who got her interested in Villa Aurora and those suitcases that were left behind. She got hurt because of me." I hear the rising edge of panic in my own voice. "She had some information she was dying to tell me about, but I've been too busy the past two days to meet with her."

Sean grips both my hands in his. "Why don't you tell me everything you think you know about her research before I call back the detectives in Summit."

Chapter 38

Morning comes too soon.

I pull myself out of bed at the sound of the twins babbling on the baby monitor. Sean will be on-duty all day with them again today, so I am taking the morning shift solo. I find them both sitting up in their cribs seeming to have a conversation with each other. There's no doubt in my mind that the two of them have their own special twin communication, and I often wonder what they're saying. Today, I suspect it must be, *Can you believe what a nut our mother is?*

As I get them changed and begin nursing, my mind goes back to all we learned last night. Sean's colleague in Summit was grateful for the information I provided, and he's going to try to track down the sociology professor Emmeline talked to. Drew is a small university, so it shouldn't be that hard to find him.

He also confirmed that Emmeline's dining room table was empty when the police arrived. The home invader must have taken her laptop and all her file folders and notes.

And he left her for dead.

By now, he must realize he hasn't finished the job. He's hoping she'll never regain consciousness. Luckily, the strict visiting rules of the ICU have protected Emmeline from this beast, but if she does improve and get moved to a regular room, she'll be in danger. I made sure Sean emphasized that to the other detective. Will they post a guard by her door? Somehow, I doubt it. Real life isn't a TV cop drama.

Sean tried to reassure me that what happened to Emmeline isn't my fault. Admittedly, I didn't tell her to go interview that sociology professor. But if I hadn't got her interested in researching the stories behind those suitcases, she would never have been harmed.

Can an 81-year-old woman recover from a smash to the head? If she does wake up, will she be consigned to a nursing home, her remaining years ruined? I can't bear that possibility. A tear slips from my eye and plops onto Thea's cheek. She releases my breast and smiles.

Not a care in the world.

I switch Thea for Aiden. Thea is the squeaky wheel and gets fed first most days. Aiden has been happily playing with his toes while awaiting his turn. Will it always be this way? Will my sweet, patient son always be elbowed aside by his bigger, tougher, older-by-five-minutes sister?

"You're a pound lighter than her now," I tell him, "but you'll surpass her one day."

Aiden rewards me with a big grin before latching on to nurse. Again, my thoughts return to Emmeline. Who else could she have told about her research? How did the attacker know what she was up to? And more importantly, why did he care?

When Sean comes into the nursery, I'm so lost in thought I'm barely aware of his presence. "Do you think Emmeline's professor friend is also in danger?" I ask as if he's been privy to my thoughts for the past half hour. "After all, he's the one who gave her the information."

"Good morning to you, too." Sean lifts Thea out of her crib. "The professor has always had the information. It seems like Emmeline's the one who must've made some connection that caused her attacker to try to silence her."

"But how did he know she had it?" I lean my head back in the rocker. "This is all my fault."

Sean caresses the top of my head. "Emmeline's a tough old bird. I bet she'll wake up today and have plenty to say."

I know my husband is humoring me. There's nothing more to discuss. But Sean's right about one thing: Emmeline does have a strong will to survive.

"I'll be home by four," I tell Sean as I hand off Aiden to get myself ready for work. "Today all prices are marked down, and anything that doesn't sell will go into the Dumpsters being delivered on Monday when the inside renovations are due to start. We don't even have to sweep up at the end of the sale."

Sean gives me a thumbs up. "I'll tell Starla to come at 4:30."

DAY THREE OF THE SALE will be quiet. There are hardly any early birds when we arrive, as almost all the valuable antiques have been sold. Today is the day for serious bargain hunters. I've over-estimated the appeal of a couple of items—apparently there's not a huge market for ginormous art deco armoires—so I'll be wheeling and dealing today, cutting prices to make sure as much as possible goes out the door instead of into the dumpster.

I let the oil painting of the prince go for a hundred bucks and allow a familiar used book dealer to take all the remaining books for thirty dollars. I suspect there might be one valuable book lurking in there amongst the old Nora Roberts and James Michener paperbacks, but it's not worth my while to ferret it out. A church that needs more plates for their weekly potlucks takes the last of the institutional dinnerware, offering me blessings for my reasonable price.

"Is Alex coming today?" I ask Donna after we finish our lunch. I'm not even trying to conceal that she'd be more likely to know his schedule than I would.

"He told me to expect him at the end of the day again. He wants to see what's left after the sale ends."

"Your nails look nice." I remark on her obviously fresh manicure—ruby red tipped with silver sparkles. "Going out tonight?"

Donna flushes and puts her hands in her lap. "I figured since we don't have to clean up after this sale, it would be safe to get my nails done. Alex is taking me out to dinner to celebrate."

I'm tempted to ask her what's going on with the Agyros family's effort to fight the coroner's ruling that Constantine was murdered, but it doesn't seem wise to go there with customers circulating in the house. Still, I worry about Donna and her attraction to Alex. I wish the police would make an arrest and put my anxiety to rest.

Charmaine wanders down the curved staircase. "What's goin' on? I haven't had a customer upstairs in half an hour."

Donna pats a chair at the check-out table. "Sit here with me if you're lonely. If someone wants to go upstairs, they'll have to pass us, and you can go up with them."

The afternoon crawls on with not enough work to keep me distracted from my worry about Emmeline. I busy myself rearranging some utilitarian items from the Center for Mindful Living, but I don't have much hope of selling an outdated scale and a grimy footbath.

I hear a commotion coming from the foyer, deep voices followed by a high-pitched scream. That's Donna!

I race through the long hallway to the foyer. First, I notice Ty and Lamar looking like they've seen a ghost. Then I see why.

Three uniformed cops block the front door, while two big guys in sports coats stand on either side of Alex. I recognize the men as detectives on the Palmyrton police force.

While customers watch wide-eyed, one detective takes out handcuffs and intones, "Alex Agyros, you are under arrest for the murder of Constantine Agyros. You have the right to remain silent—"

Alex jerks away, interrupting the Miranda warning. "Shut up! This is insane! I didn't kill my father."

The detective continues the Miranda warning without missing a beat. Then he snaps on the handcuffs and guides Alex toward the front door.

"Oh my God!" Donna sinks onto a chair.

"That's the first time I ever saw the po-po take away the rich white dude and leave the two Black dudes," Lamar says.

Ty bumps his fist.

"Stoppit, you two! This is serious." Donna puts her head down over her folded arms.

I give Ty and Lamar a warning look then turn to the crowd of customers. "Okay, folks. Show is over. Please take anything you want to purchase to the desk. We'll be closing the doors in ten minutes."

"I'll round everyone up," Ty volunteers, shoving Lamar out of the foyer ahead of him.

I leave Charmaine in charge of the desk and lead Donna into the empty library to calm her down. We sit beside each other in a deep window seat as all the furniture has been sold.

Donna clings to my hand as her shoulders shake with sobs. Her reaction seems intense given she's only known Alex for two weeks, but I figure that's not a helpful thing to say to a friend, so I pat her shoulder until she's able to speak.

"This has to be a mistake, Audrey. Alex is the nicest guy I've ever gone out with. He can't possibly have killed his father." She stretches the hem of her over-sized shirt. "Alex really wants the Villa Aurora project to succeed. He wanted his dad to be proud of him. Now, his dad will never see how talented Alex is, and that broke Alex's heart."

Or maybe the Villa Aurora project is in trouble. Could that be why Alex killed his father? But I keep that thought to myself. "We-e-ell, all I know is the police have been waiting to make an arrest until they were sure they had enough evidence. So something new must've turned up."

"No-o-o-o," Donna keens, her tears streaking black mascara down her cheeks. "Oh, ga-a-wd, no."

This reaction is awfully dramatic, even for Donna. I'm starting to feel a tingle of suspicion. Tilting up her chin so we're eye-to-eye, I ask, "Do you know something you're not telling me?"

"No." She bites her lip and tries to twist away. "Yes." She rakes her hands through her hair. "Oh, Audrey, I'm not sure what it means."

"What *what* means?"

"Something I overheard," Donna whispers. "But I can't tell you. You'll go right home and tell Sean."

"Look, Donna—this isn't middle school lunch table gossip. If Alex really is a murderer, you need to distance yourself from him. And if he's been wrongly accused..." I'm floundering here because I'm certainly not going to promise to withhold evidence from the police. "...well, he'll have a cracker-jack legal team and they'll poke holes in the prosecution's case." I squeeze her hand. "Now, what did you hear that concerns you?"

"I think Alex might know what happened to his father, and he doesn't want it to become public."

"Why wouldn't he want his father's killer to be brought to justice?"

Donna shakes her head. "I heard him take a call and he said something like, "This can't come out. Not now. Not ever.""

I don't think those words exonerate Alex himself, but I hold my tongue. Donna needs to work through this without me telling her what to think.

"What is wrong with me?" She looks at me like I'm a world-class doctor and she's a dying woman. "How can I be such a poor judge of men? I thought

Alex was one hundred percent different from Anthony. And now he's been arrested for murder! At least Anthony never killed anyone."

Anthony, Donna's ex, is currently in prison for assaulting both her and me, among other crimes. It does seem like Donna's gone from the frying pan to the fire. I pull her into a hug. "You're safe, and that's all that matters. Maybe now that he's been arrested, Alex will be more willing to tell everything he knows to the police. We'll just have to see how this plays out."

As I guide Donna out of the library, I look back over my shoulder at the room. A few random unsold items sit on the shelves: board games and puzzles with missing pieces, a box of dried out markers, a broken lamp.

What happened to the stack of notebooks from the St. Anselm's schoolgirls?

⎯⎯⎯⎯◉⎯⎯⎯⎯

AS SOON AS I WALK INTO my house, I shout for Sean, dying to learn what he knows about Alex's arrest. But the house is quiet—the dog, the kids, and the stroller are gone.

What a time to take them for a walk! I set off in the direction of the park to intercept my family.

Alma calls to me from her porch. "They left about forty minutes ago. They should be on the way back by now."

I wave my thanks, and by the time I reach the corner, I can see Sean pushing the stroller in the next block. We meet in the middle, and I distribute kisses to everyone. Then I cut to the chase. "Your colleagues came to Villa Aurora and arrested Alex about an hour ago. Has new evidence surfaced?"

My news stops Sean in his tracks. "Really? I don't know anything about it."

I can tell he's not dodging my question. He really doesn't know. "What about Holzer? Would he know what's going on?"

"Honey, it's Sunday. Neither one of us is on duty today, and neither one of us is assigned to this case."

I fall into step beside him. "What about tomorrow? Will there be scuttlebutt when you get back to the office? Donna is beside herself. She doesn't know what to believe about Alex."

"I'll find out what I can tomorrow." Sean steers the stroller up our drive-way. "But Audrey, with a high-profile case like this, the chance of a false arrest is pretty slim. You'd better prepare Donna for the worst."

At four-thirty-five, I hear a timid knock on the back door.

Who could that be? I peek out the kitchen window and see Starla's beat-up bike leaning against the fence. With all the commotion surrounding Alex's arrest, Sean and I forgot she was coming here today.

Uncertain how I'm going to feel about seeing Starla again, I take a deep breath and open the door. Starla stands gazing down at her worn-out sneak-ers, occasionally daring to glance up at me through her badly cut bangs. "Hi, Audrey," she whispers. "I came over to apologize and to see if the babies are okay."

She looks so forlorn that I can't muster up much anger toward her. "Come on in. The twins will be happy to see you."

As soon as Starla enters the family room, Aiden and Thea squeal and raise their arms begging to be picked up. Starla falls on her knees beside them. "Look at you! You've grown since I left." She pulls them into her lap and starts singing and playing.

Sean and I exchange a glance over her head. This is all very sweet, but we're not letting her worm her way back into our family. Starla came here to give us some answers, and we intend to get them. "Let's let the kids play," I say firmly. "Have a seat on the sofa so we can talk."

Reluctantly, Starla follows my directions. Her eyes dart as she tries to de-cide whether she should be more afraid of me or Sean.

My husband gives Starla a reassuring pat on the shoulder as he sits beside her on the sofa. "As you can see, the kids are fine although they certainly were very frightened and exhausted from crying when we found them."

Starla's lip trembles. "Oh my stars, I am s-o-o-o sorry. I just—"

Sean raises his hand. "We know you're sorry and that you never intended to hurt them. But we'd like to know how this happened. It's pretty clear you weren't straight with us when we hired you. We'd like the truth now."

Sean speaks in his calm, interrogation voice. He knows how to get hard-ened criminals to confess. Poor Starla doesn't stand a chance of keeping any-thing hidden. I let Sean lead the way.

Starla looks like she's hoping God will open a hole in our family room floor and whisk her straight down to Hades. She gives Sean a tremulous nod.

"What day did you leave West Virginia?" Sean asks. I know he likes to begin interrogating with a simple question that can be answered factually.

"Joo-lie fifteenth."

If Sean thought he would have to pry the truth from Starla, he was dead wrong. His first question unleashes a breathless torrent of words.

"When the trucker dropped me off in Palmyrton, I thought it was the prettiest place I'd ever seen—just like a town on TV with that nice park, and the big courthouse, and the fancy church and all the stores and restaurants. But when I walked along, I saw how much they wanted for a hamburger or a sandwich. Fifteen, twenty dollars! I only had but twelve dollars and thirty-seven cents in my pocket. I asked a lady if there was a Denny's or a Waffle House nearby, and she looked at me like I was plumb crazy. I was tired, so I rested on a park bench and a bum came and set down beside me and pulled a peanut butter and jelly sandwich out of a sack and it looked so good, I asked him where he got it and he told me about the soup kitchen. So I went there, and lunch was already over but the lady gave me a sandwich and said they were going to start handin' out groceries. I got in line for that, even though I didn't know what it amounted to and if I was gonna hafta pay, and the lady in front of me didn't speak English so she couldn't answer my questions, but then this young guy came up to me and explained everything."

Starla pauses and takes a sip from the glass of water I've set in front of her.

"And that guy was....?"

"Josh. He was there with his friend, and they were talkin' lickety-split usin' all these big words I didn't even understand but the sum total seemed to be that we could each take two big bags of groceries and even if I couldn't use all that myself, I should take it anyway. That didn't seem right to me, but Josh said just take it and I'll show you how to trade it for other stuff you need. So after I got my stuff, we all went outside and started tradin' like it was a big swap meet, and I gave away this big orange thing that I thought was some kinda squash but Josh said it was a pya...puppa...

"Papaya," I offer.

"Yeah. That. And I got some apples and some cheese and a container of chili and I ate it cold because that's how hungry I was. And Josh asked me where I was staying, and I said I didn't have a place and I realized right then that I'd run off without making any sort of plan. And that's when I started cryin' some, and Josh said I could come back to where him and his friend lived and they had another girl with them—older than me—so I thought it might be okay even though I was scared." Starla looks at me. "I can see now it was a bad decision, but I just didn't know what else to do because the sun was going down and the streetlights were coming on and I was real worried."

Oh, this poor, pathetic child! On the run from one bad situation, she landed smack into another one. I lean across and pat her knee. "Of course, you were scared. Anyone would be."

Sean remains impassive and guides the questioning back on track. "Where did Josh and his friends live?"

"Well, they took me to this house that looked pretty nice, and I cheered up some. But once we were inside, I got kinda nervous 'cause the house smelled like my grandma's place and it had a lot of little angel statues and framed pictures of weddings and graduations and little babies and Josh and his friends weren't in none of them."

"That was Mrs. Karpinski's house?" Sean asks.

Starla gazes down at her lap and twists her hands. "Yes, it surely was. I had a sneakin' feeling we weren't supposed to be there. But by that time, it was pitch dark outside and I didn't even know where I was at." A slow tear trickles down Starla's cheek.

"But you stayed with Josh beyond that first night?' Sean verifies.

"I did," Starla whispers. "I stretched out on the living room sofa. Kept one eye open all night because I was afraid—" She glances at me, looking for solidarity. "Well, you know. But Josh and his friend never touched me, didn't even try. So after that, I felt a little safer and I figured I could stay with them for a little while until I learned my way around Palmyrton and found a job."

"And what made you come to my sale at the Corrigan house?" I ask.

"That was Josh's idea. He was always looking for places where we could get good stuff free or cheap and then re-sell some of it. That's how he lived. He didn't have a regular job. He said I could do it, too." Starla furrows her brow and lays her hand on her chest. "I told him I'd just as soon have a regular job, and he laughed. Anyway, I went out there with him in his old car. And my stars! I hadn't ever seen so many big fancy houses, except on TV. When we got to the sale, Josh said we had to split up and walk around looking at everything. Then we'd get back together and make a plan. I didn't know what I was supposed to be looking for, but when I heard you talk about needing a babysitter, my ears perked right up 'cause I knew that was a job I could do."

"And what was Josh's reaction when you told him you approached Audrey?" Sean asks.

"Well, see, at first, he said being a babysitter was slave labor and all this other stuff I didn't understand. But when he found out it was you I wanted to work for, he changed his tune. He said I could work for you as long as I gave all my money to the group. Josh brought me back out to the Corrigan sale the next day and got me the bike and told me what to say when you asked where I lived and all."

"And you didn't think that was strange?" I ask.

Starla lifts her scrawny shoulders. "He said knowing more about your estate sales would help with what he does. And I didn't really see the harm in it." Her face crumples. "I wanted the job so bad. I'm sorry, Audrey. I never wanted to hurt you or these precious babies."

But she did.

I don't say that though. "What caused Josh to come here and drag you away?" I already know what Holzer said about this, but I want to hear it from Starla.

"I didn't want to give over all the money I earned from you. I wanted to save some up so I could be on my own. Josh found money I was hiding from him." Starla gnaws on her thumbnail. "The longer I worked for you, the more I could see how nice you were. I thought about telling you what was going on with Josh and asking for your help, but I was worried you'd be mad." Her sentence ends in a sad little squeak.

"What did Josh want to know? He could get a schedule of my sales from my website." There's an edge in my voice now. I feel used. "He didn't need you to spy."

"I wasn't spying on you, personally," Starla pleads. "It's just—we needed places to stay. By that time, the other guy and girl had taken off. It was just me and Josh. Josh said it wasn't safe to stay in one place too long. He thought the houses where you hold sales could be good places for us to crash for a while. But we needed to know if there would be other people around and how to get in and stuff."

I think about all the questions Starla asked me whenever I was home, and my eyes narrow. I thought she was just chatty, but she was pumping me all along. "Is there another place Josh was planning to crash besides the Corrigans'?"

Starla casts her eyes down again. "That's what I knew you'd be mad about. After you told me about about the secret entrance into the tower at Villa Aurora, Josh and I stayed there a couple nights."

"You stayed at Villa Aurora?" My voice rises so much that Aiden begins to whimper. I pick him up and bounce him on my knee while Sean takes over the questioning.

"Did you tell Detective Holzer this?"

Starla shakes her head. "He didn't ask all the places we stayed, so I didn't say. I figured I was already in enough trouble." Starla turns to face me. "I didn't like it at Villa Aurora. It was so big and creepy. And I kept hearing noises at night. I thought the place was haunted, but Josh laughed at me. Once, he left me up in the tower and went down into the house to explore. He came back with some books, and I told him it wasn't right to steal them, but he didn't care." She hangs her head. "I'm so sorr-eeee."

That explains the rearranged books in the library. Maybe they'd been missing for a while before I noticed.

Sean brings the interview back on track. "What does your staying at Villa Aurora have to do with what happened here at our house?"

"Josh found the money I had hidden in my canvas bag. When he came to get me from your house, he said it was because we had to get out of Villa Aurora."

Villa Aurora most certainly is not haunted. But if the night-time visitor who went through the suitcases returned, I want to know about it. "This is important, Starla. What night did you hear noises, and what exactly did you hear?"

"I don't remember what night it was. A while back. We were sleeping up in that room at the top of the tower, with all the windows. The moon was bright that night and I guess the light woke me up. I heard sounds down below us—bumping and banging. I thought someone was coming up to find us." Starla's eyes open wide and she clutches her chest. "My heart was beatin' so hard, I about thought I was havin' an attack. But then the footsteps got softer, like they were going out into the house, not up to the tower."

"Did you try to wake Josh?"

Starla bites her lip. "I was afraid to wake him and afraid not to. I just stayed real still and hoped whatever was in the house would go away and leave us alone."

Chapter 39

By the time Starla departs, Sean and I are reeling with all the information she's shared. Nevertheless, the kids have to eat, so we continue talking while fixing their dinner. "Starla and Josh were sleeping up in the Tower for days and you never noticed?' Sean is understandably incredulous given my usual attention to detail.

"Starla is tiny enough to fit through the trap door, and Josh is tall but skinny, so I guess he was able to squirm through also." I cut a steamed sweet potato into cubes and put it on the highchair tray in front of Aiden. "As long as they stayed up in the tower and left before we arrived, I wouldn't have noticed. Naturally, she had to be here ready to babysit before I could be there, so there was no chance we'd cross paths at the Villa."

Sean gives his head a quick shake like he's emerging from a deep dive. "You say the door from the tower into the house locks from the tower side. They could have let themselves out every night to explore the house, right? But you think nothing was stolen?"

"Josh took those books, and it was easy for me to overlook that. Once we arranged them, I didn't look at them again until the day before the sale opened. I noticed they were rearranged, but I couldn't tell what was missing. The most valuable items at the sale were large pieces of antique furniture and art. Obviously, I'd notice if any of that was missing. There's no jewelry or clothes or small electronics like there would be at a regular house sale. And no clothes that they could wear or resell. That's the kind of stuff Josh would be after."

Sean distributes cubes of chicken breast to the twins. "So you believe Starla when she says they spent all their time in the tower except for Josh's one evening of exploration?"

"Huh! I'd like to believe her, but she's lied about so much. Who can be certain she's telling the truth now? She says she and Josh were sleeping in the room at the top of the tower when she thought she heard someone else come in through the trap door down below. Josh didn't believe her when she told him she thought the house had been visited by ghosts, but then two days later he came here and dragged her away."

My phone is ringing on the kitchen table as I set a pot of water to boil for our pasta dinner. Sean picks it up, raises his eyebrows, and holds it out, an indication that I should hustle across the room and answer.

The name on the screen: Emmeline Hartnett.

My heart leaps up. Could she be well enough to call me?

"Hello?"

"Hello, Audrey." The voice coming over the line is a little raspy, but unmistakably Emmeline.

"Oh, Emmeline! I'm so glad to hear from you. I've been so worried, and they wouldn't let me come to visit because I'm not family." I rattle along breathlessly. "How are you?"

"I've been better. But I'm finally getting out of this dreadful hospital. They won't let me go home yet because I'm a little wobbly. So they're sending me to the rehab center across the street. But the good news is, I can have as many visitors there as I like." She hesitates. "Do you have time to visit me tomorrow?"

Her voice sounds so tiny and wistful. I would move heaven and earth to visit her. "Yes. Absolutely. I can get my mother-in-law to watch the kids for a while. What time should I come?"

"How about eleven? That's between physical therapy and lunch."

"I'll be there. But can you tell me now—do you have any idea who attacked you?"

Emmeline sighs. "I can't remember what happened. The doctors say that's very common when you've had a bad concussion. It's nothing to do with my age." She adds defensively.

"No, of course not."

"The last thing I remember is hearing the doorbell ring and going to answer it. After that, nothing until I woke up in the hospital." She pauses. "But this is what I've been turning over in my mind. I wouldn't have opened the door for any old stranger. I must've looked out and saw that it wasn't a salesman or a Jehovah's Witness."

"So you think it was someone you know?" I recall that she opened the door to me and Sean and the twins when we first visited, and she didn't know us.

"Possibly. But not necessarily." Emmeline clears her throat. "At my age, I'm always balancing the need to be safe with the desire to have an interesting conversation. The person who came to my door must've looked respectable enough not to worry me and interesting enough to tempt me to answer. Sort of like you, dear."

Chapter 40

Emmeline Hartnett's face breaks into a smile when I enter the visitors' lounge at the rehab facility the next day. Despite the dreary scent of canned vegetables and despair that clings to the place, she appears in high spirits, wearing sturdy sneakers, a purple velour track suit, and a jaunty turban to cover what I imagine must be a shaved spot on the back of her head.

"What do you think of my ensemble?" she asks. "All I need is a deck of tarot cards and a crystal ball to complete the look."

I sit beside her and give her fragile hand a squeeze. "I'm so glad to see you're as spunky as ever. I can't help feeling guilty for what happened to you. I never should have gotten you involved in tracing the history of those suitcases."

"Nonsense, Audrey. I'm my own woman. I do what I want to do. Always have."

I look into her twinkling blue eyes. "Me too. I guess that's why we like each other."

Emmeline rubs her hands together. "Now, let me show you what I've got." She peers into my tote bag. "Did you bring your iPad?"

I hand it to her and watch, amazed, as she taps the screen. "That brute got my handwritten notes and my laptop, but I have all my computer files backed up to the Cloud. I can piece all the information back together as soon as I log into my account."

"You're amazing, Emmeline. Did you share this with the police?"

Emmeline purses her lips. "I certainly tried. The detective was very solicitous, but I got the distinct impression he was humoring me."

Ooo—that's a big mistake.

"That's why I wanted you to come," Emmeline continues. "I know you'll take me seriously. Maybe between you and your detective husband you can make the police investigating my attack understand why the thief wanted this information."

Maybe. I'm not sure I myself understand. But I think Emmeline is right. Her attack is linked somehow to Villa Aurora and its nefarious history. "I'll try, Emmeline. Start with your visit to the professor."

She grins. "People love talking about their specialties, and this fellow was no exception. He invited me to his office and chewed my ear off for two hours. Lucky for you, I can distill the important bits down to about ten minutes."

"You're a hoot, Emmeline. Let's hear it."

She consults some notes that she's called up from her iCloud account using my device. "The story begins with a man named George Acton who owned a business in Paterson that supplied the various silk mills."

"He knew Phineas Toliver?"

"He did. And he knew all about Toliver's personal tragedies. It seems Acton was a real wheeler-dealer. During the Depression, when many other businesses were failing, Acton managed to buy out his competitors and ended up quite wealthy. He moved out of Paterson to Palmyrton, where he joined the Episcopal Church to gain some social credibility. But the old money families wouldn't admit him to the inner circle until—"

"Let me guess. Until he performed some act of philanthropy, like starting an Episcopal school."

"Exactly." Emmeline appears pleased by my accurate guess. "The Diocese of Palmer County had a plan for a girls' religious school, but no place to put it and no money for a building. Acton remembered that Villa Aurora had been sitting empty for years. He bought the mansion, probably for a song, and allowed the Diocese to put their school there."

"Thus cementing his place in Palmyrton high society. And what year was this?"

Emmeline consults her notes. "1938. So the school existed for more than a decade as a day school for local Episcopal girls."

"What happened to make it into a boarding school?"

"Oddly enough, it was the Acton family again. In 1953, George Acton's 15-year old grand-daughter was caught—" Emmeline arches her eyebrows—"*in flagrante delicto* with the family's chauffeur, who was twenty-four."

"That's rape!"

"They didn't see it that way in the fifties, dear. Remember, Elvis started dating Priscilla when she was fourteen, and Jerry Lee Lewis married his third cousin when she was thirteen and he was twenty-three."

"Ugh." I shudder, imagining Thea married off just twelve years from now. "So she got pregnant and they sent her to Villa Aurora to have the baby?" I ask, rushing the story.

"In fact, she did *not* get pregnant." Emmeline leans back, preparing to get to the heart of her tale. "I'd venture to say that if the young man had been a friend of the family and a recent Yale graduate, Grandpa Acton would've forced a marriage. You know, the young man had tasted the milk, so he was obliged to buy the cow." Emmeline rolls her eyes.

"However, he was a lowly chauffeur, and George Acton wasn't about to let his grand-daughter drag the family backward in the social standings after all he'd done to climb up."

"So why not just fire the chauffeur?"

Emmeline leans forward and taps my knee. "The family sent the girl to St. Anselm's because they didn't think she could be trusted around *any* man. I suppose when they caught her in the act, she must've been enjoying herself. Very dangerous for a young woman at that time. Since Acton owned the school building, he figured the Episcopal nuns there had an obligation to teach his grand-daughter how to keep her knees pressed together and her eyes demurely cast down. Consequently, his grand-daughter became St. Anselm's first residential student."

"Geez!" I tap my pen in agitation. "Why is it always the woman's fault when men behave badly?"

Emmeline's shrewd eyes twinkle. "Oh my dear, you know men have these urges that they can't possibly control, and it's up to us women to maintain social standards by resisting. That girl was a weak link. Once St. Anselm's accepted her as a boarding student, other families got the idea to send their weak links off to the school as well."

I tilt my head. "Wait—was this like an official mission of the school?" I'm beginning to suspect that Emmeline is reading a little too much between the lines. How much of her story is fact and how much is her resentful fantasy? "How did the other families know about the shift?"

Emmeline wags her finger at me. "That's why my chat with the sociology professor was so illuminating. It's his thesis that all of this was understood among the upper classes. In those days, schools didn't have glossy brochures. Instead, he showed me letters between the school and inquiring parents that have been preserved in the Drew University Library local history section." Miss Hartnett adjusts her turban, which has slipped sideways as she has become more excited about her story. "I took photos of these carbon copies. The originals would have been written on St. Anselm's School letterhead."

I squint at the screen. The type is fuzzy but legible.

I don't have the patience to read all these letters, but Emmeline has underlined key phrases. "The professor pointed out the code words," she explains.

We can help your daughter establish the discipline needed to be an upstanding young woman.

Emmeline taps the underlined phrase. "This was the code for anyone who was easily distracted, who didn't pay attention and follow rules, or who had inappropriate ambitions like acting or art."

You are right to be concerned about your daughter's unfortunate habits. St. Anselm's can put her on the right path.

"'Unfortunate habits' covered everything from eating too much to being a tomboy to being caught reading a racy book," Emmeline says. "I think that's the category I was admitted under." She flips to another letter.

"We are sorry to learn your daughter is proving to be a distraction to others. We can help her form appropriate responses."

"Being a distraction was the worst sin of all. The original sin," Emmeline says. "Remember, that's why Acton sent his grand-daughter to St. Anselm's. Because she—" Emmeline makes air quotes—"*distracted* that chauffeur."

"So any girl who flirted with boys could get sent away to St. Anselm's?" Even for the Fifties era, this seems extreme. "Wouldn't every teenager in town fall into that category?"

But Emmeline is relentless. "*Form appropriate responses* means learn how to bat your eyes at boys while keeping your legs firmly crossed. Lead them on without putting out."

I scratch my head. As much as I'd like to believe all this, Emmeline's story has no hard evidence to back it up. "How can your professor be so sure about all this just from reading these letters?"

"Because his mother is George Acton's grand-daughter, Diane."

Chapter 41

"Diane?" My voice squeaks in excitement. "I met a woman at the estate sale two days ago named Diane Gold. That's her latest married name. She told me she escaped from St. Anselm's to elope with her boyfriend, Antonio."

"Diane is here?" Emmeline looks startled. "She lives in California."

"Yes, in Palm Springs. She said she read about the evil eye curse on Villa Aurora and came here to set the record straight. She also said she was staying with her son, who must be your professor."

Emmeline seems a little flustered that I've pre-empted part of her story. "Yes, well...remember I told you there was a legend about a girl who got away? It turns out that was true. Diane escaped from St. Anselm's with help from her chauffeur boyfriend. It happened days after I arrived at the school."

"She said he was her grandfather's handyman."

Emmeline flips her hand from front to back. "Handyman, chauffeur—maybe George preferred to give the man a glorified title. Apparently, he drove Mrs. Acton around. She was old-fashioned and never learned to drive."

"Diane told me he was teaching her to drive when the ...er... sexual escapade occurred."

Emmeline sips from a glass of water on the table beside her. "Diane got out through the tower, and he picked her up on the road. They eloped, but that marriage didn't last long. However, it set her on her way."

"I gathered from talking to her that she's had a colorful life. She's still rather, er, flamboyant."

"According to her son, the Acton family completely disowned her after the elopement. She told him several of the older girls knew about the tower door, but none of them ever revealed the escape route to the nuns. But the knowledge of the door was passed down through the years among some girls." Emmeline presses her hand to her chest. "Although it bypassed me."

"Wasn't the escape bad for the school's reputation?" I ask.

"Diane's family were motivated to keep it quiet to avoid a scandal. They said their daughter was studying abroad and met a man in England and married him."

"Wow, things have really changed. These days, if a wealthy girl ran off from a boarding school with an older man, her parents would be all over social media blaming the school."

"There was no social media then, but a decade or so after Diane's escape, the school was becoming less popular," Emmeline says. "It was the mid-sixties. Standards of behavior were looser; girls wanted to go to co-ed schools. And the straw that broke the camel's back was another escape attempt that ended badly."

"Who—?"

Emmeline wags a finger at me. She's clearly enjoying telling her tale. "More on that in a moment. The Diocese decided the school had become a liability. They told their old friend George Acton they no longer needed Villa Aurora. And they called the parents and told them the school year was ending early and they should come pick up their daughters right away. I imagine the rush to close the school accounts for the other suitcases left behind in the basement."

"That's one mystery solved." I squirm in the uncomfortable chair of the rehab center's visitor's room. The air conditioning isn't very cool, and a trickle of sweat inches down my back. "But your attack can't possibly have anything to do with Diane. She's outlived her scandal."

"Correct. I believe my attack is connected to another young woman who was also sent to St. Anselm's for being a distraction." Emmeline shows me the next letter.

We are sorry to learn that your daughter's behavior has become a distraction to the success of your other family members. It will be best to isolate her here and redirect her interests.

I look up at Emmeline. "A distraction to the success of other family members? What the heck does that mean?"

Emmeline purses her lips and remains silent like a teacher who's confident her student can produce the right answer if she thinks long enough.

I draw my brows down, hesitating.

"A distraction to *other family members.*" Emmeline repeats the words distinctly.

"Eeew. Incest?"

Emmeline nods.

I snatch back the iPad to see who the letter was sent to. But the internal address and salutation are blurred. "Ugh! Of all the letters to be damaged, this one is illegible."

"It is. But I think I know who it was. When I came home from Drew, I started doing more research. Then I went to the library to use some of their databases. And right after I came home from the library, I was attacked." She holds up her hand. "It could be totally coincidental, but..."

"So who was the girl?" My throat is so dry I can barely get the words out.

"My research reveals that Caroline and Constance Forsyth had two older half-brothers from their mother's first marriage. Her marriage to Forsyth only produced girls." Emmeline crosses her arms across her chest. "The daughters were dispensable. And as you know, Caroline died at the school." Emmeline peers at me over her glasses. "I believe she was murdered."

I try to repress my reaction. If the letters that had been hidden in Caroline's suitcase revealed incest within the family, that would certainly explain why someone broke into Villa Aurora to look for them. I haven't told Emmeline about our nighttime prowler yet. She'll pounce on it as proof of her theory. She may be right, but I want to explore all she knows before I reveal what I know. I proceed cautiously.

"But you told me you thought her death really was an accident."

Emmeline looks at me like she's lost faith in my common sense. "Well, that was before someone tried to kill *me.*"

"Of course. But let me play devil's advocate. We have to be sure before we take this to the police."

Emmeline nods as if to say, *bring it on.*

"This letter—surely the parents wouldn't have told the school their problem was incest, even in coded language," I object.

"I suspect the parents would be careful to frame the problem as a defect in the girls' character. A pre-emptive explanation just in case Caroline or Constance confided in someone about what was happening at home."

"But who would have killed Caroline while she was at school? Did her half-brother or her father come to visit her the day she died?"

"I have no way of knowing. There are limits even to my research skills, dear."

I make up my mind to tell Emmeline the information I've been holding back.

"Constance claims her sister's body was moved, positioned to make it look like she fell down the stairs. She also says Caroline kept a diary in a tiny notebook. The diary was never found, and Constance said her sister never told her the secrets it contained. But—" I hesitate. "Someone entered Villa Aurora one night while we were setting up the sale. The only sign they were there was that the suitcases were rearranged. When Constance pried open the back of the suitcase, we found traces of notebook paper, but the diary was gone."

"More evidence stolen," Emmeline whispers. "Caroline was murdered, and someone's trying to cover it up, even after all these years."

Chapter 42

I think Emmeline may be correct, but there are still some details I need to get straight in my mind. "How do you know the Forsyth girls had older half-brothers? Constance's niece Melinda came with her to Villa Aurora. She must be the daughter of one of those boys, unless there were young children born after Constance and Caroline."

Emmeline scrolls on my iPad. "Obituaries are a great source of family information, dear. Here is the obituary for Caroline and Constance's father, Edgar Forsyth, from his death in 1980."

I skim over the professional accomplishments to get to the list of survivors. *Survived by his devoted wife Demetria, his daughter Constance and his adopted sons, Damian Forsyth (Clare) and Andrew Forsyth (Lorraine) and four grandchildren, Carl, Paul, Michelle, and Melinda Forsyth. His daughter Caroline preceded him in death.*

"So Constance never married and had children. And Edgar apparently adopted his wife's sons from her first marriage, yet they made a point of calling out the fact that they were adopted in the obituary. That's odd." I lean back in my chair. I've got the family ties straightened out, but I'm not sure how to proceed. I remember how fragile poor Constance seemed when she visited Villa Aurora. She said her sister always tried to protect her, but it seems Constance wasn't fully aware of what—or who—Caroline was protecting her from. We've got some horrible allegations here—sexual assault, incest, murder, attempted murder. We can't dump all that in Constance's lap unless we have solid evidence.

"Okay, Emmeline—I'm going to show all this to my husband, and he can share it with the detective working on your case." I squeeze her hand. "If you're right about all this, you're still in danger. How do you think your attacker discovered your research?"

She purses her lips. "I enlisted the help of my librarian friends at the Summit Library when I was doing my research. Perhaps someone overheard us talking there."

"It couldn't be a random library patron. They would've had to follow you to the library. How did they know about you in the first place?" I stand and pace our corner of the visitor's lounge. "It bothers me that Diane Acton showed up at Villa Aurora all the way from California just days after you spoke to her son."

Emmeline cradles her chin in her hand. "Yes, that is odd."

"Diane told me she read about the evil eye curse in the *Daily Record*. She claimed she likes to keep up on news from all the places she's ever lived. And she said she came to set the record straight—that evil had been done in Villa Aurora by real people, not because of some curse. But she didn't say how she intended to set the record straight." I gaze down at Emmeline in her sensible sneakers. "I'm afraid I didn't take her seriously, Emmeline. I judged her based on her outlandish appearance."

"Don't be so hard on yourself, Audrey. We all make those judgments to some extent."

A flash of insight causes me to drop back into my chair. "Emmeline, you said you let your attacker in because they must've appeared interesting and not dangerous to you. Like perhaps a woman your own age. Could it have been Diane Acton Gold who came to your house?"

Emmeline massages her temples in frustration, as if this will get her traumatized brain to remember. "I wouldn't have hesitated to let her in, that's true. But surely a woman who's even older than I wouldn't be strong enough to clobber me."

A vision of Diane Gold's heavy, carved walking stick floods my imagination. It would make an excellent weapon. But could Diane deliver the blow? And why would she? "Maybe she wasn't alone when she came."

"If you're thinking it was her son, that can't be," Emmeline says. "The police told me they checked him out. He was teaching classes all day the afternoon I was attacked."

I glance nervously around the visitor's lounge, but we're alone except for an old man dozing over by the window. "I had to sign in with the guard in the lobby—security seems pretty good here. But don't accept visits from anyone you don't know well, no matter how innocent they seem."

A nurse pops her head into the lounge. "Time for lunch, Miss Hartnett. You need to be finished by one so you can be ready for your afternoon physical therapy."

"Coming...coming." Emmeline pushes herself out of her chair with more effort than she used to display, but she shakes off my helping hand. "I've learned my lesson, Audrey." Emmeline waves to another resident who's entered the lounge. "I'd rather play bingo in the activity room than take any chances chatting with strangers."

<hr />

ON MY WAY HOME, MY head swims with all the information Emmeline has imparted. With my mind miles and decades away at Villa Aurora, I nearly rear-end the guy ahead of me when he obediently stops at a yellow light. While we're paused, another realization hits—with all the excitement of the information Emmeline shared with me, I forgot to show her the note Ty and I found in the third-floor room and the notebook from the library which proves the note was written by Caroline.

Maybe it's just as well that I didn't show her. Emmeline has a narrative about what happened at St. Anselm's firmly fixed in her mind. I should look at that note and review the notebook trying to be as unbiased as possible. I need to get all my ducks in a row before I share my evidence with the police.

With the Villa Aurora sale over and the proceeds in my account, I can afford to devote a few days to this research. I'll be working from home, and we have a week off before our next sale. I owe it to Emmeline Hartnett to discover who her attacker is.

After I pick up the twins from my mother-in-law's house and drive home, I decide I'll tell Sean only the barest details of my visit with Emmeline, keeping her theories to myself. I want to explore them further before I expose them to the cold light of his logic.

But an afternoon spent with two babies intent on learning to crawl does not lend itself to thoughtful contemplation. By the time Sean arrives home, the issue I've analyzed the most is the difference between Thea's crawl—always lead with the right and pull the left up later, and Aiden's crawl—propel forward with both forearms while dragging the legs behind. "Look what your children can do," I tell him. "Time is running out to get those baby latches installed on the kitchen cabinets."

"I'll start after dinner," Sean promises. "How was Emmeline?"

I give him an abbreviated report, and because he's preoccupied with coaching the twins to improve their crawling technique, he doesn't notice my lack of detail. "And what about your day?" I ask. "Any further news on Alex's arrest?"

Sean grins, and I'm not sure if it's because of my relentless curiosity or Thea's refusal to accept direction. But he does supply some information. "The arrest was prompted by concern that Alex might flee to Greece. They want the judge to confiscate his passport. And some new emails between Constantine and his financial advisor indicate that the old man was doubtful about the Villa Aurora project and tightening the flow of money for the renovation. They figure that gives Alex a motive to get rid of his father."

"But that's all circumstantial," I protest.

Sean looks up from playing with the twins. "Yep. Many murder cases are. The trial will come down to which team of lawyers does a better job of convincing the jury."

"Alex can afford the best lawyers." I rub the bulging eyes of an Elmo doll while Aiden tries mightily to reach it. "He might get off even if he's guilty."

"It happens," Sean agrees. "A trial doesn't always settle guilt or innocence."

And what does that mean for Donna?

⸻ ◉ ⸻

IN THE MIDDLE OF THE night, Aiden wakes up crying. I change him and rock him back to sleep before he disturbs his sister. But after I lay him back in his crib, I find myself with my eyes wide open and my mind spinning.

I slip down to the family room where I've left my laptop. Ethel leaves her doggy bed to jump up on the sofa beside me. "Emmeline says obituaries are a great source of family information," I tell the dog. "Let's see what I can turn up."

I begin by searching for George Acton's obituary. Once I find it, I get my first surprise: George's wife was a woman named Philomena Agyros. Next, I search every survivor listed in that obituary, making notes of married names. Then I re-read an obituary that I've read before, this time seeing it in a new light. Constantine Agyros's father and Philomena Agyros Acton were brother and sister. And Constantine had a brother, Basil, who preceded him in death.

With trembling fingers, I google Basil Agyros. The obituary that pops up is a photocopy of an old, printed newspaper obituary, dated November 15, 1950. Basil, twenty-eight at the time of his death, was killed in a car accident leaving behind his young wife, Demetria, and two toddler sons, Andrew and Damian.

Demetria...that's a very unusual name. A Greek name.

Demetria was the name of Edgar Forsyth's wife, Caroline and Constance's mother.

There it is—the connection between the tragedy that befell Caroline Forsyth and the Agyros family. Basil's widow, Demetria, went on to marry Edgar Forsyth and to give birth to his daughters, Caroline and Constance. And Edgar adopted the sons Demetria brought with her from her marriage to Basil Agyros. The Agyros brothers became Forsyths.

Are they still alive? One more obituary search reveals that Andrew died a decade ago, but Damian died very recently, "suddenly, at home." Only Andrew had children, one of whom is Melinda Forsyth, Constance's niece.

By the time I'm done with obituaries, I've sketched out a complex family tree with surprising connections but plenty of holes.

Then I turn my attention to real estate transactions, which are all public records.

Finally, I examine the note from the third-floor room. The words of the author, Caroline Forsyth, have a poignant meaning now:

I am banished for merely existing.
I am blamed for a sin that is not my own.
I am punished for daring to tell the truth.
I am fading away.

I page through the Algebra notebook, skimming Caroline's careful notes on how to solve quadratic equations. Like any student, she sometimes doodled in the margins next to her math problems. Towards the back of the notebook, the doodles become more elaborate, and I notice she has woven words among the little pictures and abstract squiggles. Over the margins of three pages, these words appear in tiny, neat script:

I want to escape like Diane did.

I have nowhere to run.

I WILL follow her path.

The tower is my only option.

Her words swim before my teary eyes. Did Constance try to escape and fall to her death?

But she wrote, "I have nowhere to run."

A sickening alternative occurs to me. Maybe Constance resolved her pain with the only option she could imagine: jumping from the tower.

Either way, that's why Constance saw her sister's body being moved in the lobby. The adults must've brought it inside to make the escape—or the suicide—look like an accidental fall down the stairs.

As the sun peeps through my kitchen windows, I have the answers to many of my questions, but I've also created a new list of questions.

One requires information from Starla.

And one requires Emmeline's help.

Chapter 43

Sean comes downstairs with a wailing Thea in his arms. "You're up awfully early," he says observing the bowl with a few Cheerios clinging to the sides and the empty coffee mug on the table.

"Couldn't sleep." I take Thea to nurse, wondering if I should tell Sean what I've discovered in my research. On one hand, going over all the pieces to the puzzle would help clarify the meaning for me.

But on the other hand, I fear there are still too many holes. Sean can't take this to his colleagues until I get those last two bits of information.

I owe it to Emmeline to find her attacker.

And I owe it to Donna to get some clarity on Alex Agyros and his family.

So I wave Sean off to work, assuring him I plan to take it easy today. Then I start making phone calls.

First, I connect with Emmeline, who sounds bright and chipper this morning. "I was just about to call you," she says as soon as I say hello. "A memory is starting to come back to me about my attack. I'm quite sure there were two people on my porch when I looked out the window before opening the door."

"Wow! Do you remember—"

"No, I can't recall their faces." Emmeline's voice is firm. "I'm hoping more will come back to me with time. But if it was a man with an older woman, that might explain why I felt safe opening the door."

Diane Acton Gold and who? We know her son was lecturing on campus at the time of the attack. How does this fit with my evolving theory of the passions surrounding Villa Aurora?

"But you called me," Emmeline continues. "Have you got news?"

"I've been reading some obituaries, Emmeline. I discovered a connection between two families that have been deeply connected with Villa Aurora over the years. I'll explain in a minute, but I need to know something, and I hope you can help me: what was the last name of Antonio, the chauffeur/handyman that Diane Acton eloped with? Did her son tell you that detail?"

"I'm afraid not, but I know that Antonio wasn't the son's father. Diane had him with her second husband."

A stab of disappointment deflates my excitement. "I'll need marriage and divorce records to track down Antonio's name, but I'm not sure where Diane and Antonio got married, so I don't know where to begin searching."

"If you need to know, leave it to me," Emmeline says. "My librarian friends have access to all sorts of databases. I'll call you back in an hour."

"Emmeline, wait—you need to be careful. Have you heard from Diane's son?"

"I got an email from him while I was unconscious in the hospital, but I haven't answered it. He wanted to know why the police had come to talk to him."

"Don't reply. Does he know where you live?"

"I didn't tell him my address, but it wouldn't be hard to find out. He knows I live in Summit."

"Who knows where you are now?" I ask.

"Only you and my best friend. And the detective on my case. I've been very circumspect."

"Good. Keep it that way."

WHILE I'M WAITING FOR Emmeline to work her research magic, I track down Starla at the battered women's shelter. Or try to.

The whole point of the shelter is to maintain the privacy of the residents, so I have to leave a message with a person who declines to acknowledge if Starla is there.

Stymied in my progress, I take the twins out to the backyard to swing and watch Ethel chase a chipmunk while I wait for my phone to ring. I get into a rhythm pushing the swings—one push for Aiden, one for Thea. When Aiden is up, Thea is back. Every time their swings pass in the middle, they shriek with delight and shake their chubby legs.

Such a simple pleasure!

Watching them, I think of all the sad children connected, directly or indirectly, to Villa Aurora. Children who had to work to earn their keep. Children whose behavior displeased their parents. Children who longed to be accepted and loved.

Children who were abused.

Children who grew into adults desperate for love, respect, and money.

The ringtone of my phone jolts me out of my reverie. I don't recognize the number, so I hope that means it's Starla and not a spammer.

"Hi, Audrey—you called me?" her voice sounds hesitant but hopeful.

Oh, dear—she probably thinks I'm calling to hire her back. "Hi, Starla. Yes, I have a question for you. You told us you heard sounds in the tower at Villa Aurora. Was it just bumping and footsteps or were there any voices?"

"Funny you should ask, 'cause when I told Josh about the ghost the next day, I remember that I heard the ghost say a bad word." Starla's voice drops to a whisper. "He said the F-word. And Josh said he never heard of a ghost who talked like that." Starla giggles. "Now that I think on it, I bet he bumped his head and called out."

"So it was definitely a guy?"

"Yes, ma'am. A young guy, I think. The voice sounded young."

There's a long silence between us.

"Was that helpful?" Starla whispers.

"Yes, it was." I want desperately to hang up before I do anything I'll regret. "How are things there?"

"Oh, folks have been real sweet to me. Real sweet. Except I still haven't found a job, so that's got me a little down in the dumps, is all."

"I'm sure something will come along," I say. "I'll keep my ears open." And then I hang up before any more promises leave my lips.

By now the kids have tired of swinging, and we go back inside for a snack. They're too young for library story hour, but a nice walk to the library in the stroller will put them both to sleep. And I have one more detail to check, which I hope I can track down there.

On the walk home with two snoozing babies, my phone rings. "Audrey, I found the information you asked for."

I'm holding my breath, hoping Emmeline's going to complete the picture with this one missing piece.

"Diane's first husband was Antonio Raimondi. They got married in West Virginia, where it was legal in the 1950s for a 16-year-old to marry without parental consent. Does that name mean anything to you?"

I let out a relieved huff of air. "I was right!"

"But Antonio's been dead for many years. Why is this connection significant?' Emmeline asks.

"Because Antonio had a younger brother who's still very much alive. His name is Arturo. He and his grandson are the landscapers working on Villa Aurora. And Arturo is very involved in genealogy research. I think Arturo has figured out through his research what you and I have figured out by studying obituaries, and marriage records, and property sale records: the fates of the Agyros family and the Raimondi family have been intertwined with Villa Aurora for over a century."

Chapter 44

"Are you ready?' I ask Sean that night after the twins are in bed. He looks at my notes and diagrams spread out on the kitchen table and makes a noise somewhere between a chuckle and a moan. "Do I have a choice?"

"No." I pat the chair beside me. I've already explained my theory to Emmeline over the phone, and she enthusiastically agreed with me. In fact, she was able to do some extra digging via her librarian friend to support some key points. But her support, while welcome, doesn't count for much if justice is to be done. I need Sean to accept my reasoning and take the evidence to his colleagues managing both Emmeline's assault investigation and Constantine's murder investigation.

And I know my husband will be tougher to convince than my sweet, elderly friend. He won't put his career on the line for mere speculation.

"I'm going to lay out my entire theory, and then you can punch holes in it at the end, okay?"

Sean rubs his hands together and draws his chair close to the table like he's waiting for the turkey dinner to be served.

"The story starts with Phineas Toliver and the construction of Villa Aurora using money earned in part through the exploitation of child labor in the Toliver silk factory in Paterson. One little girl, Aggie Raimondi, was maimed when her arms were caught in machinery, and her family received no recompense."

Sean winces. "How do you know—"

I glare and push paper and pen in his direction. "No interruptions. Take notes and ask your questions at the end." I settle into my task. "I know about Aggie because Arturo Raimondi, the landscaper at Villa Aurora, told me her sad story one day while we were eating lunch outside during the set-up for the sale. Except at the time, he didn't tell me that the little girl was an ancestor of his. I confirmed that fact today when I took the kids to the library and found a book on child labor in the Paterson silk mills." I point to the dusty tome amidst my papers. "You're welcome to use it as your bedtime reading."

Sean makes a note and nods for me to continue.

"The idea that Villa Aurora was cursed by the evil eye arose when Phineas's wife and newborn son both got sick with the Spanish flu and died in the house after the servants all fled. I suspect—" I hold up my hands acknowledging I have no proof for this detail—"that Phineas was not any kinder to his household help than he was to his factory workers. Arturo's grandfather, the skilled stonemason who built the walls and paths in the Villa gardens, was woefully underpaid for his work, according to Arturo. Phineas's exploitative ways may be the reason the servants abandoned him to care for the sick baby alone. At any rate, we know that after his wife and child died, Phineas moved out of Villa Aurora and couldn't manage to sell it. When the Depression came along a few years later, his factory also failed, and he was in deep financial trouble."

I take a deep breath and move forward one of my family tree diagrams. "Enter George Acton. George was a shrewd businessman who managed to profit from other people's failures. He was a supplier to Toliver's factory, and he bought it at a discount and turned it around. And here's the significant fact." I tap the first square of my crudely drawn family tree. "George Acton was married to Philomena Agyros, a Greek immigrant woman, and her brother was Constantine's father."

Sean grunts and makes a note.

"George and Philomena used their new prosperity to move their entire family from Paterson to Palmyrton, but they weren't really accepted in the social circles to which George aspired. They joined the Episcopal church, but it wasn't until George performed a significant act of philanthropy that they moved up in the world. The church had ambitions to launch a girls' school. George knew that Villa Aurora stood empty, so he bought it at a favorable price and allowed the Diocese to use it. Voila—St. Anselm's Academy for Girls was born."

I glance at Sean, worried that he might be getting restless, but he seems engrossed by my story. "The next ten or twelve years pass with St. Anselm's as a day school for local well-to-do girls. Then George and Philomena's grand-daughter, Diane Acton, was caught having sex with the family handyman/chauffeur, Antonio Raimondi."

"And Antonio's related to Arturo, the old landscaper who told you about the curse?' Sean clarifies.

"Yes, Antonio was Arturo's older brother, and the grandson of the fellow who built the walls at Villa Aurora. They were a family of gifted stonemasons. But George certainly didn't want his granddaughter backsliding with the son of Italian immigrants."

"Wait a minute," Sean protests. "Philomena was a Greek immigrant. The Actons weren't aristocrats."

"Exactly. That's why George was even more motivated to protect the family name. So he broke up the affair and sent Diane off because she was a distraction to men and he wanted her to be straightened out by the Episcopal nuns. Consequently, St. Anselm's evolved into a boarding school for *difficult* girls."

"Good thing you weren't alive then." Sean elbows me. "You'da been sent there for sure. You distracted me as soon as I met you."

I laugh and shiver at the same time. With my relentless disposition and the wrong kind of parents, I would have been doomed in the 1950s. "Diane didn't last long at St. Anselm's. She discovered the trap door in the tower and eloped with Antonio, causing the Actons to disown her."

I tap my pen on the table. "She also caused trouble for Antonio. Their marriage was illegal in New Jersey, so Antonio had to leave the area. They didn't stay married long before Diane dumped him and moved up to a better marriage, leaving Antonio in the lurch. Diane went on to marry three more times and had a son with her second husband who grew up to be a sociology professor at Drew. The one that Emmeline talked to."

I can see Sean wants to ask another question, but he presses his lips together and makes a note instead, so I continue. "Now, you know this part of the story already. Emmeline and other troubled girls were sent to the school, and they were all miserable and mistreated. Among the students were two sisters, Caroline and Constance Forsyth. First Caroline came, and then her sister followed. Their sin was the same as Diane's—they were a distraction to men. But the gross part is, the men in question were Caroline and Constance's half-brothers, Damian and Andrew. Mrs. Forsyth's first husband was their father, but Mr. Forsyth adopted them when he married Demetria, the widow of Basil Agyros."

"Whoa, whoa, whoa," Sean can't help shouting. "The creepy half-brothers were members of the Agyros family?"

Pleased by the big reaction, I relent on my no interruptions rule. "Yes."

"Does Alex know this about his family?" Sean continues.

"You gotta wait until the end for that," I say, returning to my narrative.

"Caroline and Constance's mother must have blamed the girls instead of her sons and sent her daughters away." My voice trembles with outrage even though this injustice was done so long ago. Sean grunts in disgust, but as a cop, very little truly shocks him.

"Caroline kept a journal of what happened to her at home and at school. Her younger sister never saw it. It seems Constance didn't understand why she'd been sent away. I guess her half-brothers hadn't started in on her...yet."

Sean shakes his head. "There's so much shame surrounding incest cases. Victims often can't bring themselves to say aloud what happened to them, even nowadays. It would've been worse back then."

I'm encouraged that Sean appears to believe everything I've told him so far. "Caroline hid her journals in the lining of her suitcase, and that's where they stayed until they were stolen from Villa Aurora after Donna posted pictures of the suitcases on social media."

Sean takes a breath and opens his mouth, but I raise my hand. "More on that later. Caroline died in a fall at St. Anselm's. The school said it was an accident. Her sister claims it was murder. Personally, I think she may have committed suicide by jumping from the tower. But we'll probably never know for sure."

Sean makes another note. His list of questions is growing, I crane my neck to see them, but he puts his hand over the paper. "Go on."

"Caroline Forsyth's death came too close to creating a scandal for the Diocese. They closed the school on short notice and sent the remaining students home. Once again, Villa Aurora was empty, and George Acton was eager to find a buyer."

Chapter 45

While we've been talking, the sun has gone down. I let Ethel out in the backyard for the last pee of the evening, while Sean makes us both mugs of herbal tea. A rumble of thunder sends the dog scurrying back into the safety of the house. Once we're all settled, I return to the table to tell the final chapter of my saga.

"By the time St. Anselm's Academy closed, George Acton was an old man. He and his family were established in Palmer County society. He probably wanted to unload Villa Aurora so his heirs wouldn't be saddled with this white elephant. But he must've been having a hard time finding a buyer because the Villa remained empty for several years after the school closed."

"Then right before George Acton died, it sold." I take a sip of my tea. "I know from my research that the sale was conducted privately."

Sean massages his chin. "You think there was something shady about the deal?"

"I can't be sure. But Acton wanted to sell quickly. And the buyer must've thought he was getting a bargain."

Sean chuckles. "I'm waiting for the other shoe to drop. Who was the buyer?"

I whisk my hand over another stack of notes. "None other than Paul Raimondi, son of Arturo and father of Nico and Pete. Paul was the one man in the family who didn't embrace the landscaping and stonemasonry craft. He became an accountant instead. And he turned Villa Aurora into the Center for Mindful Living."

Sean scratches his head. "I thought a shrink owned the place when it was a psychiatric clinic."

"There must've been a psychiatrist on staff, but I read an interview in a New Jersey business magazine where Paul talked about seeing a need for long-term mental health care that wasn't being met in, as he put it, 'the marketplace.' He started the clinic not out of any interest in mental health care, but purely as a business opportunity in an under-served market. And according to Betty's friend, who worked there, he ran it for many years with a close eye on the bottom line."

I shuffle the papers on the table. "Until...misfortune struck again. A patient set a fire, and the code inspectors came out in force and demanded so many repairs and renovations to the old structure that keeping the Center open was not financially feasible. Paul Raimondi stood to lose a bundle of money unless he could sell Villa Aurora for a lot more than he paid for it."

"And the place had a reputation as a loony-bin, so buyers weren't lined up at the door," Sean says. "Paul Raimondi needed some kind of deal to save his skin."

Outside, a boom of thunder and crack of lightening emphasize my point.

I lean back in my chair and lock eyes with my husband. "This is where I'm speculating. I think Paul Raimondi is the silent partner that Alex Agyros is paired with on this redevelopment project. It won't be Paul's name directly on the paperwork, but it'll be some holding company or shell corporation that he's behind. Paul needed someone young and ambitious...someone eager to prove his worth in the family real estate business. Someone he could manipulate. It can't be a coincidence that Villa Aurora has gone back to the family that bought it at a bargain price because of Toliver's problems. Paul wanted to pass the white elephant back to the people who stuck him with it. To use Agyros family money to make Villa Aurora valuable again."

Sean clicks his pen two, three, four times before he speaks. "I don't believe in coincidence."

"I know you don't." I grin and squeeze his hand. "Are you ready for the last part of my theory?"

"Hit me." Sean waves towards his notes. "But you'd better be prepared for a lot of follow-up questions."

Taking a deep breath, I begin. "I think Arturo Raimondi killed Constantine Agyros. I think it was Arturo who sent his younger grandson, Pete, into Villa Aurora at night to search for Caroline Forsyth's diaries. And I think it was Arturo, this time accompanied by his one-time sister-in-law, Diane, who went to Emmeline's house and attacked her."

Sean narrows his eyes. "Wait...are we talking about that little old Italian man who said hello to you the evening we took the kids to the Apollo diner?"

"He's strong. I saw him lift a big stone out in the garden at the Villa. And he's the one who's been perpetuating this evil eye mythology. I think he wants revenge for poor, maimed Aggie Raimondi, and for his grandfather, who he sees as exploited by the owners of Villa Aurora. He wants his son Paul to come out on top of the Agyros family. And he's willing to do whatever it takes to make that happen."

Chapter 46

Sean and I stay awake for another hour going over my notes and my family trees. I explain how either Emmeline or I uncovered each fact.

"How did Arturo know that those suitcases you pictured on your social media accounts would contain the tell-all diary of Caroline Forsyth?"

"He couldn't know for sure, of course. But I think he's stayed in touch with Diane over the years. She told me she had extended family in New Jersey. I think Diane must've seen the photo of the suitcases and recognized one of her own. After all, she was the first student to leave St. Anselm's in a hurry. Maybe she asked Arturo to check it out, so he sent his grandson in through the trap door. And he found much more than he expected."

Sean frowns. "So Arturo planned to use what he found to pressure Constantine, and when that didn't work, he killed him?" My husband gnaws on his lower lip. "The murder was pre-meditated; it took some planning. There's still a piece missing here."

Sean gets up and paces the dining room. "And didn't Arturo and his grandson come back again, while Starla and Josh were in the tower? What was he looking for that time?"

I shrug. "More incriminating evidence that he could hold over Alex's head, maybe."

Sean looks at me askance. "Constantine was already dead and Alex under suspicion. What more could he hope to find in Villa Aurora?"

Sean's tone raises my hackles. "I don't know. If you arrest Arturo and question him, I'm sure you'll find out."

Sean cradles his head in his hands "I need some concrete evidence linking Arturo to these crimes before I can take it to my boss. All this is speculation. We can't make an arrest based on this."

"What about the eye drops Arturo used to poison Constantine. Can you search his credit card records to see if he made a large purchase of them?"

Sean snorts. "It'd be very convenient if he ordered twenty bottles of the stuff from Amazon and had it delivered to his house. But he most likely paid cash for a bottle at the supermarket, two at Walmart, two more at CVS. The product is so readily available, we'd never be able to trace his purchases."

Talk of eyes causes me to picture Arturo's thick glasses. "Arturo doesn't drive anymore. Neither does Diane. She took an Uber to Villa Aurora. Maybe the two of them took an Uber to Emmeline's house the day they attacked her. Maybe Arturo took an Uber to Constantine's house. That's easy for you to trace, isn't it?"

A slow grin spreads across Sean's face. "I really would encourage you to enroll in the police academy if it weren't for the fact that you earn more as an estate sale organizer."

We turn out the lights and fall into bed. Tomorrow will be a busy day for Sean. I've shifted a load of responsibility from my shoulders to his. As my eyes drift shut, I'm feeling hopeful that justice is close to being attained for Constantine's murder and Emmeline's attack.

I JOLT AWAKE. ETHEL is at our bedroom window with her paws on the sill, barking her fool head off. My gaze finds the clock on the bedstand: 3:00.

The storm must be over, or the dog would still be hiding in the closet.

"Ethel!" I get out of bed to pull her away from the window before she wakes the kids.

"Wha'ssa madder?" Sean mumbles.

"Probably a skunk or a fox out there."

Ethel keeps straining toward the window although she's stopped barking. Then I hear it: the sound of helicopter rotors above. I get down on my knees and twist my neck to look up at the sky. No fewer than three helicopters are circling, shining bright beams down on a sleeping Palmyrton.

"Something's going on. There are helicopters circling."

Sean leaps out of bed, instantly alert, and checks his phone. "It's a big fire." His head snaps up. "Villa Aurora is burning!"

Chapter 47

Sleep is impossible now. Sean gets dressed and heads into the Palmyrton PD to learn what he can about the fire and start working on leads connecting Arturo to Emmeline's attack.

"Call me as soon as you—"

"I will." He kisses me and is gone.

I tune into the local TV news, where breathless reporters stand in front of Villa Aurora as flames pour out the windows and engulf the tower. I should feel sorrow that this architectural masterpiece that I've spent the past two weeks exploring is about to crumble into ash.

But I feel...relief.

Maybe this is a fitting end for a mansion that has brought its many occupants nothing but pain and sorrow.

The curse is eradicated.

But what strange timing!

The sale is over...Alex is arrested...renovations were due to start yesterday.

What caused the fire? The lightning last night? Embers from a worker's blowtorch or soldering iron?

Or arson?

I glance at the clock. Not even six a.m. I can't call Sean for news yet.

Patience, Audrey, patience.

Soon the twins are awake and keeping me distracted. Then my father calls and asks if he and Natalie can come to visit. They haven't seen the kids in over a week—a lifetime!

The morning passes pleasantly, but still no word from Sean. Of course, Dad and Natalie are buzzing about the fire, but I don't want to talk to them about Arturo and all the scandals associated with Villa Aurora. I simply nod and agree that it's a tragic loss and direct their attention back to the kids. When the twins go down for their nap, I figure my folks will leave, but they insist on staying. "I'm sure you must have errands to run, dear. Why not take a little time for yourself?" Natalie says.

"Yes," Dad makes a shooing motion. "Go have a couple hours of fun. We'll keep watch over the kids."

As it happens, I do have some chores that can be completed twice as fast if I don't have Thea and Aiden with me, so I take my folks up on their offer.

The bank...the drug store...the drycleaner. I'm almost done when my phone rings. I snatch it up expecting Sean, but it's Emmeline.

"Audrey?" her voice sounds tremulous and uncertain. "There are people here who want to visit me."

"What?" I'm immediately on guard. "Who?"

"They told the guard in the lobby their names are Bill and Mary. But I'm not expecting anyone, and I don't know a Bill and Mary."

In the background I hear a nurse saying, "Now, Emmeline—it'll be nice for you to have visitors. You'll remember your friends when you see them."

Emmeline's voice grows agitated. "They're not my friends! Why won't you believe me?"

"Let me speak to the nurse, Emmeline."

When I get on the line, I give the woman a piece of my mind and tell her absolutely no visitors are to be admitted to Emmeline's room. Then I tell Emmeline I'll be right over to the rehab center. We'll soon see who this Bill and Mary are.

———◈———

I BURST INTO THE LOBBY of the rehab center five minutes later. There, continuing to argue with the security guard at the desk, are Arturo and Diane.

"What are you doing here?" I snap.

The two of them spin around. Instead of looking guilty or flustered, Diane breaks into a big grin.

"Well, look who's here—Nancy Drew herself." She points at me with her knobby-headed cane.

Arturo looks less delighted to see me. "Can we sit down, please. My back is killin' me."

The two of them sit down in a circle of lobby chairs, giving me no choice but to follow them. "What are you two doing here? And why are you calling yourselves Bill and Mary?"

"We certainly knew Emmeline wouldn't agree to see us if we gave our real names." Diane squints at me like I'm none too bright. Today's she's wearing a fuchsia scoop-neck shirt over zebra-patterned leggings. "We came to apologize to her."

"How did you know she was here?"

"She wasn't home and she wasn't at the hospital," Arturo says. "This place is where they always send you in between." He makes a face like he's swallowed a moldy grape. "I've done a few stints here myself."

I'm dumbfounded. "So you admit you attacked Emmeline?" I glance over at the guard, a bald, overweight guy reading the newspaper. What good will he be to protect anyone against violence?

"Attack is a strong word," Diane says. "We went to her house to talk to her, and Arturo got a little carried away when she wouldn't listen to reason."

"I regret it." Arturo wrings his work-worn hands. "I've always had a temper."

I turn on Diane, who seems utterly unperturbed. "And you—why did you go along with him?"

She smiles and lifts her hands. "One last adventure. The Raimondi boys have always been good for some excitement."

I feel like I've stumbled onto the set of some surreal drama. "Excitement? You call clobbering an elderly woman exciting?"

Diane huffs with impatience. "Emmeline was collateral damage. I came to help Arturo execute his plan for revenge."

Arturo is relaxing in his chair, looking like he's waiting for someone to bring him a cup of espresso and some pignoli cookies. "Are you going to tell me about that?" I ask.

"Sure, if you wanna hear."

I certainly do! "What are you two trying to accomplish?"

"I had a plan," Arturo begins, "to screw the Agyros family, get revenge for Aggie and Caroline, and end the curse of Villa Aurora once and for all. But I had to do it in a way that my son Paul didn't lose out."

"He's a gambler," Diane interjects. "All the Raimondis are."

"Not all," Arturo corrects. "Not my grandson, Nico. He's a hard worker and a saver."

Diane makes a face as if she thinks these are dubious qualities to boast about.

"And Emmeline interrupted your plan? So you assaulted her?" My voice rises in indignation, causing the guard to briefly glance up from his reading.

"You and Emmeline had to stick your noses in where they don't belong." Arturo's face darkens. "All I asked of Emmeline was to keep her trap shut for a while to give me the time I needed. I only got a few weeks left."

I cock my head. "A few weeks until what...?"

Arturo thumbs his chest. "I got end-stage pancreatic cancer. The docs said I shoulda been dead months ago. I hadda get this done before I go."

That explains his brazen admission of the assault on Emmeline. Arturo has nothing left to lose. Will he continue his confession? "And Constantine—did you poison him?"

Arturo smiles and closes his eyes but says nothing. Having Alex take the fall for his father's murder must be part of the revenge scenario. But Arturo did it. He must have.

"Does Alex know about all this?" I ask.

"He knows what a scumball his Uncle Damian was."

"I made an anonymous call and told him," Diane interjects. "I disguised my voice. I used to be in the theater, you know."

"Alex didn't want that to come out, for sure." Arturo smiles like the sweet old grandpa he is to Nico. "But Alex has no idea it's me behind all this. You're gonna tell the cops. That's okay. It's enough for me to know Alex Agyros spent a few nights in jail scared to death."

"And the fire burning right now at Villa Aurora?" I continue.

Arturo opens his eyes and shrugs. "Accidents happen during renovation projects."

A lightbulb clicks on for me. Of course, Arturo can't admit involvement in the fire. If it's proved to be arson, his son won't be able to collect on the insurance. That's how he's going to bail Paul out of his financial troubles. Looking at Arturo's smug face, it dawns on me that the visit to Villa Aurora overheard by Starla might have something to do with the fire. Could they have rigged something to ignite remotely?

I turn to Diane. "What's your part in all this? I thought you were whooping it up as a rich widow in Palm Springs?"

Diane pats her bouffant, which is a little flat on one side today. "I got one foot in the grave just like him. Congestive heart failure. I can see the writing on the wall. Arturo and I have always stayed in touch." She taps his shin lightly with the tip of her cane. "Just like I stayed in touch with some of the girls from Villa Aurora. I heard about Caroline's death at the time it happened. And my son has made a job of studying that crazy school. So when Arturo told me he and his grandson were back working at Villa Aurora and that you found suitcases belonging to the girls I went to school with, I decided it was time for a visit to New Jersey." She pats Arturo's knee. "Then when Arturo found Caroline's diary telling about the awful things her half-brother Damian did to her, I knew I wanted to be part of setting the record straight."

Arturo gives Diane an admiring look. "She's a good planner. Helped me a lot."

Diane nods. "I said to Arturo, 'Men like Damian never change. Caroline was the first girl he hurt, but you can be sure she wasn't the last.'" Diane shudders. "I'm ashamed Damian is a cousin of mine. Getting disowned by that family was the best thing that ever happened to me."

My eyes shift from one old person to the other. "Are you saying you killed Damian Forsyth?"

"Damian Agyros Forsyth, Constantine's nephew who he always protected," Diane elaborates.

"We made sure the cops found him with his pants unzipped and his collection of kiddie porn all around him," Arturo adds.

I recall Damian's recent obituary. It read 'died suddenly at home.' "You used the eyedrops on him, too?"

Arturo's satisfied grin returns. "The cops figured he drank himself to death. They don't look too close when a scumball dies. Constantine, on the other hand, was a very prominent, well-respected figure." He coughs, the words catching in his throat. "Also, not a heavy drinker. He took care of himself, I gotta give him that." The old coot actually winks at me. "Still, I was surprised the cops figured out he was murdered. And then they pinned it on his son!" Arturo kisses his fingertips.

These two are like an elderly Bonnie and Clyde. I can't believe how casually they're talking about murder.

Arturo struggles but succeeds in pushing himself out of his chair. "It's been good talkin' to you, Audrey. Give Emmeline our apologies and tell her I hope she gets outta this joint soon."

Then he and Diane link arms and head for the door.

Should I try to stop them? Enlist the help of the drowsy guard? I move to follow and then fall back in my chair, too stunned to pursue.

It's not like they can get far.

I pull out my phone and call Sean. Then I head upstairs to talk to Emmeline.

Chapter 48

Sean mans the monster gas grill I got him at the beginning of the summer as his first Father's Day gift, flipping burgers and turning shish-kebob skewers.

Quite a crowd of people have turned out for our Labor Day barbeque. The summer has been far too eventful, and I'm looking forward to a peaceful autumn, especially now that our nanny, Roseline, has returned from helping her sick daughter in Texas.

Thea and Aiden get grass stains on their knees as they crawl around the backyard, periodically pulled onto the laps of their grandparents, Alma Bannerman, Grandma Betty, and Starla.

"Come here, you cutie pie!" Starla bounces Aiden on her knee after he plops into a flower bed and can't get out. "You're still the handsomest boy I know!"

Sean's mother is cool to Starla, but Alma has forgiven her transgressions. "Where did you say you're working now, dear?"

I wander off to offer more drinks as Starla explains that she was hired by the battered women's shelter to watch the clients' children when they have job interviews or are out apartment hunting. Starla has found a tiny furnished apartment with another girl and has upgraded her bicycle and her wardrobe through careful purchases at garage sales and my estate sales. She's made Palmyrton her home.

"Beer, wine or margarita, Alex?" I ask at the picnic table.

"Oh, get the margarita, honey," Donna advises. "Audrey makes a great one."

Alex does as he's told, smiling affectionately at Donna. The two of them have been spending a lot of time together since he was released from custody. She's even met his little boy.

Arturo passed away two days after he confessed to me, and Diane died a week later. My information, in conjunction with the stolen diaries and other evidence Arturo left behind at his home, was enough to spring Alex—Arturo really didn't plan for Alex to be arrested. Sean admits the prosecution's case was weak, and the district attorney was happy to close the investigation with the death of the elderly murderer.

With his grandfather gone, Pete quickly admitted his role in breaking into Villa Aurora to rig some wires that would lead to an electrical fire. The insurance companies and their lawyers are still arguing over whether Paul Raimondi knew about his father's plans to torch the mansion for the insurance money, but I hope Alex will get his fair share of the pay-out. Donna says he talks a lot about the pressure he'd felt to prove himself to his father. He's now working on a small-scale condo development, a low-key project which gives him time to coach his son's soccer team and have fun with Donna.

With an empty tray, I return to the kitchen where I find Ty mixing gin and tonics while discussing with my father when to start his nephew playing chess.

"Is one of those G&Ts for Emmeline?" I ask.

Ty slides a fizzing glass with a big wedge of lime toward me. "That's her second. Maybe hold up on anymore until she's eaten a burger."

"I'll tell her you're monitoring her intake."

Ty raises his hands defensively. "No, no. I don't want to be on the wrong side of that woman. She's too smart."

Bearing two drinks, a G&T for Emmeline and a lemonade for her companion, I cross the backyard to the chairs in the shade of our old maple. Emmeline and Constance Forsyth share their own bowl of guacamole and chips and watch with great interest as Charmaine tries to teach Sean's sister a dance move.

"Thank you so much for inviting me to the party, Audrey. I love to see all these different people having fun," Emmeline says.

"Yes, it's delightful," Constance agrees. She looks much younger than the first time I met her. With the perpetual anxiety erased from her face, she's a different person. Telling Constance what really happened to her sister was one of the worst tasks I've ever undertaken. But despite the horror of the facts—her half-brother abused her sister, her mother sent both girls away to St. Anselm's, her sister probably jumped from the tower, Arturo killed her half-brother—Constance was relieved to finally know the truth. Although she's heartbroken that her sister committed suicide, Caroline believes their mother sent them to St. Anselm's for protection because she was powerless to control Damian and too ashamed to ask for help.

Constance is more forgiving than I would be.

"We're happy to see you both having fun," I tell the ladies. "We were worried about you there for a while."

Emmeline rubs the spot on the back of her head where her silver hair is still patchy. "I've got a little dent, but I'm no worse for wear. You know, it's my curiosity about people that got me into trouble. When I saw Arturo and Diane on my porch, they looked so interesting, I couldn't resist opening my door."

"Maybe you should focus on meeting new people in larger social settings, not alone in your house," I advise.

"You're right, dear. I've renewed my friendship with Constance, and that's been so rewarding." She sips from her gin and tonic and her eyes twinkle over the rim. "But just imagine—I met a murderer and his moll!"

"Arturo believed in the evil eye. I wonder if he believed in God and heaven and hell?" I muse. "He might not be in such a good place right now." I take a chip from Emmeline's bowl and nibble the edge. "Still, it's hard to feel sorry that Damian Forsyth is no longer doing evil on this earth."

"I'm afraid my time at St. Anselm's Academy for Girls destroyed my faith in God," Emmeline says. "I believe in justice. But it's very dangerous for individuals to administer justice single-handedly."

Emmeline takes a big swallow of her cocktail and faces me with a benevolent smile. "However, when I think of Damian Forsyth's death, I am reminded of that famous quote often misattributed to Mark Twain but actually penned by Clarence Darrow, 'I have never wished a man dead. But I have read some obituaries with great pleasure.'"

I HOPE YOU ENJOYED *Treasure in Three Acts*. Please leave a review to help other readers discover this book. Thanks for your support! Join my mailing list to be notified of new releases: https://swhubbard.net/contact

Read all the Palmyrton Estate Sale Mysteries, available in paperback, Kindle, Kindle Unlimited and audiobook:

Another Man's Treasure
Treasure of Darkness
This Bitter Treasure
Treasure Borrowed and Blue
Treasure in Exile
Treasure Built of Sand
Rock Bottom Treasure
Treasure Under the Tree

———◉———

Life in Palmyrton Women's Friendship Fiction Series
Life, Part 2
Life, Upended
Life, at Last
Life, Revealed

———◉———

If you've read all the Palmyrton Estate Sale mysteries, it's time to try the
Frank Bennett Adirondack Mountain mystery series:
The Lure
Blood Knot
Dead Drift
False Cast
Tailspinner
Ice Jig
Jumping Rise

About the Author

S.W. Hubbard writes the kinds of books she loves to read: twisty, believable, full of complex characters, and highlighted with sly humor. She is the author of the Palmyrton Estate Sale Mystery Series, the Life in Palmyrton Women's Friendship Fiction series, and the Frank Bennett Adirondack Mountain Mystery Series. Her short stories have also appeared in *Alfred Hitchcock's Mystery Magazine* and the anthologies *Crimes by Moonlight, Adirondack Mysteries*, and *The Mystery Box*. She lives in Morristown, NJ, when she's not traveling and hiking with her husband and her rescue dog. Visit her at http://www.swhubbard.net.

Printed in Great Britain
by Amazon